Also by Ronald Tierney

The San Francisco Mysteries

DEATH IN PACIFIC HEIGHTS *

The Deets Shanahan Mysteries

THE STONE VEIL
THE STEEL WEB
THE IRON GLOVE
THE CONCRETE PILLOW
NICKEL PLATED SOUL *
PLATINUM CANARY *
GLASS CHAMELEON *
ASPHALT MOON *
BLOODY PALMS *

available from Severn House

DEATH IN PACIFIC HEIGHTS

DEATH IN
PACIFIC HEIGHTS

Ronald Tierney

This first world edition published 2009
in Great Britain and in the USA by
SEVERN HOUSE PUBLISHERS LTD of
9–15 High Street, Sutton, Surrey, England, SM1 1DF.
Trade paperback edition published
in Great Britain and the USA 2009 by
SEVERN HOUSE PUBLISHERS LTD

British Library Cataloguing in Publication Data

Tierney, Ronald
   Death in Pacific Heights
   1. Women private investigators - California - San Francisco
   - Fiction 2. Private investigators - California - San
   Francisco - Fiction 3. Murder - Investigation - California
   - San Francisco - Fiction 4. Pacific Heights (San
   Francisco, Calif.) - Fiction 5. Detective and mystery
   stories
   I. Title
   813.5'4[F]

ISBN-13: 978-0-7278-6728-5   (cased)
ISBN-13: 978-1-84751-109-6   (trade paper)

All Severn House titles are printed on acid-free paper.

Typeset by Palimpsest Book Production Ltd.,
Grangemouth, Stirlingshire, Scotland.
Printed and bound in Great Britain by
MPG Books Ltd., Bodmin, Cornwall.

To Chat. All too brief.

Acknowledgements

Thanks to brothers Richard and Ryan and to Karen Watt, Jovanne Reilly and Lisa Phillips for their keen insights.

Pacific Heights is the place where many of San Francisco's old-money families live and die. Among its many mansions, Pacific Heights has two beautiful public parks. Alta Plaza, the more regal of the two, has formidable grand steps leading up to a windy hilltop park, where it occupies four square blocks of expensive real estate. Lafayette Park, smaller, friendlier, sits at the edge of Pacific Heights where home values begin to diminish little by little as the neighborhood descends east to Van Ness Avenue.

On the rare occasions when the sun is out and the temperature is above 65 degrees, sunbathers occupy the western slope of Lafayette Park, as do dog walkers and children with their nannies. The eastern slope has more trees, more brush. There are places to hide in the night, as a few sleeping homeless would attest. This morning a dead body will be found there.

One

This was important to her. A couple of mental health days. Why shouldn't she? She hadn't taken sick days in several years. None. She dropped her large bag and jacket on the bed, went toward the glass doors that opened on to a balcony. What a week.

She slid the doors open and caught damp cool air. Stretching out in front and below her were wetlands. Pools of still water glistened in the low grassy marsh – tall grasses, short grasses. A white crane walked stilt-like in the silky shallows. Beyond and to the left was the Pacific. No horizon line. Gray faded into gray at some distance. A scraggly beach separated the ocean from Bodega Bay. The falling sun cast a gold light tinged with salmon pink.

She felt a pleasant and fitting sadness.

She went inside, retrieved a bottle of Merlot from her bag. The Inn had provided an opener and glasses. They provided wine as well, but she could have better wine for less if she brought her own. She opened the wine, plucked a glass from the table and went back out to absorb the sights, sounds, and smells in a place where land stopped.

She took a sip.

'So,' she said in a conversational tone, 'here I am.'

She fought against the forces in her mind that insisted she traipse back through the painful wounds that brought her here. In the end, it was this: Peter had left her. She didn't want to look at it like a bad invest-ment. She hoped she wasn't that cold and calculating. The thing was, though, when her eleven-year relationship came to an end, it wasn't just losing him, was it? It was losing hope. Opportunity. The odds change. She was now toward the end of the timeline, wasn't she? By generously interpreting middle age, she could fit the description. So was he. But he was still prime in a culture that valued older men more than older women.

She sipped her wine, stared out.

She must not have loved him. She wasn't lost without him. She didn't cry. She was stunned. She felt like she'd been slapped and didn't see it coming, didn't know why it came. Still she didn't know. But it fell short of real tragedy.

They had been comfortable. They knew each other, could finish each

other's sentences. Liked many of the same things. No stress. Very little
anyway. A little dull, yes. At times. But there was some comfort in that,
after all.

She was doing it again, withdrawing into the inside of her brain, dismissing
what went on outside of it. She looked out into the slice of world in front
of her.

Her eyes caught something white flutter into a row of pines. She set
down her glass, went to her bag again, this time to get her binoculars. She
came back out, eyed the white spots on green, lifted her binoculars and
scanned until she found them – two elegant, pure white egrets. She had
never seen them in trees. Didn't think they did such things. Yet there they
were, just the two of them, basking, almost shimmering in the last of the
light.

She was jealous. When she realized it, she laughed.

'And I'm here because?' she asked herself, smiling. She nodded. 'To
think about what I want.' She toasted the air. There was humor in all of
this, she was sure.

That was the purpose. To re-evaluate her life, her profession, to determine what was valuable and to hold on to it or if she didn't have it,
pursue it. Start a new life. Not just because Peter decided to move to
Seattle and thought this was as good a time as any to dissolve the relationship. It was work too. No longer easy to work up the enthusiasm for
the cold corporate approach. The work had become boringly routine, and
the routine was only broken by bitter backbiting. The environment had
become toxic.

She reminded herself she wasn't lost without Peter. But she would have
to admit that she didn't know how to spend her time without him to fill
in most evenings and weekends. She needed to do something. She needed
to develop a plan, just as she would do for the clients assigned to her. Only,
with her own life, she didn't know how to begin.

The killer put an ear to her breast. The damp air coated the flesh. Her heart was beating ever so slowly, lightly. The killer's head raised, looked around, eyes combing the foggy early morning landscape for any sign of movement. Nothing. In the eerie silence of the city, the sound of breath escaping – a long deep sigh – signaled the killer. Ear to breast. It was certain now. It was over. The incredible, beautiful wave of sadness was overwhelming.

She woke up early. She didn't want to. She fell asleep just after the last of the Merlot. The fire was out. The room was cool and gray. Her head was thick with last night's alcohol, but it didn't hurt. She went back to sleep. When she awakened again, the light carried a wisp of gold. She slipped out of bed, went to the bathroom, returned to the main room, gathered her binoculars and went out on the deck. She realized she had left the doors open and that on the second floor she had left herself vulnerable to harm. As a professional in matters of security this was inexcusable. But it made her smile. Forgetting the rule book was something she should consider.

The fog appeared to be backing off, letting light shine down on the world closest to her. She'd take a drive this morning, check out the little town of Bodega, see the coast, maybe drive along the Russian River. In the afternoon, if it were warm enough, she'd go to swim, sit in the whirlpool and sauna. She would force her senses to come alive if she had to.

Vincente Gratelli, Inspector of the San Francisco Police Department's Homicide Detail, was on his own. Looking close to eighty, the gaunt, pale cop was in his late sixties. He wore a lined raincoat as he worked in the dreamlike haze and damp chill of a San Francisco summer morning. His partner dead now for a few months, Gratelli worked solo, though he was not alone at the edge of the park. The medical examiner and her team were there as were others trying to make sense of the body of a pretty, slight young girl in the damp undergrowth.

Gratelli had already dispatched several uniforms to canvas the nearby buildings. They were all residential. Unfortunately it appeared that the murderer used the section of the park with the least exposure. And given the time of night that the girl was likely killed or placed there, he expected little if anything to come of it.

She ordered breakfast in her room. Breakfast on the balcony was relaxing, calming. She believed she was getting a grip on calm. The coffee was excellent. The chicken sausage and lightly fried eggs were just what she wanted. The food made up for the surprisingly coarse towels and the room itself, which, while clean, was a bit worn. The chair arms were frayed. The glass in the sliding doors wasn't clear. That was one reason she kept the doors open, despite the chill. The place was giving away its age. It needed to be freshened up a bit.

She took a shower, dressed and drove inland from the area known as Bodega Bay to Bodega. She didn't know if the town was named after the Bay or the Bay after the town. She remembered both from Hitchcock's *The Birds*. The town was small. Very small. The schoolhouse, she recognized. The church she thought she remembered from the movie. Other than those strong presences, there was a surf shop, a couple of galleries and a place called 'The Casino.'

There was nothing to stop for. There was nothing there. Whatever she was looking for, she couldn't find. She drove back toward Bodega Bay, through the area targeted to collect tourist dollars – restaurants, spas, shell shops, galleries – and up along the coast. It was beautiful and desolate. She pulled off the road at one of the spots created for that purpose. She got out of the car carrying her binoculars, and walked to the edge of a small precipice. She could go down to the beach. She took a deep breath and decided just to look. Nothing propelled her to walk down in the sand or wade in the cold water.

She could see the marsh and the ocean and the bay. With the binoculars, she could see the beach and the small gathering of buzzards – she wasn't sure they were buzzards, but what else could they be? – feeding on some gray flesh. Seagulls kept their distance from the big birds.

Life goes on and it doesn't, she thought, whether you like it or not.

She skipped lunch, inquired at the front desk if they could seat her at dinner.

'How many?' the desk clerk asked brightly.

'One,' she said.

'You're a guest, right?' the clerk asked, perusing the reservations book.

'Yes.'

'Well, even so,' the clerk said, speaking sympathetically, 'I can only seat you at six. Is that too early?'

'No, that's fine,' she said. Did it matter? Six was fine.

'Name, I'm sorry.'

'Carly.'

The clerk's face suggested she wanted more.

'Carly Paladino.'

The sun was out now. Warm enough to go to the pool. The room had been straightened, clean towels, fresh soap. A new log for the fireplace.

She changed into her swimming suit, checked herself in the mirror. The lighter highlights worked on her dark hair, softened her face and camouflaged the few gray strands that had begun to appear. She had put on a few pounds since last she wore the suit. But it was all right. That belief that she had to look just perfect eroded, bit by bit, as the years passed. She understood there were changes that diet, exercise, make-up, and surgery for that matter, couldn't reverse.

She slipped on one of Peter's old shirts, tucked her feet into yellow flip-flops and, gathering her sunscreen, sunglasses, bottled water, and book, left. She found the path that led down to the pool.

No one was there. Perhaps it was the wrong time of the year for a spa crowd. It was midweek. That was how she got a discounted rate. And wasn't this what she wanted? A place to be alone. Solitude. Getting in touch with herself. A re-evaluation, without the stresses of work, and away from the familiarity of home, where little things would distract her?

She took a deep breath, put her belongings near one of the lounge chairs, took off her shirt and headed toward the pool. For a split second, she had the urge to just dive in. She thought about it. Perhaps it was too cold or too shallow. She didn't know if she could take the shock of anything that sudden. And, she found as she thought about it, she didn't know what her body was capable of these days. She rarely used it in this kind of way. She went to the shallow end where she could walk down the steps and immerse herself in the water gradually. She wasn't sure she wanted to get her hair wet.

She swam a few laps, sat in the whirlpool. She would have gone in the sauna, but it was barely warmer than the moderate temperature outside. It might not be wise to come into the office on Monday with a nice, healthy tan, after feigning illness on Thursday and Friday. On the other hand, what did it matter? She stopped accumulating sick days because she never took them and she maxed out.

People saw her as solid. Management did as well. Dependable. Perhaps because she was a woman or maybe because her boredom was recognizable . . . whatever the reason, she had gone up the corporate ladder as far as she could, and as she was beginning to realize now as far as she wanted. She tried to settle into the book. She couldn't. It wasn't the book. It was her. She was edging toward something. What. She wasn't sure.

Gratelli parked in the lot behind the Thomas J. Cahill Hall of Justice on Bryant. He walked up the ramp that led to the building. The Medical Examiner's Office was part of a newer addition tucked behind the old building. Off to the right was the new other-world looking jail.

Unlike the original building, which faced a main street and housed the courts, the police, and the DA, the examiner's offices were clean and modern, but also pretty much hidden from public view. He knew where to find it. He'd been there too many times already.

The chief medical examiner was a woman with more initials after her name than anyone Gratelli had ever met before. Unlike the crime scene investigators, who he would also talk to, she didn't report to the police, but to the mayor.

'I don't know much, really,' she said. 'There is a probable needle mark on her right arm and a cut on her left ankle. I won't wait long, but I'd like to have an ID before I do anything too invasive. Any chance of that?'

Gratelli followed her into the room. She pulled out the drawer. He looked but turned away quickly. In terms of blood and gore, he was used to much worse. However, he could never get over this kind of thing – a kid, innocence even more striking in death. Someone should have protected her.

'A few hours and I might have something,' the examiner said. 'Some of the tests are going to take longer.'

He nodded.

'There's going to be a lot of heat on this one,' she said.

He nodded again.

'It's not just where she was found, but this girl grew up wealthy,' she said.

'You know that? How?'

'Just do. That's why I think we'll know who she is very soon.'

Carly Paladino never minded dining alone. It was a fact of single life in an urban setting – and in many ways she had been single all along. Here it just seemed sad. It wasn't so bad at first, but halfway through her meal, others showed up. A big party at one table, celebrating something. A number of couples. A couple of businessmen. The light was too dim to read and it seemed wrong to read in this elegant setting anyway.

She had crab cakes over buttery pasta. A few grilled shrimp decorated the plate. It was well prepared, grilled on wood she guessed. The wine was delicious, but the fine dinner nevertheless failed to bring joy or satisfaction. She thought she ought to have rented an escort, some handsome, younger man. Dowagers did this without shame in Palm Beach. She'd read that anyway. Now she understood why.

She made her way up the slight grade toward her room. A few lanterns emanating golden light were scattered amidst the darkness. If you were to ask her what she was thinking, she wouldn't have been able to tell you. A full stomach, and a mix of wine and regret, deadened conscious thought.

A quick shadow movement and the sound of something sweeping into the brush brought her back to full alertness. She was frightened, ready to fight or flee. But there was nothing. A deer she thought. They were around. She had seen one earlier from the balcony come to the edge of the tended grounds and then slip back down the slope to the wild. She probably frightened it as much as it frightened her.

Nonetheless her heart was beating fast, and breathing was an effort. She stopped, looked around, found a sliver of a moon and nothing else. She had been startled, maybe frightened, possibly thrilled. It was as if a light clicked on in her brain. She felt alive. She looked at the sky, felt the breeze, smelled the ocean.

'Yes,' she said.

Two

This wasn't where Noah Lang wanted to be. Last night, he was parked in front of a home in Sea Cliff until three in the morning, watching a garage door. It never opened. No one came out of the garage door or the house and no one came by. The lady of the house stayed in the house. If there were clandestine lovers meeting there, they would have had to beam in.

He didn't want to be here either.

This morning he was in court at 10 a.m. as requested. Unrelated to last night's marathon stake-out, he was in court to testify that a witness to a corner store robbery in the Western Addition couldn't have been a witness to the crime because he was in a bar in the Mission when the incident occurred. Both neighborhoods had tough areas, but they were in different parts of the city.

Lang sat in the front pew, as he called it, as the trial ran late. He sat there, wanting, needing to be in bed. The starched collar to his only decent dress shirt scratched his neck. Sadly, the top button couldn't be buttoned. Instead he tied the tie to hide the small non-traversable gap. He told himself that he hadn't grown fat. In fact, he was in great shape – no belly anyway – for a man closing in on, but still a few years away from the half-century mark. It was just that as he aged, his shoulders got bigger and his neck got thicker. Like most men, he put on about ten pounds a decade. And there weren't *that* many decades since he was in his skinny twenties.

The defense attorney, Chastain B. West, gave Lang an apologetic look. Or maybe it was a pained look. Not about the collar, but about the delay. West, a tall, thin, elegant black man, was paying for Lang's time. And Lang, because of last night and today, was doing better than usual in the income department, but worse than usual in the sleep department. He had another long stake-out in Sea Cliff tonight.

Lang looked at his watch. Even though he was up next, there was no way he'd testify before lunch. He spent a lot of time in courtrooms – and he didn't know a judge that would start a new witness when it was this close to noon.

'How are you doing?' Lang asked West shortly after the judge announced Lang's predicted recess and asked the participants in the drama to return at one thirty.

'I don't know. Toss up. You'll make the difference. Sorry about the delay,' West said.

They talked in the cold, drab marbled hallway lined with Superior Court Rooms.

'Who are you sorry for?' Lang asked.

'Me.' He smiled. 'You're like a taxi. Whenever I see you, I know the meter is running.'

'And what did you say you did for a living, Mr Billable Hours?'

West grinned. 'When it comes to invoices, it's like Christmas. It is better to give than to receive.'

'Appreciate the work,' Lang said. 'See you at one thirty. He headed out for a quick cup of coffee at McDonald's. He did appreciate the work. West, who worked as a criminal defense attorney, wasn't exactly getting rich. He was, however, the source for maybe fifty per cent of Lang's income. And West was a decent guy who never tried to screw him over and took cases even when it was unlikely he would get paid.

West was among those people Lang called 'distant friends.' Easy to be around, but no real need to be around them. Sometimes their business conversations leaked into broader discussions, usually about music. Every once in awhile they would have drinks on Fillmore, where there were heroic attempts to revive the city's jazz community. West and Lang shared an interest in Blues. The difference between them was that West knew what he was talking about. He knew the historic details, could recite the cast of characters, understood the nuances of their relationships, musical and otherwise.

As it was about most things, Lang just knew what he liked. And that was just about anything slow and sad. He liked music that stretched time out, made it go slow. He liked that about New Orleans. He liked a lot about New Orleans except the heat and the fact that it was in Louisiana. That's why he was in San Francisco.

Outside the Hall of Justice, it was a familiar neighborhood. In Union Square you could find all the famous shops within walking distance of each other – a luxury shopper's paradise. Here was where the crime business was consolidated – courts, morgue, criminal attorneys, cops, prosecutors, jail and a gaggle of firms willing to bail out those caught accidentally or purposefully in the web. And all of them existed within a few blocks of each other.

There were also places to eat. A few weren't so bad. Even so, he just wanted coffee, and McDonald's would fill the bill for now.

By himself again, he picked back up on the thoughts he had while the case was being tried. His thoughts were heading toward a conclusion, a solution. Business was good. He was putting in a lot of hours. But, and this was a big 'but,' he wasn't really getting ahead. What he would do, he decided, is clean out his office. He used to live there, but now he had a small place of his own to escape to. If he removed the extraneous junk – that is leaving only the essential junk – there was room for someone else to set up shop.

Lang ordered his coffee. Large. Black.

He would share this space, hopefully with a criminal attorney – that could be helpful – or another investigator. Rent would bring in some income – steady income. He could put this aside for his old age.

'That's it then,' he said to himself, but loud enough to be heard by the graying, balding man behind the counter who slid the cup of coffee toward him.

'That's it,' the man said. 'You want a drum roll?'

When she heard the President, CEO, Chairman of the Board and all-around Grand Poo-bah of Vogel Security, was out of his meeting and about to leave for his usual hour at the gym, Carly Paladino moved from her office, cutting through a sea of cubicles like a cigarette boat, to his office. She gave his secretary a smile and went in. She was high enough in the organization that she could enter unannounced.

'Carly?' the retired general said, slipping on his navy blue Brooks Brothers suit jacket. He went to his desk, searching through papers.

'General?'

He looked up at her, quiet for a moment, then blandly said, 'My, my. Good color. A spring in your walk. Illness becomes you.' He went back to fiddling with the papers.

'I wasn't really ill.'

'You don't say.' His voice did not give the hint of the sarcasm he intended.
'There they are,' he said, grabbing a set of keys from the desk. He faced
her again. A thin smile on his old face. 'If you have something to say, please
say it. I'm late for my workout.'

'I've decided to resign,' she said.

He didn't look at all shocked. But then he never did. You could tell him
the world was ending in twenty minutes and he'd nod that he'd heard and
wonder what you expected him to do about it. One never knew what he
was really thinking until he told you. And if he wanted to tell you, he would
– whether you wanted him to or not.

'I can give you a month, if you like,' Carly said, but she really wanted
to leave right away. 'If you need more . . .'

'Well, I think we can work it out for this afternoon,' the general said,
not missing a beat. 'Arthur what's-his-name and Sinclair can pick up the
slack.'

Done. Problem solved.

While she knew this ought to be received as good news, it wasn't.
It was what she wanted, but the sudden acceptance stunned her. Had
she brought so little to the organization that she was so easily replaced?
He didn't ask why. He didn't want to know if there was anything he
could do to keep her. He didn't even think it was something he should
think about.

'Yes, well,' Carly stammered. 'I can do that.'

'Good,' he said. If she had any doubts that this was now settled, they
were gone. 'Talk to Sarah. Tell her I said to give you the silver. She'll know
what I mean. You want a farewell party or anything?'

She tried very hard not to laugh. She didn't succeed.

He looked at her, confused. She stepped in.

'Oh, no. Let's not make a big deal out of it,' she said, not caring if he
picked up on her sarcasm.

'Precisely,' he said. He looked like he might ask her what was so funny.
He didn't. He really didn't care what she thought.

If it hadn't been for her days in Bodega, this might have destroyed
her, having removed any vestige of self-worth that Peter hadn't already
taken with him. But now it all seemed extremely silly. She would
throw her own fucking farewell party. She was ready to move on with
her life.

As she walked toward Human Resources to talk with Sarah, she thought
about what moving on really meant. She was supposed to go somewhere.
Where was she going?

'There, smarty pants,' she said to herself, echoing the words of her mother who would say it whenever Carly took a particular action her mother advised against and it ended badly.

Logic told her to worry. Why couldn't she wipe that smile off her face?

Pamela Hanover, the victim's mother, wore a blue blazer and cream slacks. Her blonde hair was pulled back. Her posture was perfect.

The medical examiner had done her best to make the environment as warm as she could.

Inspector Gratelli stood at the foot of the body, which was draped in a white sheet. When the orderly pulled the sheet back from the face, he noticed Mrs Hanover nod in confirmation. It was barely noticeable. She continued to stare. She didn't move, but there was something Gratelli saw or perhaps just sensed. She was doing all she could to keep it in. He could imagine shards from her porcelain face flying everywhere any moment now.

She did not explode. After a long and increasingly awkward silence, she looked at Gratelli, gave him a sad smile, nodded again. She turned and left.

He caught up with her outside. She wasn't sure which direction to go.

'Someone driving you home?' he asked.

'Yes. He's parked in front.'

'I'll walk you there.' He touched her elbow and guided her to the front door of the building, through the lobby. It was easier getting out than getting in. A line of folks were waiting at the metal detector to get in – gang bangers, lawyers, prostitutes, members of juries, rapists, drug sellers, witnesses, reporters, clerks and others emptied their pockets and opened their purses, backpacks and briefcases for a city cop who no doubt saw the assignment as punishment.

Outside on the front steps, a white Land Rover pulled to the front.

'Thank you,' she said.

'I'll need to talk to you.'

'Yes, of course,' she said, but she was already heading down the steps to the sidewalk.

Gratelli knew there were people – family, friends, witnesses, even juries – who judged grief on the ability to cry, weighing even the volume of tears. But he knew grief had many faces. Anger. Disbelief. Panic. Hysteria. He had also seen shock. No reaction. As if someone had merely commented on the weather. Somehow the brain protected the heart, stayed coldly sane, until the details were taken care of and the shock wore off. He thought that about her.

While Gratelli did not judge her, he knew he had been too respectful. He needed to talk with Mrs Walter Hanover. Family members are the first suspects. He had allowed her to get away. Was he slipping?

He would go home for dinner, freshen up, and would see Mrs Hanover in the early evening whether she liked it or not. And unfortunately, he would have to do more than merely interview her.

Thanh, Lang's part-time, long-time bookkeeper, friend, occasional special operator, and technological bridge between Lang and the twenty-first century, had put a Martin Cruz Smith novel on Lang's little Apple Nano. It was a device he had bought at Thanh's urging for the kind of long, boring stake-outs in which he was about to engage. The plugs in his ears would deliver the story, while his eyes remained free to observe, if need be, the very unlikely departure of the woman of the house or the equally unlikely arrival of a suspicious visitor.

Lang had the feeling he was working for an obsessive, a control freak. The bad taste in his mouth got worse the more he talked to his client. But he had committed to the task. One week's observation while his client was, of career necessity, out of town.

He stopped at his place, grabbed a couple of hours of sleep, fed his four-footed roommate, showered and was out on the street again by five.

Lang had a quick dinner at the Mandarin Villa on Fell and Franklin. Good, inexpensive, fresh Chinese. He ordered his usual, unimaginative Kung Pao chicken. Hot. It wasn't a good idea to have a beer considering how long he'd be in his car, but how could you eat spicy Chinese without a chilled brew? He opted for the Sapporo rather than the Tsingtao, hoping he wasn't offending the Chinese owner.

Today the parking gods were with him. Not only did he find a space near the restaurant, he later found a great spot close but not exactly in front of the home he was watching. He was a few yards up the slight incline but had a view of the front door, the garage and the gate that went around back. Fortunately he was far enough away to avoid discovery if she left or someone came. The only thing he had to worry about was a neighbor as nosy as he was. In his years at this, he'd had local security or the police called on him more than once. It was a pain and attracted unnecessary attention to his task.

Once in his spot, he called Thanh and explained how he wanted to rent out half his office. Thanh thought it was a good idea. 'Consider it done.'

Lang put the little earpieces in place, put on his glasses to read the small type on the screen. He selected the book rather than one of the several dozen albums Thanh had loaded for him. He sat back and relaxed. It was still early summer. It would start getting dark around eight. He settled in the old leather seat, and switched on Smith's *Havana Bay*. This was great – Smith and Cuba. Two of his favorites.

He half hoped the woman behind the door was having an affair. It would serve her prick of a husband right. He'd watched her before – for a couple of days now. The stake-outs during the day while her husband was at work. Lang had followed her as she'd done her errands. She'd picked up groceries, dry-cleaning. She'd had lunch one day at Beetlenut on Union Street with a person Lang imagined to be a pal. Lang had noted the friend's license plate, but didn't follow it up. All seemed innocent enough. They had separated after lunch.

The wife, attractive in a demure way, didn't seem to be playing around. It was the husband who had the problems. Over the years he'd learned that it was the cheating spouse who was the most suspicious of the mate, just as it's the liar who can't trust anyone else to tell the truth.

Three

A sliver of butterfish, roasted potatoes and a salad was about to be consumed by Carly Paladino. She retrieved an open bottle of Chardonnay from the refrigerator. The kitchen window faced south. The fog hadn't arrived yet, so she had a view over the rooftops bathed in the warm early-evening light just before sunset. On clear days San Francisco morning light was usually silver. In the evening it was gold.

She sipped her wine before sitting at the small counter in the kitchen. She would have invited Nadia over to celebrate this strange rite of passage, but her friend was in Italy. Her only other close friend, Michael, was at his restaurant on Valencia. She could only commandeer him on Sunday nights and Mondays. She didn't mind dining alone. She didn't really miss Peter. Yet.

The phone rang.

She almost didn't answer it. Opinion poll. Wrong number. Charity. The ringing got to her as it always did. It was like a baby crying. And what if it was an emergency? Peter calling to say he made a mistake. Would she take him back?

'Hello,' Carly said. She moved back to the counter to get her wine.

'This is Frank,' the general said.

Two surprises for Carly. One, that he had called. Two, that he had referred to himself as 'Frank.'

'Yes, Frank, what can I do for you?'

'I have a little situation,' he said.

'Is everything OK?'

'Well, one of our clients has requested you personally.'

'Oh. OK.'

'So, Carly, we're thinking you could come back on for as long as you like or maybe work for us freelance.'

'Who is the client?' she asked.

'I can't reveal that until we have some sort of agreement here. You understand. It's not just for our protection, it's also client confidentiality.'

'I'm sorry, Frank,' she said. Sometimes she didn't know what she was thinking until she said it. 'I'm moving on.'

'Carly, we could pay you handsomely, maybe for this one case. You know, in addition to the severance. Get you started in your . . . ah . . . ah . . . new life.'

'Thank you for thinking of me,' she said, knowing full well that this wasn't his idea. This would be the last thing he wanted. It had to be an important client putting the pressure on him. Maybe she could figure out who. 'I'm going out on my own.'

'Your own?'

'Yes. Start my own agency.'

'Really, Carly, you don't mean that. You have that kind of backing, that kind of money?'

'Start small. Build.'

'Maybe we took you too much for granted. You did good work for us. Today, I just took you at your word. You wanted to leave.'

'I did.'

'I can't convince you otherwise?'

'No.'

After she clicked off, she nibbled at the fish. It had cooled off and wasn't quite as tasty. She lost her appetite, but not her thirst. She took another sip of the Chardonnay. It was buttery. That was good. She thought about the general's offer. Had she been stupid twice in one day? Nope, she was still smiling inside. This sudden sense of insecurity was energizing.

She looked around her two-bedroom condo – one that she had lived in since she was twelve, when her parents had moved there from a small place in North Beach. After they passed away, she'd inherited it. It was a nice place, large for the average single person in the city. A big, comfortable living room with high ceilings and a fireplace. With two bedrooms she had the room to set up an office. But did she really want clients in her home?

She'd have to find space somewhere. Cheap space. Sure, she thought, in San Francisco that ought to be as easy as . . .

*   *   *

Gratelli waited in the hall only a few moments before Mrs Hanover appeared. She wore the same clothes she had when she identified the body. Her eyes were red. He hoped she had cried. It would make it easier on her. Also easier on him.

'Thank you for seeing me,' he said as she approached.

'I didn't have a choice, did I?' She didn't mean it. Just a statement of fact. This wouldn't have been her choice.

'Am I keeping you from dinner?'

'Not hungry.' She went down the hall and into what looked like a den. It was masculine, though not dramatically so.

'Your husband?' Gratelli asked.

'He's on his way back from New York.'

'He was in New York yesterday?'

'No. He was here. He flew out around noon. He had to turnaround at the airport.'

'I see.'

She looked at him quizzically.

'You see what?'

'I am trying to understand where everybody was. I have some questions, Mrs Hanover. I hope none of them are impertinent or insensitive, but as a police matter I hope you will understand that sometimes . . .' She looked at him coldly. 'Actually more than sometimes the victim knew the killer. You know that. In cases like this, the first thing we do is rule out family, then friends, then known associates. It's not personal.'

'I understand. I'll cooperate.'

Pamela Hanover was incredibly composed. It wasn't likely she had had anything to drink. No sedative. She was toughing it out. He admired her. He was taken with her. Even so, he couldn't allow his feelings to change anything. If he could choose, he'd rather she be a friend, not an adversary — for reasons beyond just admiring her. A woman in her position in the community could make life miserable for the department. But she was, at this moment, a suspect — as was her husband, stepsons and friends.

Gratelli took out his notebook. He would ask about these people. He would ask about the victim's habits, state of mind. Did she drink, smoke pot, do any other drugs? Was she troubled about anything? Grades, romance, sex?

Carly must have dozed off on the sofa. The ringing of her phone aroused her. She was disorientated for a moment before glancing around to see where she was and what had happened. There was an empty wine bottle and glass on the coffee table.

'Oh,' she said, stirring. If I'm not careful with the wine, she thought, I'll be pushing a grocery cart in the park before long. By the time she got to the phone, it stopped ringing. She looked at her watch. 11.15 p.m. She heard the voice.

'This is Pamela Hanover. I need to talk to you about a very serious problem in my family.'

Carly didn't pick up.

The voice left a phone number and the instruction for Carly to call as soon as she possibly could. Later that night would be fine, the woman said.

Carly didn't pick up. She wanted to make sure she had her wits about her. She was aware of Pamela Hanover of course. The firm had done work for her husband; but moreover, she now *knew* who Pamela Hanover was.

The general's phone call began to make sense. What appeared to have happened was that the Hanovers wanted Carly more than they wanted the firm.

Carly would return the call early in the morning. She wasn't sure she had the clarity to deal with whatever it was at the moment. What she was sure of was that she had mourned or celebrated, whatever she was doing, long enough. She'd get down to serious business tomorrow, first thing.

Lang listened to a couple of hours of *Havana Bay* and switched over to music. The Rolling Stones' bluesy album, *More Hot Rocks (Big Hits & Fazed Cookies)*. His friend West might laugh at him, but he was alone, in a car, on a lonely street in the dark. No one would know his guilty pleasures.

The fog had crept in, but it stopped short of hiding the home he was watching. There wasn't much beyond it that he could make out. The house went dark. He checked his watch: 3.20 a.m. He would stay until 4 a.m., thinking that surely any amorous adventure would surely have begun by then. He was hungry again.

'Standing in the Shadow' finished and he had just clicked on to 'Let it Bleed' when he saw the flash of light in a second-story window. He pulled the plastic earpieces out – thinking maybe he should have been listening as well as looking. He rolled down the window.

He continued to watch. Nothing. No movement. No other flashes. All was quiet.

He understood that it could have been a TV turned on and off quickly. Or a light mistakenly turned on. A camera flash? There were reasonable explanations. But the hairs on the back of his neck stiffened. His gut confirmed it, telling him something was wrong. Seriously wrong.

In the seconds that followed, he thought about what he should do and what the ramifications of each action would be. He got out of his car, walked over to the home. The air was cool and damp. He pulled the lapel of his sport coat up over his neck. He rubbed his hands together. He rang the bell and stepped back to see if a light came on anywhere in the house.

Nothing happened. He prepared a story. He would ask for some woman . . . Caroline, he decided, and then beg forgiveness for getting the wrong address when his client's wife answered the door.

Nothing. He rang the bell again. Stepped back on to the lawn again. No light. No movement in the neighborhood. He leaned on the bell. Nothing. He thought he heard something behind him. He turned quickly, thought he saw a blurred form pass under the hazy light of the street lamp and disappear into the foggy darkness.

In a split second, he had another decision to make. Call 911? Go after the person he might have seen or go in? What if someone was dying upstairs?

Four

Lang stood outside the residence on the street. Activity swirled around him. Firefighters, waiting for further instructions, stood by their trucks. Police and crime scene investigators came and went from the house as the flashing lights from the various emergency vehicles bounced against the fog. The wetness in the air made everything seem slightly out of focus.

Behind a yellow ribbon were neighbors, a surprising number considering the hour. But all the sirens and lights called them from their slumber. Sea Cliff, as its name implies, was a very quiet, safe, and wealthy neighborhood with homes either on or very near the ocean. For the people who live there, this kind of crazed attention in the middle of the night has to be disturbing in its strangeness.

Lang was told to wait. And to wait outside. The directions were clear and firm.

He had broken a window earlier to get inside that set off the alarm. He found the body upstairs where he saw the flash. A woman Lang could clearly identify as his client's wife was on the floor between the bedroom door and the bed. She was naked. A bleeding hole in her temple. Blood and brain had skidded on the floor on the opposite side of the wound and a .38 was just inches away from her open right hand.

It didn't take an experienced medical examiner to know she was dead and to think first of suicide. It made sense to Lang on an emotional level. The husband was an asshole. If he was as controlling as he appeared, maybe she thought this was the only way she could escape. Lang wasn't thinking kindly of himself. He almost didn't take the job because he didn't like the guy, but in the end, money won out. Now he felt complicit.

No. He was just there to report the facts, whatever they were, wasn't he?

He called 911 immediately, though she was clearly dead. He examined the scene without disturbing it. He touched nothing and moved carefully back into the hallway. He went downstairs to wait on the doorstep, wondering if he had really seen someone leaving. It was a shadowy image that lasted less than a second. Could have been the wind and a branch or a bird. He was tired, excited. There was so little light.

He sat on the trunk of one of the police cars, wishing he had a cup of coffee and weighing how much responsibility he had in whatever happened upstairs. Beside him was an attractive, but uncommunicative policewoman who was, no doubt, told to keep him there until homicide inspectors interviewed him.

'Lang?' The question came from a big white guy in a black raincoat. He was accompanied by a small black guy in a beige trench coat and an all-weather, mock-fedora.

'Well, if it isn't Fric and Frac,' Lang said.

'Bric and Brac would be nicer,' the little one said. His real name was Inspector Rose. His bigger Caucasian friend was Inspector Stern.

'What's with you and dead bodies?' Stern asked.

'It's been a few years since I've had the pleasure,' Lang said. They weren't bad guys. A little silver in Rose's hair that wasn't there before. Stern had put weight on a body that already had enough. 'You guys are aging gracefully.'

'We think you're cute too,' Rose said.

'I don't,' Stern said. 'Never did. I don't know, something about him. Maybe it's his constant proximity to death. Makes me queasy.'

'Well, it's just me then. We don't agree on coffee either,' Rose said, looking sympathetically at Lang. 'He's Starbucks, I'm Peets.'

'You still hanging around with the shemale?' Stern asked.

'I see you aced your sensitivity training class,' Lang said.

'You have no idea what I have to put up with,' Rose said, with a feigned sigh.

'Well, dammit, Rose, are you Black or African–American? You keep changing.' Stern stopped pretending he was angry and turned to his partner.

Rose decided to end their familiar and predictable banter.

'Let's talk about the late Mrs Kozlov,' he said. 'But let's do this inside.'

'We should take him downtown,' Stern said.

'It's depressing down there. All those ne'er-do-wells.'

Rose won the argument if there was an argument and Lang followed the two inspectors into the victim's house. They moved to the big room at the back. It was lined with windows that faced the Pacific. The ocean, however, was a force hidden by the foggy night.

Lang sat on a huge upholstered chair that would have a helluva view if he could see anything, but all he saw was himself sitting on a huge upholstered sofa. Rose sat on the arm of the sofa. Stern stood. Lang told them, moment by moment, the story of the flash in the window and what followed.

'So you say you saw someone run from the house?' Rose asked.

'No, I didn't say that. I said I saw something, a shadow, a branch, a bird pass underneath the street lamp. Maybe just the wind blowing the fog around. Or maybe I just imagined it. I wouldn't swear it was a human form.'

'You shouldn't swear anyway,' Rose said.

'Maybe it was her soul. You know, the victim's soul running like hell?' Stern asked.

'I love it when you get all spiritual on my ass,' Rose said.

'You guys should go on Letterman,' Lang said. He was tired and wanted to go home and sleep. But he knew this would go on. Ten years ago, when they were investigating a case he was involved in, they were around so often they almost became family, and not in the good sense.

'We just want to make sure your interview experience is as pleasant and entertaining as we can make it,' Rose said. 'How are we doing?'

'So, if you took a lie-detector test you would pass it with flying colors?' Stern asked.

'I don't take lie-detector tests,' Lang said. 'Remember?'

'Thing is you could have been hired by your client to kill his wife and at the same time provide an alibi for him,' Stern said, not playing dumb any more.

'Look at it this way, Lang,' Rose continued. 'Your story about rushing into the house to save the damsel in distress would give you cover for any mistake you might have made in the actual killing. A stray hair – and I want to compliment you, you've got a lot of hair for a man your age – could be attributed to your attempt at saving her. Clever, don't you think?'

'It would be clever,' Lang said. 'You remember this blame the PI idea didn't work for you last time.'

'All the more reason . . .' Stern began.

'Sorry, guys,' Lang said, standing up. 'I've been up for almost two days. If you want me, here's my card.'

'Did we offend you?' Rose asked.

'No. Listen, the husband wasn't exactly a saint.'

'Giving up your client?' Stern asked.

'No. I did what the client asked. He asked me to see if she was cheating on him. I did that.'

'Was she?' Stern asked.

Lang thought about whether he should answer that. Decided he would. 'Not that I could see.'

'One more question,' Rose said, moving across the room. 'Where's Mr Kozlov? Out of town?'

'Yep.'

'Where?'

'Sacramento,' Lang said. 'He's up there all week, said he didn't want to commute. My guess is he wanted her to have a window of opportunity to cheat.'

Lang left them in the room. Their work was far from done. His was.

Carly Paladino watched the early-morning news as she sipped an orange juice and slipped into her running clothes. It was 6 a.m., and the hard news led. She sat on the edge of her bed, watching as the identity of the dead girl found in Lafayette Park was explained. It was the sixteen-year-old daughter of Mr and Mrs Walter Hanover.

She stopped tying her running shoes, stared in shock at the screen. Pamela Hanover was calling her about her daughter's death. 'The police,' the anchor said, 'have not indicated whether foul play was involved, however an official who did not wish to be identified, said it was clearly a suspicious death.'

Carly took a deep breath. It was early, too early to call Pamela Hanover. She would think about this as she got in her morning run. She peeked through the window. Despite the fog, she could see that the sun had risen and the black was slipping slowly into an illumined gray.

She descended the stairs from her second-story flat and said hello to Mr Nakamura, her downstairs neighbor. He was retrieving his newspaper. He smiled and nodded. They had known each other for years. Nakamura had to be in his seventies. He had known her parents and had known her since she was a teen growing up in the flat she'd inherited from them. A sweet man whose life was a mystery to her.

Out on the sidewalk, she looked around. No matter which direction she went, she would confront hills. However, this morning, choosing a route wasn't difficult. She would run the few blocks up to Lafayette Park. She would run around it, through it, get a sense of it as it might relate to the girl's death. She didn't really know what Mrs Hanover wanted, but it was likely related to her daughter's death.

A damp morning wasn't a bad thing for a runner. The moisture in the air was a coolant and the coolness a motivator. She ran three mornings during the week and once at the weekend, usually in the afternoon. The morning runs were close to home. On the weekend she might drive out to Golden Gate Park for a serious run. Or she would go down to the Marina and run along the Bay to Crissy Field – a stretch of reclaimed nature that not only served naturalists but runners and kite flyers.

She saw the yellow crime scene ribbon around the north-east corner of the park. A cop stood guard. She ran the perimeter, taking note of any place where one might have a view of that section of the park. Not many. At the west end of the park, she could look down steep Laguna and see the piers of Fort Mason Center out on the Bay. On Washington, there were only a few homes – very big ones, including the imposing mansion of a world-famous, high-society, bestselling author. Further east was a tall, elegant building, apartments or condos, but with formally dressed doormen. Perhaps, someone could have seen something from the upper floors, but the tall, old trees might obscure the view.

She was getting ahead of herself. No doubt the police knew a whole lot more than what the news program revealed. She'd stop speculating, at least until she'd talked to Mrs Hanover.

Carly was home by 7 a.m., put the coffee on, and jumped in the shower. As usual she cranked up the hot as high as she could bear to warm not just her cool flesh but also her cold bones. Sometimes it was hard to get the cold out of the bones any time of the year.

She forced herself to wait until exactly 8 a.m. before making the call. Before punching in the numbers, she put a pen and notebook on the kitchen counter, and refilled her coffee. Rarely intimidated, Carly Paladino nevertheless felt a bit of trepidation calling. She was one of the Hanovers.

'This is Carly Paladino returning Mrs Hanover's call,' she said, when the male voice announced, 'The Hanover residence.'

She waited.

'This is Pamela,' a voice said.

'Carly Paladino returning your call.'

'Thank you for calling. If you are available I would like to talk to you about a situation. I need some help and Walter said you were excellent at what you do.'

'That's very nice of him to say,' Carly said, feeling a little phony. 'What would you like for me to do?'

'Could we talk at your office?'

She thought for a moment. Office? Her home?

'I'm kind of between offices. Could I drop by there or meet you some place?'

'I understand. Here is fine,' Hanover said with a tone of resignation. 'Eleven?'

'That would be fine.'

Carly put her laptop on the counter that divided the kitchen from a small dining nook and clicked it on. She poured herself a cup of coffee and keyed in Craigslist, then clicked 'office/commercial.' After narrowing down the list to San Francisco only, she found hundreds of listings. Some had photos, some didn't. Most were out of her price range.

But an ad did catch her eye. Private investigator looking to share office, some phone, clerical duties included. She wasn't sure about the 'sharing' idea, but having worked so long for a large security firm, she hadn't even thought about logistical support. That could be helpful.

It was listed with a SOMA location description, which meant south of Market Street, an area that could be a little rough, but was currently in the midst of rapid gentrification. It wasn't necessarily a bad address any more. And it was affordable compared to the others. After a few minutes searching the list, she knew she couldn't afford the Financial District or the Embarcadero.

Why not look into it? She checked her watch, retrieved her cell from the living room and made the call about the potential office space.

Carly was prompt, arriving at the Hanover residence on Broadway. There were two TV trucks and a couple of what Carly guessed were print reporters gathered outside. A San Francisco police officer stood at the walkway to the Hanover home. She gave him her name and she was permitted to pass. A reporter called out something, but Carly kept walking.

She was met at the door by a young, blond man, whom it turned out was neither a butler nor relative, but Mrs Hanover's secretary. He ushered her into what appeared to be a den, somewhat masculine in decor – no boar's head, but deep leather chairs and ancient maps in heavy frames.

Mrs Hanover got up from the desk, moved around and the two of them went to the sofa and chairs grouped for conversation.

'Coffee?' Hanover asked. She was dressed in a handsome pantsuit – probably Chanel – light olive on top and pale olive below. The style was meant to imply luxurious comfort. She seemed rigid and uncomfortable in it.

'No, thank you,' Carly said, not wanting to interrupt the meeting with a bathroom break.

'You're a native, aren't you?' The question was assumptive more than inquisitive.

'Yes,' Carly said, knowing that being a third generation San Franciscan was a point in her favor.

'High school? Lowell?'

'Yes,' Carly said, acknowledging high school, not college, was the true native test. San Franciscans didn't care whether you went to Stanford or Cal, as long as you went to the right high school in the city. But there was also a clique that required attendance at the University of San Francisco for membership.

'What does your family do?'

'They're gone now. Restaurants. Paladino's was in North Beach. It's gone too.'

'I remember,' she said, with a slight smile. 'You didn't want to follow?'

'Too much for me. But very much part of my life. I'm at home with pots of boiling pasta, and the smell of garlic, fennel and oregano.'

Hanover didn't go any further with questions about Carly's pedigree.

'What I need is for someone with investigative experience to represent our family while the police sort this out.'

'I'm very sorry about your daughter,' Carly said.

Hanover nodded. It was an appropriate statement and a nod was the appropriate answer.

'You want me to investigate the incident?' Carly asked.

'Maybe. That might become necessary. But for now, what Walter and I desperately need is to keep this from becoming a JonBenét Ramsey media circus.'

Carly remembered how the parents of the murdered little beauty pageant child were raked in the press. Did they do it? Did they kill their own daughter? The case was reported everywhere, from network news and talk shows, to the tabloids. Because the murderer was never caught, suspicion hovered maliciously over the Ramseys for years, until finally, after Mrs Ramsey died, they were officially cleared.

'We need to have someone work as much as possible with the police. We need to know what they know. We need to keep the media off our front lawn and out of our lives. We have other children to think about. Their lives. We don't want them destroyed to feed the press's insatiable appetite for titillation.'

'I'm honored that you've asked me, but wouldn't you be better served by a large firm with unlimited resources?'

Hanover smiled.

'Whoever works with us will have a window into our lives. As you might guess, we are uncomfortable with that. We are private people. And we are not perfect. We have skeletons, of course. Any family does. They have nothing to do with this. You will be privy to information the public has no right to know. You'll no doubt see us at our worst as well as our best. We need to have the utmost discretion. Having twenty or thirty people involved is not the way to keep our lives private.'

'I understand.' While the newspapers would report a drive-by shooting that killed an innocent bystander, the coverage would be done in days. The death of the daughter of people as prominent and powerful as Walter and Pamela Hanover would be news for days and months. And it was likely it would never go away. Not completely.

'You'll have to sign some papers, promise not to write a tell-all,' she said with that same faint smile. The meeting was coming to an end. 'Our attorney is drawing up the agreement, primarily a non-disclosure contract. You'll work with her as well.' Hanover again smiled weakly. 'This will be our team. You, me, and Hannah Rodriguez.'

The three of them would meet in the morning. This afternoon Carly would research the Hanovers, call a few people she knew who traveled in those circles, and stop by the office for rent South of Market at four. If Lang wasn't there himself, someone named Thanh would show her around.

Five

'You have a Carly Paladino coming by this afternoon at four,' Thanh told Noah Lang as he came in to the office.

'Really? A client?'

'She's looking for office space,' Thanh said. Thanh, late thirties, Vietnamese, wore a leather jacket, charcoal T-shirt and jeans. Slender and good looking, today's attire would puzzle anyone trying to guess gender. This ambiguity about his long-time friend, Lang knew, wasn't an accident. Thanh could change his look daily from male to female and often did. Today it was androgynous – somewhere in the middle.

'You're quick.'

'I'm worth my weight in gold,' Thanh said. 'So far she's the only one to express interest, so be on your best behavior.'

'It's already four,' Lang said, looking at his watch. He was surprised how much of the day was gone; but then he shouldn't be. He'd slept most of the day, from 8 a.m., when he'd left Rose and Stern, until 2 p.m. when the newly minted widower had called to ask Lang what he knew about his wife's death.

The man hadn't seemed all that upset. He'd just wanted to know what Lang had seen, what the police had asked him, what he'd told them. After he briefed his client, he was simply told to send an invoice and the account would be settled. All business, no sentiment. That made Lang uncomfortable, but not uncomfortable enough to forgo a bill. He didn't bother offering the man his condolences. Seemed as if he didn't need them.

A knock on the office door came promptly at four. When Carly Paladino came into the office she tried to hide her disappointment.

'Mrs Paladini?' Lang said, standing up, noticing his attractive visitor's initial reaction as she glanced around the room.

'Paladino,' she said. The correction was friendly.

'Are you related to Jack Palladino, the big-time PI?' Lang asked.

'Maybe fifty generations ago in Italy. Who knows? Anyway he spells his name with two Ls. I only use one.'

'Why waste an "L" I always say.'

She looked around. She wasn't liking the place any better.

'Not what you expected?' Lang asked.

Thanh made a face.

'I'm Noah Lang, this is Thanh, my assistant.'

'Nice to meet you.' Her eyes left neither of them out. 'You know, I'm not sure I even know what I'm looking for.'

She had dark hair, falling straight down toward but not quite touching her shoulders. The hair was in just enough disarray to make it right. Lang didn't like looks that were too perfect. She was about his age – give or take – maybe a pound or two beyond the ideal. That showed him she wasn't starving herself to look good. That was in her favor too. He was wary of too much sacrifice in the name of vanity. A little? Fine. Her eyes were alive, but they still showed amused disappointment.

'But this definitely isn't it,' Lang said. 'Right?'

'He's a remarkable sales person,' Thanh said. 'Look around, see all the signs of prosperity.' Thanh had already given up on closing the sale.

Carly tried to imagine Pamela Hanover in this room with a battered old wooden desk, a stiff wooden chair, a couple of beat-up filing cabinets, and a brown vinyl sofa.

'What do you do?' Lang asked.

'Investigation, security consultant.' She smiled, catching his surprise. 'Not what you expected?' She unslung the cloth satchel from her shoulder and dropped it on the sofa.

'I didn't know what to expect. The rent is reasonable,' Lang said.

'Yes, I suspect it is.' She was sounding snooty. She didn't want to sound snooty.

'What is the rent?' Lang asked Thanh.

Thanh explained the rent and what kind of clerical support could be provided.

'I work Tuesdays and Thursdays and I'm available for other kinds of assignments at an additional hourly wage,' Thanh said, ever the entrepreneur.

'I see,' she said.

'There is another room,' Lang said, leading her to the small, window-less room where he had stored his belongings during the time he'd lived in his office.

She looked and smiled. It was clear she wasn't buying any of it.

'It says Tracker Investigations on the door,' she said.

'Yes, it does,' Lang said.

'That's the name of your company?' she asked.

'No, it was the name of the senior partner.'

'And where is he now?'

'In a jar on someone's mantle, I believe,' Lang said. He intended to shock. He wanted a read on this woman who seemed a little cold on the surface.

She laughed. She wasn't easily thrown. She knew what he was doing.

'Position of honor. We should all be so lucky,' she said, heading toward the exit. 'Thank you both for your hospitality.'

'We could redo the sign on the door. Needs to be done anyway.'

'Well . . .'

'You could be on top.'

'What?'

'On the door. Your name could be on top.'

'That won't be necessary.'

'I could move my desk over there, and you could have the window,' Lang said, noticing the layer of soot that made the office light gray. 'We could even wash the window.'

'Does the peeping Tom standing on the fire escape come with it?' Carly said.

Lang looked back.

'Yes, he does. That's actually peeping Barry. Barry Brinkman. They won't let him smoke inside his office. We have the good fortune of sharing a fire escape.'

'We could not only clean the window, but create a no-smoking zone.'

'That's all right,' she said. 'We wouldn't want to remove the character.'

He could see she was begging off.

'I'm open to sprucing the place up,' Lang said. 'A plant or two.'

'Some paint,' Thanh said.

'This is the first place I've looked,' she said. 'I've got to get a little perspective. I know how to reach you.'

'Don't you want to know about restrooms, who else is in the building?' Lang asked.

'You want me to be polite?'

'No,' Lang said.

'No,' she said, moving toward the door. 'Good luck.'

She waved. It was a kindly if not slightly dramatic wave – a happy 'ta ta' kind of gesture. She left.

'It's tough saying goodbye,' Lang said to Thanh.

'If this line of work isn't your thing,' Thanh said, making a sweeping gesture of the office and no doubt Lang's career, 'you could always sell Girl Scout cookies. So smooth. And the window. How could she turn down that kind of offer?'

'I know. I try to be charming and . . .'

'And you end up being . . .'

'Shhhhhhh. No need to state the obvious. Thing is I liked her.' He went to his desk and sat, put his feet up, and looked at the door. 'Anyway, she'll be back.'

'Why would she do that?' Thanh asked.

'She forgot her bag.'

'Oh, the private eye thing again,' Thanh said. 'You're good.'

The door opened. Carly peeked in before she entered.

'I would have just left it, you know, but my life is inside.'

Lang and Thanh smiled. Lang gestured with a 'ta ta' kind of wave.

'She's too good for you,' Thanh said.

'Isn't everybody? I liked her. Knows how to dress. The loose blue shirt and Ralph Lauren slacks. Nice. More casual and more fun than you'd think.'

'You know all that?' Thanh asked.

'Colors her hair, but subtle, just enough to soften the black.'

'Sounds like you're trying to sell a car or a condo.'

Lang looked out of the window, down at the narrow street, saw her get into her Mini Cooper.

'See, she'd fit right in,' Lang said. 'Little car, little street.'

'It's an alley,' Thanh said.

'No, it's a street. San Francisco has no alleys, or rivers.'

'What?'

'Maybe an alley or two. But no rivers. Not one single river, not even a little one.'

Carly went light on the wine. One glass as she nibbled on some grapes and some old, hard stinky cheese. She forgot what it was, but it was good. She had stopped at the library, picked up some books – some history, some gossip – about the old San Francisco families and what they were like then and now. She knew a lot simply by living in San Francisco all her life, their lives touching hers from time to time. But she knew more by reading about them in the society pages of *7X7 Magazine, The San Francisco Chronicle* and the *Nob Hill Gazette*, as well as the occasional tell-all.

She did some Google searches. She keyed into Lexis-Nexis. She had a password through Vogel Security, which they hadn't cancelled yet. So she got a thorough financial picture of the Hanovers – their assets, charities, giving patterns. They were major donors to the San Francisco Opera, Ballet and Symphony, as well as several nonprofits devoted to women's health, starving children, and international education. They were generous with their money and with their time. The Hanovers were no doubt courted by every major charity in the city.

Nothing negative in the press. Their sons, 21 and 23, had no police record, but then they might not if they had committed any crimes before they reached 18. Carly wondered about the skeletons Pamela Hanover mentioned. It was true though. What family didn't have secrets?

Her mind drifted from the Hanovers from time to time. She revisited her afternoon appointment at Tracker Investigations. There was something about Lang, something she found attractive. No, she corrected herself. Interesting, not attractive. She found him easy to be around, but in a way that seemed contradictory she was also very wary. He was a little too 'street' for her. She wasn't a snob – she hoped she wasn't a snob – but he could do with a little refinement. Why was she even thinking about him? It was the wrong place for her to set up business, wasn't it?

She plucked a piece of cheese from the plate, followed it with a sip of wine. She thought she might like being her own boss. It wasn't easy talking herself out of a second glass.

Gratelli returned to the Hanovers at 10 a.m., this time with two additional, very groggy homicide inspectors – Rose and Stern. Gratelli took Walter Hanover aside. He was a young sixty, older than his wife by twenty years, tall, casually but expensively dressed in a gray sweater, pink shirt, and gray slacks. He wore an old Rolex – the discreet model, not the one that looked like it belonged to a submarine commander. The two of them went to what Gratelli imagined to be the library. Walls of books, many of them leather-bound. So far, the Hanovers were living up to the stereotype of old, established, rich families.

Gratelli sat on a comfortable, worn leather Chesterfield sofa. Hanover sat on a high-backed leather chair. He crossed his legs as gentlemen do, at the knees. He seemed comfortable.

While Gratelli talked with Walter, Rose and Stern would separate Walter's two sons by an earlier marriage – Evan and Jordan – and ask questions about their relationship with their stepsister, what they knew about her life, and what they knew about the hours she was unaccounted for.

Gratelli, though he got a little tired of their constant banter, had respect for his fellow homicide inspectors' abilities. They'd been on homicide detail for at least twenty years, much like Gratelli. This wasn't unusual. Homicide was a desirable assignment and once assigned, inspectors tended to remain until they self-immolated, retired or died. But the assignment also usually went to cops who did well in their previous assignments, so Gratelli was comfortable his case wouldn't be compromised. The three of them would meet afterward and compare notes.

At that moment, Gratelli focused on the father. Walter Hanover reminded Gratelli of an eagle. He had shoulders that slanted down from a strong neck, a powerful nose, and cold, piercing blue eyes. He was a man who was comfortable in his own skin and no doubt made others uncomfortable in theirs. He was an investment banker – but the source of his wealth was a few generations old. His ancestors benefited from something less abstract – diamonds, or sugar, or railroads, or paper. He wasn't sure.

'I was aware that Olivia was around until around ten, I think,' he said when asked about his daughter. 'Then I guess she went to bed or at least to her room.'

'She doesn't say goodnight, give you a kiss goodnight?' Gratelli asked.

'No,' he said. It was an impatient 'no' – a short, one syllable word that he managed to make shorter.

'You have any idea who might have killed her?' he asked before Gratelli could ask him the same question.

'Do you?'

'No idea. But that's your job, isn't it? Should I expect something of substance any time soon?'

'That's what we're doing now, Mr Hanover. We're gathering information, just as I'm sure you do before making an investment. One thing leads to another usually. Was your daughter dating? Mrs Hanover didn't believe she was.'

'We're very busy, Pamela and I,' he said, acknowledging the suggestion that they hadn't taken enough interest in their daughter. 'We may not have known as much about her day-to-day activities as we should have. I regret that now.'

'Who would have known what was going on in Olivia's life?' Gratelli asked, trying to keep any disapproval from his voice.

'She was close to Pamela's secretary, Gray, and she has some friends from school.'

'Gray his first or last name?'

'Last. Gary Gray, I think.'

'Does your wife run a business from home?'

'Why do you ask?'

'She has a secretary,' Gratelli said.

'No,' Hanover said with a little too much patience in his demeanor. 'She's very active in charities. She's on various boards. It might surprise you how much work is involved.'

'And you didn't miss your daughter in the morning, the morning she was found?'

'I'm afraid not. In the summer, the children sleep in. They have activities. I had an early flight.'

'You left around noon, right?'

'Yes. The plane left around noon. I left about eleven.'

'Your own plane?'

'Used to. I charter if I need to.'

'I'll need the details of the flight,' Gratelli said. 'And what were you doing the previous night – before going to bed?'

'We had dinner around eight. I . . . I went over some proposals until maybe ten. Read a few chapters of a book and I was asleep.'

'All night?'

'Yes,' he said with exaggerated patience.

'You know of anyone who might want to harm you?'

'What do you mean?'

'Someone trying to get back at you . . . maybe for some deal you made or didn't make.'

'I can't imagine it.'

'What about Olivia's real birth father?' Gratelli asked.

Walter's disengaged expression didn't change.

'What about him?'

'What was his relationship like with his daughter?'

'Non-existent,' Hanover said. 'He lives an adventurous life, I'm told. Lives in Tahoe, but travels the seven seas.'

There was sarcasm, but not a lot of bitterness. Distant amusement.

Gratelli had already contacted the man and he was in Dubai. Reached him in a hotel there, which solidified his alibi. And there was no apparent motive. He paid no child support and had nothing to do with her. No point in killing her.

Gratelli gathered as much information from Walter Hanover as he could about the family and about Mr Hanover's business. Outside, he called the Hall of Justice and ordered background checks on Gary Gray, Mrs Hanover's secretary, and Anna Mendoza, the housekeeper.

Six

At eleven, Carly Paladino was back in Pacific Heights. Parking was difficult just about anywhere in the city, but the upscale neighborhood was a little less problematical. She parked her Mini Cooper in a space too short for Land Rovers and top-of-the line Mercedes.

The fog lifted early. Clear blue skies accentuated what would appear to be the ideal lives of those living in such a fine neighborhood. It was this that nagged at her. Something was wrong here. There was something missing or something that didn't fit.

Pamela Hanover's secretary brought her back to the office where the two had conversed the previous day. Despite its slightly masculine look, it was, it finally dawned on Carly, Mrs Hanover's office. Mrs Hanover introduced Carly to Hannah Rodriguez, a thirtyish, pregnant, Hispanic woman who was simply but stylishly dressed.

A woman brought in a silver service with a coffee pot, three cups and a plate of pastel-colored macaroons Carly recognized from her occasional trips to a local French bakery. They sat at a round table that fit well in the five-window bay. Light filtered through stained glass. Mrs Rodriguez, after general and understandably humorless pleasantries had been exchanged, talked about the 'plan.'

In just under an hour, Rodriguez and Carly learned their roles as the story played out. The only people authorized to talk to the media were the Hanovers. All questions would be referred to Gary Gray, who would in turn, contact the Hanovers, who would in turn, refuse an interview.

Rodriguez would be the liaison to the mayor and to the District Attorney. Paladino would be liaison to the police and instigate additional security for the house and set up the security for the services and the burial. If it appeared that anyone in the family was being investigated by the police,

Carly would be asked to conduct an investigation of her own and would be provided additional resources if required.

'No surprises,' Mrs Hanover said. She lifted her cell, pressed a button and Gary Gray appeared.

Carly wasn't quite sure, but there was something odd about all of this. All of this seemed less family – a member of it was dead, a young girl – and more corporate. It seemed as if this were a process set up to minimize the damage done to a product. She couldn't quite put this into concrete terms, but she felt quite capable of working in that environment. It just didn't seem right.

On the other hand, she understood what the family faced – an attack on them that would be extremely personal and public. Nothing was clearer to Carly than the notion that the US in general (and San Francisco in particular), despite protests to the contrary, was a very class-oriented society. The class the Hanovers inhabited certainly had its privileges, but there was also no doubt that it had its vulnerabilities. Their status, in this situation, was not altogether a good thing. Preparing against the onslaught by curious minds that want to know was a matter of self-defense. Still, Carly was uneasy.

Lang allowed the morning to become a guilty pleasure and was thinking about doing the same for the rest of the day. His evening stake-out gig was over. He had completed his work for Chastain B. West. And there was nothing else in the pipeline.

Buddha, a small-framed brown Burmese cat, crawled across Lang's shoulder. Having a cat was one of life's lessons. He came to San Francisco a couple of decades ago with knowledge of all the male taboos: never use an umbrella; never cross your legs at the knees; never use more than one hand to shake hands with another guy; never wear shoes with tassels; and never, never have a cat.

Some of the taboos were still in place. He'd never owned an umbrella even in wet San Francisco and had never bought a pair of shoes with tassels. However, before his sister died of cancer a year ago, she'd made him promise to take care of her three-year-old cat. He had promised. And he was determined to honor her last and only request.

It was touch and go for the first few weeks. Buddha had hidden away, refusing to eat, and Lang hadn't been sure the cat was drinking any water. One day he'd shown up on Lang's bed. Buddha blinked his big gold eyes and that was it. The two had become fast friends. Lang, though he would keep it to himself, believed the two actually communicated in a fashion that Lang would admit was psychic only if someone threatened to pull out his fingernails.

The cat was one of the reasons Lang finally broke down and rented a place to live. Like everything else in his life, it seemed, his place wasn't traditional. It was an old dry-cleaners. It had a Chinese name in gold on the storefront window. Behind the window was a wall of glass blocks so that although passers-by would see nothing inside, some light would filter in.

Inside was one large, generally untidy room that had a makeshift kitchen and the old restroom, remodeled to include a primitive shower.

The ceiling was high. No doubt the tracks for customer's dry-cleaning had run up to the top, while most of the ground floor had been used for cleaning and pressing. Fortunately there was a skylight in the center and there were windows in the back that overlooked a small walled-in patio to relieve that hiding-in-a-cave feeling. Inside, Lang had scrounged a long, primitively constructed table with mismatched chairs, a worn gray corduroy sofa and a few scattered chairs and side tables. One wall held CDs and DVDs. On the other wall was a large, wall-mounted television screen and a decent stereo system with a turntable. He had built a small loft in the back, where a mattress and small table resided and Buddha presided.

If he'd get some food in, he could hide out for days if need be.

Lang showered and walked to Koret, a recreation center that was part of nearby University of San Francisco. He didn't work out, but he did take some serious laps at their Olympic-sized pool. He tried to do this three times a week. He had spent his college summers as a lifeguard and this was one of the few physical activities he could subject himself to, and as much as he was willing to do to keep inevitable decrepitude at bay.

On his walk back, Carly Paladino kept popping up in his mind. He liked how she looked. She had a kind of casual elegance that didn't seem pretentious. She had a quick wit and a spirit that seemed to bubble just under the surface. There was something left to be tapped. He tried to figure out her age. He agreed with his previous guess. Hers was close to his — give or take a few years. There was no doubt in his mind that emotionally he hadn't gotten too much beyond 14 until recently when slowly he began to accept the fact that hanging out at a bar all night to have a one-night stand with someone he didn't know or particularly like was unfulfilling. He no longer did that. He wondered what her life was like. What did she do in the evening? Did she have a lover?

Night was still a few hours away. He stopped at a nice little bar on Fulton across from Lucky's Market and had a shot of vodka with a beer chaser. He'd have to make up his mind about dinner. He had nothing at his place. By his second drink, he noticed that the bar's clientele was younger and hipper. Unlike his younger self who would have felt the crowd off-putting, he decided that didn't matter one way or another.

It was dusk when he finished his walk home, mellowed a bit by the alcohol, but in the dim, depressing light, the suicide nagged at him. It was just one of those things that wasn't finished. And it needed finishing.

Gratelli had agreed to meet Stern and Rose at Tosca at eight that evening to debrief. Extra hours meant overtime and the only way for a cop to afford living in the city was to put in as much overtime as possible. While technically, they were still on the clock, that didn't prevent them from ordering something to drink.

Stern and Rose ordered something serious, Gratelli a glass of red wine. Age and worry complicated his digestive system. So no hard stuff. Tosca, a legendary North Beach hang-out for celebrities and eccentrics, wasn't a known cop favorite. Probably a good thing since no one would spot them drinking. But it was really that Stern and Rose gave in to Gratelli who lived in the area and had a fondness for the opera that played on the bar's jukebox. An old wooden bar, low light, leather booths and checkerboard floors created an old-world environment, which also pleased Gratelli. He blocked out the high-tech, slick, modern world whenever he had a chance.

'What did you get from the kids?' Gratelli asked.

'The older one's a piece of work,' Stern said.

'Evan?'

'Yeah. He seemed to regard his sister's death as a major inconvenience.'

'Where was he when it happened?' Gratelli asked Stern.

'In his bedroom, he said.'

'Any verification?'

'Problem is that at that time of night or morning, whatever, no one's wandering around the house doing bed checks. And you could get lost in that house anyway – front and back stairways, front, side and back entrances.'

'Why the insensitivity to the sister, do you think?' Gratelli asked. He was taking notes. Stern wasn't referencing any in his answers.

'One thing came out. They weren't real siblings. The two boys were Walter's kids by a previous marriage. And Olivia was Pamela's by a previous marriage. Apparently Walter's family is . . . uh, well . . . I don't know how to say it . . . more important.'

'His lineage?' Gratelli asked.

'That might be the right word,' Stern said.

'What are you getting?' Gratelli turned to Rose who interviewed the younger brother.

'Not so cold,' Rose said. 'But not broken up as far as I could tell.'

'Anything at all that rings false?'

'He was nervous. Could be because he's talking to a cop. Could be because he's talking to a black cop. Don't know. But what Stern said, you know, that is one big, fucking house. Somebody could come and go or go out and come back without anyone knowing it that time of night.'

'But alarm systems.'

'There's the rub,' Rose said, taking a sip of Scotch. 'Even if the girl wandered out by herself, she would have to use the code. I think it makes it unlikely that we're talking about some kidnapper off the street.'

It was highly likely, Gratelli thought, that the victim knew her killer. In the morning, he would probably learn how she'd died and if she'd been raped.

'The kids work?' Gratelli was pretty sure he knew the answer but asked anyway.

'You shittin' me,' Stern said. 'Evan was just home for a few days to prepare for a trip to Spain for the summer. He's a student at Stanford.'

'Studying what?'

'Philosophy. I mean who else could get a degree like that and not worry about his future?'

'What about Jordan?' Gratelli asked Rose.

'Jordan's studying literature at Stanford.'

'Both at the same university?'

'Yeah. They're close. They're both going to Spain.'

Stern looked at his notes.

'Evan said something about Olivia seeing some little street urchin. That's what he called him, a street urchin. Didn't know his name. Just that he had dirty hair and dirty sneakers.'

'That's it?' Gratelli asked.

The two cops nodded.

'Evan's the leader then?' Gratelli said.

'We didn't see them together,' Rose said. 'We each took one. But based on what I'm hearing, that'd be a good guess.'

'The girl?' Rose asked. 'What's her story?'

'Just back from high school, some private school. Planned to head east to a university out there,' Gratelli said. 'We're still filling in the blanks on her.'

The three cops separated in front of Tosca after another drink. Though it returned later than usual, the fog was heavy. One could still make out the lights of Vesuvio's and City Lights Bookstore across the street. Even so, a person could vanish in the mist half a block up the street.

Gratelli walked home, back up Columbus and then right, past the bawdy strip joints on Broadway. The streets were lively. A couple of scantily clad girls stood in front of one club, one smoking a cigarette, while a young man tried to lure pedestrians inside. There was no smoking inside, of course. That would be criminal.

The clubs were just one part of North Beach and Gratelli didn't mind them. His place was up the steep incline that ran alongside Enricos. One of these days he would no longer be able to make the climb home. In the interim, it helped him keep in the shape he was in, such as it was.

Carly put logs in the fireplace and lit them, grabbed a light blanket and climbed into the big, old comfy sofa with her books and laptop. It was a great night to be inside. The weather was part of the summer pattern, which often confused tourists who came to San Francisco in June and July bringing Bermuda shorts and tank tops. One could see them waiting for the cable cars, shivering, and wondering if they were really in California.

What she learned from the light and harmless gossip in the *Chronicle*'s society section and in *The Nob Hill Gazette*, the society newspaper of record, and juicier gossip from the tell-all books was that Pamela Hanover was Walter's second wife, twenty years younger. His first wife Katherine remarried one of Walter's former business associates, but he got custody of the kids. Carly discovered that of Walter's two good-looking sons, the older one, Evan, was out and about at all the right clubs and dined at all the right restaurants with beautiful young women who either came from the 'right' families or from the acting and modeling scene. Jordan, the younger brother, was involved in the arts and tended to hang out as anonymously as possible with young writers and painters. If there were romances, they were kept quiet.

Katherine did not like Pamela, blaming her for the break-up of her nearly thirty-year marriage. There was some hesitancy on the part of her peers to invite the two women to the same events, though it was difficult. Katherine came from old money, one of the city's unofficial first families. And Pamela, while only of a slightly lesser rank, had married into one. Tough times for those holding gala fund-raisers.

There was little mention of Olivia in any context, perhaps because she was still young. Perhaps there would have been some introduction to the public once she turned eighteen or twenty-one. Perhaps not. Unlike her siblings her photographs didn't appear in either the *Chronicle* or *Gazette*.

But in the photo Pamela had given her of the young woman, Carly thought she saw pain. The eyes expressed something sad. If it wasn't pain exactly, perhaps it was disillusionment. Whatever it was, the photograph was compelling. There could be no justification for the taking of Olivia's life.

Seven

The medical examiner and crime scene investigators had done their jobs. When Gratelli showed up in homicide, the medical examiner was there with two cups of coffee – one for Gratelli.

'We've got a lot here,' she said. 'Olivia died of hypoventilation, that is respiratory depression.'

'Because?'

'Morphine overdose. But there were slight traces of ketamine.'

'The rape drug. Was she sexually abused?' Gratelli asked.

'Let me finish. The morphine was likely introduced by needle through her arm. This could have been an accidental overdose. There are no other needle marks. Nothing to suggest this was a pattern. Or she could have had a low tolerance so that a normal dose turned fatal. The ketamine is disturbing but can be taken recreationally.'

'Semen?'

'Yes. We're running DNA now. Thing is there are no signs of bruising or any kind of real force anywhere on the body.'

'She knew her killer,' Gratelli said. 'Time of death?'

'I'll send all of this up to you, but probably no more than two hours before she was found. That puts it at about three in the morning.'

'Thanks,' Gratelli said.

'Let me know if you need anything more.' She left.

He sipped his coffee. It wasn't office-brewed. She'd brought it from across the street. Bless her, he thought, sitting down and opening the file someone had placed in his chair. It was from CSI.

The bad news was that they had found nothing in the area where her body had been placed. The good news was that they'd confirmed the death had not occurred there, but was dumped afterwards. They'd found no computer and no cell phone. Odd, they had thought, considering her age.

They had also searched her phone records and found that while there was no cell phone on her or in her room, she had not one cell phone but two and the phone calls were predominantly back and forth, one to the other. They were in the process of seeing if they could track down the phones by triangulating the various cell phone towers.

Gary Gray was twenty-eight, had no police record. He'd graduated from San Francisco State with a degree in business. He lived in Noe Valley.

There was another male registered at that address. Other than an old DUI, the roommate had no police record. He worked at a nonprofit.

Anna Mendoza, originally from Mexico, was legal. She had a green card. She worked for the Hanover family and had gone with Walter when he divorced Katherine, presumably because of the children. She had worked for them for almost all of her time in the country, probably before she was legal. That's how these things go.

Gratelli suddenly knew considerably more than he did fifteen minutes ago. He didn't want to jump to conclusions. But he felt that if the phones had not been tossed, they would lead to someone, if not the killer, then someone who knew a whole lot more about Olivia's life than her family.

This was good. He hoped this could be settled quickly. There was the political angle, the press issues, and the fact that he had a number of other homicides to solve, most of them gang-related and almost impossible to close. There would be public pressure too. Another wealthy white girl getting all the attention, while African–American and Latino kids were whacked by ricocheting bullets from half-blind gang bangers.

The ringing of his phone diverted him from mentally listing all those things that required 'immediate' attention.

Carly's conversation with Inspector Gratelli was no more or less than she had expected. He wasn't very forthcoming, though he did say they were making progress. He thanked her for letting him know she would be involved with the case. After a gentle warning to not get in the way, he acknowledged the extra difficulty a family like the Hanovers faced with this kind of tragic incident.

She could cross that off her list of things to do that morning. She would call the General, or Frank now that they weren't employer-employee any more, to see if they would be available to work with her on the security of the house and provide security for the funeral. She bore Vogel Security no ill will and genuinely believed they were the best in the Bay Area in these kinds of matters. She thought it best, given her new circumstances, to build rather than burn bridges.

In a brief phone call to the General, she was reassured they would be happy to do the work. This was no surprise. The Hanovers were the Hanovers. Just working for them was a high recommendation of Vogel Security. Carly would meet with one of her former colleagues, a specialist in this kind of work, to go over the Hanover house and grounds the same afternoon.

Carly felt good. She was barely a day out of her regular job and she had a good gig. She checked Craigslist again for potential office space. She found reasonably priced space in Hayward, Redwood City, South San Francisco, and Milpitas. She needed to be in the city. She needed to have a city address. And inside the city, the neighborhood is important. She wanted clients who could afford to pay a decent rate. That wouldn't happen in Daly City or Bayview or in the Richmond. Again, she confronted the possibility that she was a snob and decided that in some ways she was. She wanted to do higher-end work, not repos and bail skips.

She managed to find a couple of San Francisco possibilities, but she soon found out that some of those who rented out office space had expectations of their own. Private investigators, especially those without an established reputation, a financial statement and a business plan, weren't welcome. She found she wasn't the only one who was choosy.

Lang went into the office in the afternoon to check the answering machine. It was the number listed in the Yellow Pages. He hadn't quite figured out how to do it remotely. An envelope had been slipped under the door. A bike messenger, according to the form attached, delivered it.

He opened it. A check from the recent widower. Lang hadn't billed him. Didn't matter. The check was for more than Lang would have billed him. The guy was clearly moving on and he wanted to tie up his past. While money was always welcomed – all the more so because he had no job lined up – the hurried nature of it all added to Lang's discomfort with the situation surrounding the woman's death.

Lang checked the answering machine. No calls. There was a note from Thanh saying that he sent out an email to all of the security firms he could find on the Internet, listing the office space. So far, Thanh wrote, no takers.

There weren't a lot of private eyes any more. Or at least, it wasn't an expanding field. Most worked for established firms.

One of the problems with this kind of work was that it was either too busy and he was exhausted or there was nothing to do and he was left twiddling his thumbs. He would cash the check. He would catch a movie, grab a bite to eat and get home in time to watch Letterman.

Gratelli told the cops to hold the kid for questioning until he could go through the apartment. They had called both cell phones and found them in the same place. A young man had both phones in his possession. Gratelli put a search warrant into the works and headed to the Tenderloin, where the young man was found.

The neighborhood was rough – a domain for the down and out, the victims of pain and the addiction to drugs that promise relief but in the end cause more pain. More recently, Vietnamese immigrants were settling in the area. Increasingly the Tenderloin was becoming 'Little Saigon.' Things were looking up.

He didn't immediately talk to the suspect who was handcuffed and in the possession of a large patrol officer in the hall outside the room. The boy looked sad and confused.

Inspector Bonita Morrow accompanied him inside the tiny studio. With her partner on sick leave, they paired her with him. Gratelli had no problem with it. He liked her. She was by-the-book, but not obnoxious about it. She was serious about her work, but had a sense of humor. A uniformed cop let them in.

The only light came from a window that looked into a light well. A mattress was on the floor, bed unmade. There was a small desk, but surprisingly no computer. No phone. No TV. A Sony Walkman was on a crumbling bureau, and a stack of CDs. The kid was well behind in the technology department, Gratelli thought, but then again the kid was ahead of him. There was a pile of notebooks on the floor beside the bed.

Gratelli picked up the top notebook, flipped it open. All in Chinese. At least he thought it was Chinese. He gathered the rest and put them in the bag that would be taken back to homicide.

The small bathroom was clean, not sterile, but clean. Toothbrush, toothpaste, soap, brush, safety razor and shaving cream were on the edge of the sink. Gratelli wondered how often the kid had to use them. Inside the medicine cabinet, there were no prescription drugs, just a bottle of Aleve, some Neosporin, cotton swabs, and deodorant. No cologne. A bar of soap and a plastic bottle of shampoo were on the ledge that surrounded the tub. A towel hung over the shower bar.

Nothing. Just the necessities.

The toilet tank contained only water. Nothing behind the tiny radiator.

Morrow was still in the kitchen, if you could call a 3-foot refrigerator and a hotplate a kitchen. When Gratelli came in she looked at him. He shrugged. She nodded toward the kitchen cabinet, shook her head. Nothing.

'Cheerios, soy milk,' she said.

The young man's lack of interest in material possessions would keep things simple, Gratelli thought. They found no drugs. There would be no phone records to comb through. And from the lack of mail or a computer, there wasn't likely much of anything to connect him to the outside world – no bank accounts, no correspondence from family, no trails through the Internet.

The apartment manager didn't have the boy's application on file. Didn't fill out one. Paid first, last and deposit. The manager didn't see the boy hanging out with anyone. He caused no problems. He paid his rent on time. In cash.

With the exception of the cell phones, which weren't even his, the kid was completely off the grid. Complete anonymity.

The two homicide inspectors continued to look, this time checking for hiding places. They didn't know if he was hiding anything, but he had to have money to pay the rent, to eat. Nothing underneath the mattress, no way to stash anything inside. The small closet held a few pairs of jeans and a couple of black jackets of different weights. His black running shoes were empty. The bureau drawers yielded black socks and black underwear. Gratelli smiled. It didn't take Morrow and Gratelli long to run out of real estate to search.

'Let's talk,' Gratelli said to the kid in the hallway.

The uniform gave Gratelli a plastic bag. It contained a wallet, keys, and some change. Gratelli removed the wallet, fished through it. Not much in it. Some ones and a five. He had two driver's licenses, both with his picture and different birth dates and different names. One listed his name as Daniel Lee with an address that may or may not exist in New Mexico. Gratelli would have to check to see if this was even a good counterfeit of a New Mexico License. The other license was in the name of Byron Siefert. It was unlikely that this dark-haired boy with pecan skin was a Siefert. Could be, but for now Gratelli would call him Daniel Lee. There was a piece of paper with a series of numbers written on it tucked in the wallet with a twenty and three ones. Nothing else.

Gratelli couldn't make out the nationality. The kid had a mixed heritage, he guessed, Asian and something, maybe black or Latin. Dark hair, longish. Brown eyes, Gratelli had noticed in the brief glance he'd had when the boy looked up. Nice looking in a waifish way.

'What's your name?' Gratelli asked him.

The kid continued to look down.

'Gotta know your name.'

No response.

'You know Olivia's dead, right?'

The kid looked up. His eyes were sad, but there was fire behind them.

'You do it?' Gratelli asked.

Nothing.

'Let me tell you something. We have semen. You know about DNA, right?'

Nothing.

'If you and Olivia had sex, we'll know it. If you're eighteen or older you are guilty of statutory rape. And, frankly, that may turn out to be the least of your worries. You're on your way to a murder charge. You have any idea what that means?'

'We're only a year apart,' the kid said.

'Might as well be twenty. She's under age and you're not. That's the way it goes.'

'I didn't kill her.'

'When did you last see her?' Gratelli asked. Maybe he should ask these questions at the Hall. Maybe this was less threatening.

The kid shook his head.

'Are you going to talk to me?'

The boy looked at him squarely, then shook his head.

'We're taking you in, you know.'

He nodded.

Eight

'I didn't wake you, did I?'

The voice on the other end of the phone was familiar, but it took Lang a moment to figure out who it was.

'Chaz, what's up?' It was Chastain West. Lang had drifted off on the sofa. He looked at his watch. It was only 9.10 p.m.

'You working?'

'Not at the moment,' Lang said. 'I'm trying to stay awake until bedtime.'

'No, I mean do you have a job?'

'No, you need me?'

'A young guy was arrested for the murder of Olivia Hanover . . .'

'That going to be yours? Jesus!'

'At least for the moment. I'm going to meet him at ten tomorrow morning. I'd like it if you could come along.'

'Done.'

They agreed to meet at 9.30 a.m. at a place across the street from the jail. Chastain said there wasn't much to tell because he wasn't told much – just that the kid doesn't have a name that checks out and refuses to talk.

Buddha eyed Lang from his perch on the table. He sat in the small pool of light coming down from a pin spot, a perfect pose, tail curled around the front as if he was modeling for a formal portrait. He did that a lot.

Lang went to the refrigerator, pulled out the plastic container that held the roasted chicken he got from Costco a couple of days ago. He prayed it was still good. He wasn't encouraged when Buddha declined an offer to share, but Lang made a sandwich with it anyway. Buddha was more particular than he was. He looked for a beer. Out.

'I need to talk to the family,' Gratelli said.

Carly had put down one of the tell-all books she'd gotten from the library and picked up the phone. She thought it might be Nadia, who was due back from her trip at any time.

'Thank you for checking in with me.'

There was a moment of silence.

'How urgent?' Carly asked.

'Tonight if possible. Very early tomorrow, if not. We have a person of interest. I need to know if any of them have seen him around.'

'I can come pick it up, show it to them,' Carly said. She was pretty sure she wouldn't get by with it. There was another long silence. Gratelli was an experienced cop. He wasn't buying it. 'OK. Just checking.'

'Pushing until you know where the line is,' Gratelli said.

'Yes.'

'So you know where the line is now?'

'Yes. I'll get right back to you,' Carly said.

'Thanks.'

She called the Hanovers. Instantly voicemail clicked on. She called Mrs Hanover's cell phone. Same thing. She called Gary Gray.

'Gary?'

'Yes.'

'This is Carly Paladino. Something's happened on the case and I need to get in touch with Mrs Hanover or Mr Hanover, somebody, but nobody's picking up. Are you there?'

'No, I'm at home.'

Carly tried to measure the coolness in his voice.

'Ms Paladino, they pretty much shut down after seven or eight. I mean that's when they shut down to the outside. We're all out of there by seven unless they're hosting something at the house. This is their time.'

'I see. When do they open back up?'

'Anna's there before seven in the morning. I arrive at ten.'

'Could you be there early tomorrow? The police will be there at eight.'

'I think you need to reschedule them,' Gray said.

'Oh, good,' she said, flipping her phone closed. She knew that this was precisely why the Hanovers had hired her. She knew it, but now she understood the full impact. As it turned out, she wasn't a liaison to the police exactly; she was supposed to control them.

Gratelli didn't accept the polite refusal and counter offer. He reminded her in a calm but firm way that he wasn't a member of their staff and that this wasn't a sales pitch.

'Have them down here at nine a.m. tomorrow morning,' he said as if he were discussing the weather. 'All of them. Mom, Dad, and the kids or we'll be there at nine fifteen with sirens and a SWAT team.'

'I'll relay the message,' she said. She didn't look forward to a confrontation with any of the Hanovers at this first task. Yet, she kind of liked the idea, as erroneous as it was in contemporary America, that at least in this case they stood equal to others in the eyes of the law. She also hoped that Gratelli wouldn't lose his pension.

She called Gary back, told him the repercussions. He resisted at first. But she convinced him that they should show a passionate interest in finding out who killed their daughter. Most parents would. She didn't add that.

Concessions were made. Carly joined Gratelli, the Hanover family and the District Attorney in one of the DA's conference rooms. The DA, a striking black woman who, like most San Francisco mayors and DAs, was a celebrity. She remained standing and introduced herself with a short speech about how much she appreciated the Hanovers coming in and hoped they would understand that the police had certain protocols and responsibilities.

A man in a gray pinstriped suit, a little too tailored for Carly's taste, came in and the DA introduced Howard Dane, an assistant DA who would handle the case personally. Dane went to the window as his attractive boss smiled and excused herself. Gratelli sat on one side of the large table poker-faced and quiet. The Hanovers – Walter, Pamela, Evan and Jordan – sat in a line on the other side of the table.

Carly stood by the door with Gary Gray.

Dane repeated much of what the DA said, vowed that both the police and the DA's office would not rest until Olivia's killer was found. Then he turned the meeting over to Gratelli.

'Thank you for coming down,' he said. 'It is important that we move as quickly as possible. The longer a crime goes unsolved, the less likely it will be solved.' He looked at the parents.

Pamela gave her subtle nod.

'What is the code you enter to disarm your security alarm?' Gratelli asked in the general direction of the Hanover clan.

'I beg your pardon,' Walter asked. It was a more polite way to ask 'Why?'

'Please humor me,' Gratelli said, unfolding a worn piece of paper he had plucked from the kid's wallet. 'You can change it when you get home. In fact, I suggest you do if you give me the series of numbers I expect you will.'

Walter recited the code.

'You'll need to change it.'

Gratelli refolded the paper. He opened a file that was on the table in front of him. It was a photograph.

'Have any of you seen this person?' Gratelli slid a photograph across the table. The older boy picked it up first.

'That's the street trash Olivia was seeing on the sly,' Evan said.

Walter and Pamela seemed surprised or annoyed. It was difficult to tell.

'Why don't I know about this?' Pamela asked.

Evan's look seemed to dismiss her. His grin was barely perceptible, but Carly caught it.

'Jordan?' Gratelli asked, aware that the young man showed no surprise.

He looked at his brother briefly.

'What?'

'You know him?'

'Yes, I've seen him around.'

'You think he's responsible for Olivia's death?' Walter asked.

'At the moment, the signs point toward it,' Dane said. 'We're trying to nail some things down. Meanwhile, we are holding him.'

Gratelli noted Dane didn't tell the family what they were charging him with. Statutory rape, most likely, not murder. But the boy had the Hanover house security code in his wallet. He had the phones. He admitted he'd had sex with her. He, whoever he really was, wasn't exactly a pillar of the community, or at least the Hanovers' community. But what Gratelli really wanted was motive.

'Anything else?' Walter asked. He seemed eager to leave.

'Olivia,' Gratelli said, 'apparently had sex at some as yet undetermined time before her death.'

Four frozen faces, five counting Pamela's secretary.

'Do we know with whom?' Pamela said.

She was the only one who showed any emotion and that was only in her eyes. She continued to sit straight as a rod.

'We will,' Gratelli said.

'You will let us know,' Walter said stiffly. He stood. 'Are we through here?'

'I would like for Mr Gray to stay behind and chat with us,' Gratelli said. He looked at his watch. He and the assistant DA had another appointment at ten – this time with the public defender, some investigator and the boy, himself.

Gary Gray's eyes darted nervously from the police and DA to Pamela and Walter.

'We'll take the car, Gary,' Walter said, 'if you don't mind taking a cab when you leave.'

Gray nodded.

'I'll drop you back,' Carly said, using her voice for the first time since they gathered together. She could discuss the meeting with the Hanovers afterward. The best use of her time was to be around when they questioned Gray. 'I'll sit in, if you don't mind.'

The statement was directed at Gratelli.

'Sure. Just let him answer the questions. OK?'

'Absolutely.'

After the family filed out, Gratelli got up and gestured for Gray to take a seat, which he did.

'The guy in the picture,' Gratelli said, 'was in the house during the day?'

'You know, this is family business. I'm hired help.'

'They may make those distinctions. We don't. And bear in mind, there is an officer picking up Anna and bringing her in. We will be asking her the same questions.'

Gray looked at Carly, who took a deep breath, but remained quiet.

'Yes,' Gray said. 'He and Olivia hung out together.'

'How often?'

'Lately, just about every day. School's out.'

'What's his name?' Gratelli asked.

'Daniel.'

'Does he have a last name?'

'I'm sure he does,' Gray said. 'I'm sorry, I don't mean to be a smart ass. I don't now his last name. He and I weren't close. The two of them went up to her room. I would only see him come and go.'

'And Mrs Hanover never saw him.'

'Olivia went out of her way to keep him away from her. It wasn't hard. She never went to her daughter's room.'

'But Evan saw her.'

'Evan sees everything, knows everything.'

'Evan didn't like the boy.'

'Evan doesn't like anyone.'

'Olivia. Did Evan like Olivia?'

'No.' Gray folded his hands on the table as if he were the good student in third grade.

'Did Walter like Olivia?'

'Walter doesn't know – didn't know – Olivia existed.'

'You did. You knew Olivia existed.'

'I did. I felt sorry for her.'

'Why is that?'

'She was always an afterthought to the family. Jordan was civil to her, but not close. She talked to me. And she talked to me as if I were another human being.' He looked back at Carly, shook his head. 'I'm sorry. I'm talking too much.'

'You know, Mr Gray,' Gratelli said, 'this is more important than most anything you can think of. We appreciate your candor.'

'I'm supposed to keep some of these things private. It's my job.'

'No one is speaking for Olivia right now. She deserves a voice.'

Gray looked down. He cried.

Nine

Lang was surprised to see Carly Paladino leave the DA's conference room. She was with a youngish, stylishly dressed blond guy. They were followed by a gaunt-looking man with dark circles under his eyes. She obviously saw Lang. Eyes widened. Lang smiled and waved.

'Hello, Mr West. Good to see you again,' Gratelli said, and then introduced himself to Lang.

'Mr Lang is going to help me prepare for the defense,' West said. 'We thought it important to make the introductions since your paths might cross.'

'I appreciate that,' Gratelli said. 'You're licensed?'

'I am,' Lang said. He was going to let West do all the talking.

The three of them went into the conference room where they met the dapper Assistant DA, Howard Dane.

The discussions, mostly between West and Dane, centered on potential plea bargains. What would happen to the young man if he confessed? Dane was clearly eager to wrap everything up quickly. The DA and the police were eager to have a solved homicide. The murder rate was up. But not many were solved. The Hanovers wanted it to be wrapped up as well. They didn't want the public scrutiny. And they had strings to pull and knew how to pull them.

West no doubt sensed that but the DA, he said, was premature. They didn't have any evidence of murder. And that while technically based on his own admission, the young man might be guilty of having sex with an under-aged girl, no jury in San Francisco would convict him of it.

'We're talking about less than a year difference in their ages,' West said. 'I mean you've got the law on your side, but a jury is not going to buy it.'

Dane, who had not bothered to sit down, smiled. 'One thing we know is that the morphine wasn't self-administered. The victim was right-handed and the needle mark was in her right arm. We have DNA. When we have the semen match, we won't be worrying ourselves about statutory rape except as an example of his character. We'll be going for murder. He was the last person seen with her. He had the secret access code. He had both of the phones. Both of them. He has no alibi. And between now and the trial, we'll find out who he is. His silence about his past suggests we'll find a gold mine.'

'You've got a few facts mixed with a lot of speculation,' West said.

Lang knew West was blowing smoke. The evidence, circumstantial as it was, was overwhelming.

'And from what you've said,' West continued, 'both sides have their work cut out for them. In the meantime, the young man is young and vulnerable. You'll take care to protect him.'

'For now,' Dane said.

Standing up, West said, 'We'd like to spend some time now with . . . uh . . .'

'Daniel,' Gratelli said. 'It's as good a name as any.'

Carly's debriefing with the Hanovers took very little time and didn't include Walter, who was off pursuing one of his potential investment projects.

'Why wasn't Mrs Rodriguez there?' Mrs Hanover asked Gary Gray.

'She was unavailable.' Gary said it with a tone that said he would fill her in later.

Mrs Hanover, not wanting to wait for a further explanation, demonstrated her feelings with the tiniest expression of displeasure. And that, Carly began to understand, was her nature. It was if she could only afford a partial payment on her feelings.

'Unavailable?' she asked.

'She was having her baby,' Gary said.

Carly wasn't sure, given Mrs Hanover's stone face and lack of comment, whether that was a suitable excuse. Mrs Hanover looked to Carly.

'What did you make of it?'

'It's moving surprisingly quickly. It seems as if the police have a solid suspect. They are willing to move quickly. They are keeping the press away. This could be resolved in the next few days.' Carly thought better of leaving it like that. 'Not a promise, just a possibility.'

'Anything happen after I left?' Mrs Hanover asked.

Carly thought for a moment. This was dangerous territory either way it went. 'Nothing out of the ordinary. They asked Gary some questions about the young man and he mentioned that he had seen him – as had your son.'

'Why didn't I know about this boy, Gary?' she asked.

'It didn't seem important enough to bother you with. I'm sorry, obviously it was. I should have been more alert.'

He didn't look at Carly, or she at him.

'What are the next steps?' she asked.

'Finding out just who the young man is,' Carly said, and then thinking it was important to pave the way for the obvious. 'They will try to determine the nature of the relationship between Olivia and the boy.'

'You mean of a sexual nature?' Mrs Hanover asked.

'Yes.'

'Oh God,' she said.

'Depending on the circumstances, this may not go to court. A plea agreement would mean that the public part of this would be over fairly quickly.'

'Let's hope you're right,' she said. 'We need to try to make that happen.'

Carly picked up on the tone. It wasn't a suggestion. It was an order. And it became clear that the small gestures and the understated tones of her remarks weren't marks of a humble personality, but of unmitigated arrogance. She didn't have to say 'off with their heads.' All she needed to say in her world was 'their heads are no longer useful.'

'We only have fifteen minutes,' Chastain West said as the young man in orange clothes was led into the room. The prisoner was handcuffed and a single short chain insured that his steps would be short. It wasn't only to keep him from running, it was also to keep him humble. He looked like a bumbling Geisha.

The boy stared at West as if the attorney had just killed a puppy. He glanced at Lang with less hostility.

'We need to talk. I need to get a lot of information in a short amount of time, so please cooperate.' West no doubt picked up on the attitude. 'Your name is Daniel?'

If it was Daniel, it didn't matter, the boy refused to answer. West looked at Lang and shrugged. 'I've got to make a call.'

Lang knew what West was doing. He struck out. He hoped there would be something a little more positive between Lang and the young man.

'The other night,' Lang said, 'I was on a stake-out. I was hired by some guy to make sure his wife wasn't cheating on him. I didn't like the idea because I didn't like the guy, but it was work. It's what I do for a living. The woman killed herself while I was outside in the car. Or somebody killed her. I'm not sure. At any rate I feel really crappy about it. I feel responsible.'

'You're not,' the young man said. 'You couldn't have done anything.'

'That doesn't change how I feel. The fact of it I mean. If it is a fact. I feel rotten and I'm not sure there's anything I can do about it.'

The young man was quiet for a long time. Lang didn't want to press him. He'd let the silence go on for a while.

'I didn't kill Olivia.'

'You're going to have to help us help you then. We're the only thing you've got. And I'd feel even crappier if I fail on this job too.'

At first, Lang read distrust in the boy's eyes, but it seemed to dissipate.

'I would never have killed Olivia. The only thing of value we had was each other.'

'How did the two phones end up at your place?'

'She came over. We went for a walk,' he said. 'Then when we realized we needed to call it a night, we were closer to her house than mine. I walked her home. We forgot the telephones.'

'Makes sense. She sneak out a lot?'

'Yeah. Sometimes I sneak in.'

'They have a security system, I'm sure.'

'Olivia gave me the code.'

'You have sex with her?'

He nodded.

'Was it consensual?'

He nodded again.

'Do you have any idea who would have killed her?'

He thought for a while. Lang thought it too long.

'No. She felt very alone in that house. But she didn't say she thought someone would kill her.'

He was fighting back tears, stopping at times to hold it back before his own words got the best of him.

'Where are you from?'

He shook his head. He was done talking.

'You hiding something?'

He nodded.

'You don't like Mr West?'

'The black guy?'

'Yes. You have something against black guys?'

He shook his head. 'Suits,' he said. 'I hate suits.'

'Well, I hope you'll make an exception. I've worked with him. He's not going to make much on your case, I promise you. He's just trying to do the right thing. He's a good guy. Trust him.'

The young man looked at Lang, measuring him.

'I'll tell him to wear a sweatshirt next time,' Lang said. The kid shook his head again. 'I don't like to be the one telling you this. You're up against professional lawyers and homicide police. They want to close a case quick. The victim's family has more money than Argentina and if they think you did it, they will be hard to stop. And you? You got nothing.'

'I never did,' he said. He smiled a sad smile.

Carly slumped in her sofa. Pamela Hanover's parting words still ringing in her ears.

'While I have every confidence that Gary can handle the protocol of my social and charitable engagements,' she said, 'I never intended for him to deal with the police, nor is he capable of it. That's why I brought you on. And I want to make it clear to you that I do not ever want to be at the beck and call of a public employee again.'

By 'public employee' she meant the police department. Carly kept calm. She said nothing in return, but she questioned whether she wanted the job. 'Quit again?' she asked herself out loud. She wanted a drink, but it was way too early. She didn't want to start down that road.

When Carly asked Gratelli about Lang's presence, the inspector said he didn't know the guy, but that he was with Chastain West. West, Gratelli told her, was the public defender assigned to the young man alleged to have killed Olivia. It wasn't difficult for Carly to make the leap. The man who wanted to be her landlord was, in fact, working on the case as well. On the other side.

The 'small world' phenomenon was nothing new in San Francisco. If you removed the vast numbers of folks who came into the city in the morning to work and who left in the evening and if you removed the hundreds of thousands of tourists who visit the city at any given time, you would have a surprisingly small world indeed. The official city is roughly seven miles by seven miles and has a population roughly the same as Columbus, Ohio. The probability of people in the same line of work running into each other is high. A coincidence? Yes, but not a big one. Knowing who was going to pick through the Hanovers' garbage was also a leg-up. Then again, he probably figured out what she was doing there as well.

Maybe she should arrange lunch.

* * *

After Lang and West put their heads together on their problematic client, they decided Lang would take the lead with the young man until trust could be developed with West. West laughed when he was told that the basis for Daniel's enmity was that West wore a suit rather than anything racist.

'Can't win for losing,' he said, smiling at the humor not only of the moment but most likely of the universe.

They would have more time with Daniel when he was moved from the booking jail to slightly more permanent quarters. They would have more than fifteen minutes for the interview.

Lang's cell announced a call shortly after the two separated. Lang agreed to meet Carly for lunch – her treat – and after Carly turned down fish and chips at Edinburgh Castle, they agreed on Brenda's, a tiny place between Civic Center and the Tenderloin, that served genuine Creole.

The noise level was high when crowded, as it nearly always was, with many employees from the nearby federal building. He shouted over the din.

'I'm betting you're not here to talk about sharing an office,' Lang said, eyeing the fried oyster po'boy delivered to another table just inches away.

'No –' she kept her eyes on the menu – 'I'm not.'

'You want to know what I know about Olivia's death.'

'You could just let me tell you.'

'That would take all the fun out of it,' he said. 'But OK.'

'I want to know what you know about Olivia's death.'

'Nothing. Well, unless you have something else to talk about we've just exhausted lunch conversation.'

They were interrupted by the waiter who took their orders, an omelet for her and a po'boy for him. Seemed fitting, he thought. But he also ordered beignets. Too rare to pass up.

'I realize that one of the ways a defense attorney casts doubt on the guilt of his client is to make someone else the killer.'

'My thinking exactly,' Lang said.

'You're smug,' she said.

'It's the least of my bad traits. And you? You think that you are somehow superior because you have very moneyed clients.'

'My superiority has nothing to do with them,' she said, smiling. 'What I'm trying to do is find a way to work together professionally. We're all interested in making sure the person responsible for her death is the one who pays for it. And we'd all like for this to be over as quickly as possible.'

'Not if you're paid by the hour,' Lang said.

'C'mon,' she said, pretending to beg.

'Look, you and I can agree to be nice – and we should be nice – but in the end there's a whole lot of power going to fall on a young, power-less, isolated suspect. If you're going to get mad if I want to find out just what kind of family Olivia belonged to, you're going to get plenty mad.'

'No,' she said. 'I understand. But let's not do something underhanded. I don't want the media to get rich off of exploiting either of our clients. Let's work to get justice here. I expect you to dig into their lives and I plan to do what I can to protect them.'

'I'm not in the business of supporting the tabloids,' Lang said. 'Beyond that . . .'

'OK, this is a start,' she said, wanting the conversation to cool off. 'That's done. Let's talk about you.'

'Not a lot to talk about,' Lang said.

'What do you hate?'

'I don't hate much.'

'Surely something.'

'Sprouts.'

'That edges out war, famine and floods and –' she smiled – 'sprouts.'

'Alfalfa sprouts, bean sprouts.'

'Brussel sprouts?'

'It's a sprout, isn't it?'

'What else would you put on your list of things you don't like? Wait, are you a dog person or a cat person?'

'I'm kind of a person-person, if we're talking romance, especially.'

'My mother said she didn't trust a man who owned cats.'

'Add your mother to the list.'

'What?'

'Right after sprouts and before pillaging.'

'You own a cat,' she said. 'I'm sorry. My mother was a nice woman, really.'

'Nobody *owns* a cat anyway,' Lang said. He forced back a smile.

'You're serious?'

'Well, yes, I'm serious. But I don't take my seriousness too seriously.'

The food came.

'Just in time,' Carly said.

Carly had breakfast and Lang lunch. She decided she liked him and wanted to undo the results of her twenty questions game. The thing was, she always struggled with small talk. She talked about her family and her mostly corporate work for the security firm.

'I envy your connection with real people,' she said.

'Yes, it's incredible, all those wonderful bail jumps, unfaithful spouses, insurance cheats, bunko artists. I miss them too when I have a dry spell.'

'OK, OK. I'm having a hard time here. Why don't you talk about foot-ball or ask questions? Tell me about your life.'

'Question then. What do you think of me?' He grinned.

'Well . . .'

'I was kidding.'

'No, let me answer that. You are a smart ass.'

'You're quick with the obvious.'

'Deep down I think you are a happy guy.'

'Now, I'm insulted,' Lang said. 'I want to be dark, brooding. That's much more romantic.'

Truth was, Lang admitted to himself, that he'd passed through years of angst and bitterness. He was angry about being an outsider, someone who for some inexplicable reason couldn't fit in. Now, in his general reclu-siveness, he wasn't happy in a bubbly way but found pleasure in many small moments.

'You're looking for romance, are you?' she asked.

'No. I appreciate it as an abstract concept.'

'It's the second time in our short conversation you've mentioned romance.' She smiled wryly.

'But then, who's counting?'

'Counting to two wasn't a challenge.'

'I'm sure you were very good at math.'

'I wasn't.' She took a bite of beignet. 'What do you think of the case?'

'I want to be clear here. I work for the defense attorney. Anything I find out goes to him and him alone. That's the way it works.'

'I meant generally. What does your gut tell you?'

'Gut speaking. He didn't do it. But what do I know about these things?'

He thought about the suicide and how his gut told him it wasn't what it looked like. And it probably was what it looked like.

'You?' he asked.

'At this moment,' she said, 'it's hard to imagine that it's anyone else.'

Ten

Lang was engaged in opposition research. It wasn't likely that he would get to conduct an interview with the Hanovers. They had no reason to talk to him and every reason not to. However, there was a former Hanover who agreed — Walter's first wife, mother of Evan and Jordan. Thanh, playing the role of dutiful secretary to the principal of Lang Investigations, arranged it on short notice.

It was a little after three when Lang arrived to talk with Katherine Wexford, widow of real estate tycoon Winston Wexford. Katherine came to the door herself, a tall woman with sharp features and the face of an attractive horse. The smile was large and genuine, revealing slightly yellowed teeth. There was no evidence that she defied nature with needles or scalpels. She looked to be the fifty she probably was. She was attractive in her way, so different from the tight-skinned, plump-lipped, heavily made-up woman he expected.

'It's a shame that a sad death is the only way for us to have a little excitement these days. Please come in.'

'You're here by yourself?' Lang asked.

'I have a pistol hidden in every room,' she said, smiling. 'So don't get any ideas I don't find interesting.'

'OK,' Lang said. She flirted, but he suspected that was just her way.

'That nonetheless gives you a lot of latitude.'

She led him down a long hallway, well-dressed rooms on either side. At the end was what in middle-class homes would be called a family room. He had no idea what something so grand would be called in a home like this. Less formal than a living room, it was still a bit intimidating. A wall of windows overlooked the bridge and bay.

'Something to drink?' she asked.

'I am fine, thank you.'

'Well,' she said, settling in next to him, 'let's get right at it then.'

Closer now, he could see her weathered face. From some of the photographs artfully scattered about, he guessed heavily lined flesh came from hours on the high seas and that her lanky, fit body, came from toting barges or lifting bales or hoisting sails or whatever they have to do on those boats. There was a photograph of Winston and her two sons, Evan and Jordan. Evan stood tall, but had more of a smirk than a smile on his face. Jordan slouched slightly. An intellectual posture, sensitive and less certain, Lang thought. He wondered why Walter got custody.

'Tell me about Walter,' Lang said.

She got up quickly. 'This does call for a drink,' she said. 'You sure I can't twist your arm?'

'Nothing for me,' Lang said. 'I'm on the clock.'

'Yes, but you are the Lang in Lang Investigations. I'm sure you could without having your pay docked.'

'I try to set a good example for my employees,' he said, thinking of Thanh, who wasn't exactly an employee and certainly wouldn't follow any example Lang set.

She went through the elaborate ritual of making a Martini.

'Walter is all brain, very little heart,' she said. 'That doesn't mean he's unkind, at least not intentionally. But he is so busy trying to show his father – who is still very much alive at eighty-four – that he is just as capable a business man as he was. It was Walter Senior's constant mantra that Walter would squander the family fortune. So Walter has quadrupled it. And of course, he hasn't convinced his father of a damned thing.'

'Nice to the kids?'

'Not nice, not unnice,' she said, straining the Martini she had just shaken. 'They were, I suppose, in his eyes property for which he was entrusted to manage.'

'Are you bitter?'

'Because he left me for a younger woman?'

'Is that what happened?'

She laughed.

'Mr Lang, I need attention. Not an inordinate amount mind you, but some. He married me to satisfy his father, to show that he was a responsible son who could continue the name, which he dutifully did. And I was picked not for my extraordinary beauty and sexual allure, but because my family was . . .' It was clear she'd come upon a thought she didn't really want to share.

'Was what?' Lang said. They both knew she was treading on what was known but unspoken.

'My family was very established.'

'And very rich.'

'And very rich. That meant I wasn't a gold digger. That meant there wouldn't be an introduction of his family to a group of people living in a double wide. That meant the wedding would go on without incident and all future children would be welcomed.'

'I thought that only happened to English royalty.'

'Don't you believe it,' she said. 'This little game is played out in New York and Chicago and God knows where else. It's a little more complex that what you might imagine. It's not all snobbery. There are trust issues and power issues.'

'Power?'

'The power of endowment carries with it the power to significantly influence how, for instance, the city operates.'

'And the kids?'

'What would you like to know?'

'Usually the mother has custody in a divorce.'

She slipped into an upholstered chair across from him, the spectacular view now behind her. The fog was in the process of making the great Golden Gate Bridge disappear.

'I was having a few problems,' she said, toasting him with her Martini. 'Drugs. Affairs. I was reverting to my wild-child days in South America and Morocco. I wasn't fit at the time and being mommy doesn't fit me now.'

'What do you think of the new Mrs Hanover?'

'She's not all that new any more. We've all tried to come up with something original, but "ice queen" remains the best description.'

'Who is "we"?'

She shook her head and laughed. 'The editorial "we."'

'And there is an editorial board?'

'Of sorts. She married up.'

'She was poor, middle class?'

'Oh, no, she comes from some wealth. And that wealth has been around awhile. Just not . . . You know where I'm going. And I know what you're thinking. Privileged and pompous asses. I don't blame you. On the other hand, all those who would have us empty our bank accounts and hand out money on the street corner need to check their own impulses. What would the average person do after winning the lottery? I promise you they wouldn't turn into Mother Teresa.'

'I wasn't judging.'

'Yes, you were, but that's OK. We were fortunate. Genes and money. I think Walter and Pamela were made for each other. They share the same values. And Pamela was young and beautiful and Walter's tastes seemed to gravitate toward younger and younger women as time went on. I think it had to do with his lack of emotional development. I always anticipated there would be a third and even younger Mrs Walter Hanover.'

'And Olivia?'

'Poor little thing. I never met her. She was completely overshadowed by Evan and Jordan. Overshadowed is probably the best word, now that I think of it. She seemed to like staying in the shadows.' She looked down a moment, then up. 'You know Pamela changed Olivia's name so she could become a Hanover.' Katherine Wexford gave a little laugh and shook her head. 'Poor Olivia.'

'You really never met her?'

'No. Why would I? My boys come over for special occasions. She's never along. She's not even Walter's daughter, but a daughter by Pamela's previous marriage. She and my boys have nothing in common.'

'What did the boys say about her?'

'Nothing. She didn't come up.'

'And your boys?'

'And my boys? What do you mean?'

'Would they have wanted Olivia out of the way for any reason?'

Her look scolded him.

'I have to ask.'

'And what reason might that be?'

'Inheritance,' Lang suggested.

'My boys will have what I leave and they will have all but a fraction of what Walter leaves.'

'Wouldn't Pamela get most of Walter's money?'

'Prenup. Evan and Jordan were protected. So money is not much of a motive. Evan wouldn't have given her the time of day, so he would hardly go out of his way to kill her.' She smiled at her own wit. 'And Jordan? Jordan is a peacemaker. He lives to remove enmity. He wouldn't have the stomach to kill anyone, not that Evan would. Any other thoughts?'

Everyone knew that prenups didn't always hold up. Contracts, like any other promise, were meant to be broken.

'Jealousy?'

'You have to be kidding. She had nothing they wanted. What? Obscurity? What are the motives for murder? Jealousy, revenge, greed? None of that fits.'

'Rage.'

'And what could possibly anger them about someone whose life didn't intersect theirs.'

'Maybe she knew a secret.' The thought hadn't been in Lang's head before now. Could be. He was pleased as she ran through the traditional motives for murder that there was one not so easily dismissed.

Katherine was quiet.

'All right. Who would have a reason to have her out of the way?' Lang said, breaking the silence.

'You're assuming,' she said getting up and heading back to the bar, 'that someone wanted her out of the way. The police have someone, some young drifter. He had the code to their security system. He was in the house unbeknownst to Walter and Pamela very late at night into the early morning.' She began to fix a drink, the second he knew of. 'You sure?' She lifted her glass.

'Sure. Nothing.' Lang thought that maybe not all of the lines on Katherine's face came from sailing.

'Don't give me that worried look. You aren't responsible for me falling off the wagon,' she said.

'You were on the wagon?'

'Yes, but I fell off awhile back. But it's not so bad this time. I take my liquor straight now. No barbiturate chasers.' She grinned and came back, but didn't sit. 'Do I need an attorney?'

'Only if you shoot me with one of those hidden pistols.'

'I lied,' she said. 'I'm totally defenseless.'

'I doubt that,' Lang said, getting up from the sofa.

She followed him down the hallway to the door.

'Come back anytime,' Katherine said.

It had been a long time since anyone considered him a potential toy boy. Life was crazy, wasn't it?

'By the way, Mr Lang, don't use slick innuendo to suggest my boys had anything to do with her death. I understand the need to create reasonable doubt. But don't use them. I don't want their names bandied about in the news.'

'You'll have to talk to the defense attorney. I'm just an investigator.'

'You will pass the word along, won't you?'

The scolding look she gave him earlier paled alongside the cold, steely and confident glare in her eyes as she spoke.

Eleven

Carly Paladino spent the afternoon checking out leads on office space. If it was nice, it was too expensive. If it was affordable, then it wasn't nice. Having had the benefit of inheriting her parents' flat, she hadn't followed the ballooning housing prices in the city in the last couple of decades. Not having a lot to do with the budget at Vogel Security, she wasn't aware of the price of office space. What she was experiencing was sticker shock. Maybe she had been a little too impulsive on this out-on-my-own business.

She met Nadia at three at a coffee shop on Upper Polk. There was a lot to talk about. Nadia's trip. And Carly's new career.

'Not bad for a couple of old broads,' Nadia said. Nadia was a size 2, looked younger than she was, ran a public relations firm dedicated to artists' organizations because she loved the arts and fortunately didn't need the money. Most of her work ended up *pro bono*.

It was nice to have someone to talk to. Carly was beginning to feel alone in the world. While she wasn't all that close to her co-workers at the company, the environment offered some level of socialization. Her time with Pamela Hanover barely qualified as human interaction.

They caught an early dinner at a place with no vowels in its name –
SPQR. While it didn't go trippingly on the tongue, the food and wine did.
And the more trippingly the wine played on their tongues, the more they
talked. There was a lot of catching up to do.

By bedtime, Carly Paladino felt better about the job she left and the
temporary job she took on. She promised herself she would be a little
more adventurous in her search for an office. 'Be open,' she told herself,
as she drifted off to sleep.

Her dreams weren't as encouraging.

Lang wanted to see the widower's place again – at night. If he could figure
things out, he could stop the constant nagging at his conscience. And this
night was identical to the night she died. Little, cold pinpricks of water on
his face and hands made him uncomfortable. The heavy drizzle and fog also
limited visibility and again the lamplight could only pierce a small space
around it. The house was dark. Either the widower was out or was in
asleep, where most sensible people were this time of night.

Flashlight in hand and hope in his heart – it was closing in on four in
the morning and his actions were more than a little suspicious – he stood
for a moment in the same spot where he saw something go by him. There
were two bushes and a space between them. Anyone passing there would
have been visible for a fraction of a second on his way to . . . What? Nothing
manifested itself.

He went around the side of the house, walking between the widower's
place and his neighbor's place. Behind his client's home was a wall. He
pulled himself up far enough to see that it was a long drop down to sharp
rocks. Beyond the rocks was sand and beyond the sand the ocean.

No one could escape from the house that way. He came back up between
the homes, went between the bushes crossed in the direction the mystery
person would have to have gone. He crossed the lawn of the neighbor's house.
He could be arrested as a prowler. He was, in fact, the very definition of a
prowler. He had no legal reason to be there.

Maybe he was obsessing. What would happen if he found out the guy
killed his wife? Could he prove it? What ate at him was the possibility that
he had been set up. He would be the witness to confirm that no one came
or went from the home at the time the gunshot was fired, answering any
lingering doubts about whether her death was suicide.

Going between the next two houses, he found not a wall, but steps that
led down to the beach. He went down, his feet sinking in the soft sand.
He could hear the waves washing in. It was a lonely sound, but a restful
one. There was no way his eyes could puncture the foggy soup. The killer

could have just walked along the beach far enough to get out of sight and then go back into the neighborhood farther down the beach, where his car was parked.

He heard a jingling sound. It was coming toward him. He felt threatened until he looked down to see a black dog nuzzling his leg.

'I see,' Lang said. 'You get lucky tonight?'

He retreated, going back the way he came. Maybe that's all it was. A dog, a cat, a raccoon. He was making something out of nothing. And, worse, he wasn't getting paid for it. What he could do was take advantage of the time to check something else out.

Lang went from this ritzy neighborhood to an even ritzier one. It took him awhile to find a parking space around Lafayette Park. He walked up the damp steps into the darkness. Lang was pretty sure that the police canvassed the neighborhood trying to find out if anyone saw or heard anything. He wondered if they came down here in the middle of the night to talk to some of the park's temporary, more mobile residents.

Fortunately Lang knew the layout of the park, where the concrete paths went and where they didn't go. Where they didn't go was a patch of the park that was used for trash bins, lawn clippings, broken branches. His flashlight caught the glimmer of aluminum and he made out the shape of a grocery cart.

Just beyond it was a lump under a blanket. Lang moved the flashlight around the area, as far as it could go in this weather. The lump was alone.

Lang kept his distance. Some of these folks weren't happy campers. And even if this guy wasn't a threat normally, being awakened by a stranger in the darkness might make anyone dangerous.

'Buddy,' Lang called out.

Nothing.

Lang thought he could make out which end was head and which was foot. He kicked the guy's feet lightly. The lump moved.

'Buddy,' Lang called out. 'I've got to talk to you.'

'Go away.'

'I can't. Not until I talk to you.'

'Can't you people leave me alone? I don't want no fucking shelter. Can't a man just live his life?'

'You're fine. I just need some information,' Lang said.

'I don't have any information about anything anywhere at any time. This is a public park. I got a right to be here.'

Lang kept the beam of light on the head of the beast in the blanket.

'I'm not a lawyer, or a cop, or a social worker. I can give you a few bills if you help me out.'

The man pulled the cover from his bony face. Eyes were sunk deep in his skull. Teeth weren't readily apparent. His flesh looked yellowish and damp, as if he were coated in some film substance to protect him from the world he was in but not part of.

'Take that light off me. I ain't puttin' on no show.'

Lang aimed the flashlight down so that just enough light spilled on the man to see what he was up to.

'What's your name?' Lang asked.

'What's yours?'

'Lang.'

'Well, Mr Lang, what words of wisdom would you like in exchange for your fucking generosity?' He got to his feet. It was more a work of determination than skill.

The man saw nothing on the night of Olivia's death. Nothing at all.

'The night was so bad you couldn't see even if you looked. But,' he said after some prodding and a ten, 'I heard a scooter just before dawn.'

'A scooter. You're sure it was a scooter, not a car or a motorcycle.'

'No, I can tell one engine from another. This is like a little Vespa engine.'

'Could have been on the street?'

'I know where the sound came from. Down there. You could hear it come up and then the engine went off. There was some shuffling.'

'You could hear all of that?'

'I could. At night . . . I mean in the dark, you'd be surprised at how keen your hearing is. Then after a few minutes, the engine started. The rider must've wheeled it away a little before starting it up. It zipped off.'

'What direction?'

'That way.' He pointed west.

Carly Paladino lurched awake, sweating. Around her was pitch darkness. It took her a moment to realize where she was, that she had been asleep, and that she had been dreaming. If she could have verbalized her feelings, she would say she wasn't frightened, just deeply, deeply sad.

The dream cast her younger self, a girl left alone in the middle of a large, empty public swimming pool. The place was familiar, but she had never seen it this way. No sounds, no people, no water. The sun set quickly, chased by heavy, smoky clouds. She couldn't remember how to get home. Soon all the light was squeezed out of the sky and a heavy dampness settled over her.

That's what she remembered of the dream. Perhaps there was more. She had had lovely, caring parents, but she'd always felt alone. Her shyness turned to practiced indifference and eventually coldness. She saw this in

Pamela Hanover. Carly got out of bed, went to the hallway and switched on the light, feeling slightly but also desolately insane. The lights didn't change the purgatorial mood, just steadied her mind in its place.

How quickly moods could shift, she thought. Only hours ago she'd sat with Nadia. They'd been out, among people, laughing at Carly's daring career foolishness and Nadia's wonderfully silly fantasy crushes in Tuscany. Nadia could bring her out of it. Michael, whom she hadn't seen for so long, could make her laugh, could melt the ice. But moods are fragile. Lives are fragile. One minute, then another minute.

She went to the bar in the kitchen, clicked on her laptop. She went to the most popular social site with young people. She keyed in 'Olivia Hanover' and 'San Francisco.' The victim's page came up immediately. Of course, she thought. She'd have to have a page. She went to the refrigerator, again raided the aged Cheddar and the bag of grapes. She hoped they would change her body chemistry to lift this fugue. She sat down with her snacks at the side, and focused on the page.

'Let's get to know you, Olivia,' she said.

There was a photograph of Olivia. Her long hair fell straight down. Her eyes suggested she had seen too much of the world and was weary of it. She wore a gray sweatshirt. She described herself as a 'caged soul wanting its freedom.' There were other places for the website subscriber to put in information.

> Turn-ons: People who read
> Turn-offs: People who know everything
> Hobbies: Poetry, dance
> My Friends: Gary and Daniel
> Job: Student
> Smoke: No
> Drink: Sometimes
> Religion: None
> Orientation: Straight, probably
> Dating Status: Sort of
> Body Type: Skinny
> Birth Sign: Pisces
> Favorite Group: The Doors
> Favorite Book: The Bell Jar
> Favorite Movie: Cement Garden

The Bell Jar, Carly remembered, was about a young and suicidal woman. There was probably a whole lot more to it, but that's what she could dredge from that long ago memory. In fact, the author, Sylvia Plath, killed herself. Carly didn't know the *Cement Garden* movie, but she doubted it was in the same vein as *Mary Poppins*. Choosing The Doors was perplexing. Olivia was far too young to know them. Carly only knew of them because some of her older friends referenced them. But she knew the lead singer, Jim Morrison, had come to a tragic end. Overdose. It was often difficult to tell if an overdose was intentional or not. Two doesn't a pattern make, but was it possible Olivia killed herself?

Maybe, Carly thought. But probably not. Olivia would have had to shoot up at home and then find her way to the park. That would be several blocks. If she shot herself up at the park, there were no needles left behind. And what would be the point in placing her in the park?

There was something else. She listed only a few friends. She appeared to have a very small social circle. She was a lonely girl.

When Carly was a teen, she confided in a journal that she kept hidden. Today, all of this was on the Internet and anyone anywhere in the world could read it. Strangers could know deeply personal things, figure out how to get to you.

This opened the frightening possibility of an unlimited number of suspects.

There was a link to a video. Carly clicked it. A little box appeared with an out-of-focus image. She clicked the arrow that appeared. The arrow disappeared and the image came to life.

It was Olivia. She spoke: 'Sleep. My other world. Monsters and Angels. The same as not sleeping, only richer, more fantastic. Sleep. Sleep. Sleep.' Her smile seemed blissful.

That was it. No more than ten seconds. Her gentle face and soft voice signified resignation. Acceptance.

What all that meant eluded Carly. She looked at the clock in the kitchen. 3.12 a.m. She would try to get some sleep. Maybe Olivia's ghosts would be kinder than her own.

Twelve

She got a couple of hours of sleep, dreamless as far as she knew. She put the coffee on and got into her running gear. Outside, the sun wasn't strong enough to penetrate the fog, but had enough luminescence to make the air translucent. Hood up, she ran up the slight incline toward Lafayette Park planning to run around it five times. That would give her twenty blocks or two miles. She would go no longer. She was already exhausted.

Carly didn't recognize him the first time around – the man sitting on the steps leading up to the grassy knoll. He was bent forward talking on his cell. The second trip around the park he called out to her.

'Paladini!'

She stopped. 'Paladino,' she said. 'Mr Lang, what are you doing here?' She stopped. It was a little awkward being seen before she put herself together. She also regretted the 'Mr' bit. More than a little stiff, wasn't it? Running into him wasn't all bad. She got to stop running.

'Gathering information for the case,' he said, standing up.

'You're at work early.' Yes, it was the place the victim was found. It wasn't stalking nor even much of a coincidence.

'I am. I see you are disciplined as well.'

'It's a losing battle,' she said.

'I don't think so.'

'You don't know where I started. You're gathering information how? Questioning people who go by?'

'You have to admit I get people to stop and talk. You live near here?'

'Just down the hill a bit.'

'I'm impressed. No wonder you didn't like our down-on-our-luck decor.' She grinned. 'It didn't scare me. It's just not my market.'

'The Hanovers?' he said.

'They may be too upmarket for me as it turns out.'

'You'll reconsider then?'

'Don't turn down any offers,' she said.

'I'm on my way,' he said. 'I'd give my kingdom for a cup of coffee.'

She thought about inviting him to her place. It was tempting. He was doing something here at the park and she wanted to know what. She thought no.

He extended his hand.

She shook it, giving that slightly phony half-smile that said she bore him no ill will. It was, though, a signal not a genuine emotion. She wanted to be real with him, but it seemed she was only pretending to be herself.

'I could make the cup of coffee a little more economical. I've got a pot brewing.' She said it. She hadn't planned on it. How did it come out? It was good though.

He thought he would take her up on it, realizing that there might be more brewing than a cup of coffee offered as a friendly, collegial gesture. He had an ulterior motive as well. Maybe he could convince her to take the space. Lang thought she'd be good for business.

'Got things to do, sorry,' he said, amused at this sudden reversal of his own intention. Maybe if she offered again.

She didn't.

Lang ran into Barry Brinkman in the street just outside the building where they each had an office. Brinkman, in addition to being a fire escape lurker, was a private investigator who occupied a small office down the hall from Lang. There when Lang moved into the building, Brinkman had to be in his seventies now. He was stubborn, misanthropic and technology averse.

He used to always have a pretty girl at the front desk. There must have been dozens while Lang knew him. He couldn't afford them any more.

'Take the elevator,' Brinkman said. 'Keep your legs young. Some day you'll need them.'

'What's going on?' Lang asked as they waited for the slowest elevator west of the Mississippi to arrive.

Brinkman gave him a dirty look.

'Research shows, I'm told, that people are happiest when they are very young and very old,' Lang said purposefully needling his old friend.

'And to think people get paid to come up with that crap,' Brinkman said. 'Did they ask any fucking old people? They didn't ask me. I would have told them how fucking thrilling it is to witness one's own decomposition in real time.'

'That didn't come out in the report Diane Sawyer gave on *Good Morning America*.'

The elevator door opened. They stepped in. Brinkman looked a little bit like Larry King with a flat top. The old detective used to wear a bow tie, but now went tieless. He drove an '86 maroon Buick, chain-smoked cigarettes, sometimes a cigar, and sipped whiskey most of the day.

'You lose your teeth, you lose your hair, you lose your muscle, and then slowly you lose your fucking mind.'

'If I could avoid growing old, I'd thank you for the warning,' Lang said. 'But I'm not sure I need to know.'

'You brought it up, kiddo.' Brinkman winked, pulled a cigar from the inside pocket of his sport coat. 'Want one? Cohiba.'

They stood quietly in the elevator, standing and staring straight ahead. Lang had used Brinkman a few times. He was good for surveillance. An older man like Brinkman could sit on a bench for hours reading a newspaper and no one would suspect anything. As Brinkman reminded him once, 'When you get old, you get invisible.'

Inside Lang's office, Thanh was at the computer.

'You look like death.'

'Thanks,' Lang said. 'I think the theme has been established for the day. You look like Audrey Hepburn.'

'Thanks. Why don't you go home and get some sleep?'

'OK. I need you to find out everything you can on Theodore Kozlov. The husband of the suicide case I was watching,' Lang said.

'His check bounce?'

'Not that I know of.'

'What's going on?' It was clear by his friend's attire Thanh was in touch with her feminine side. Tomorrow he might be in touch with his masculine psyche. However, the mannerisms never changed. Thanh was Thanh.

'I don't like him,' Lang said.

'So?'

'I've been hired to find out if he killed his wife.'

'Who hired you?'

'Me?'

Thanh nodded, smiled.

'How much are you paying yourself?'

'I'm doing it *pro bono*,' Lang said.

'Anyone tell you that you are a nice person?'

'Are you telling me that?'

'No. Just asking if anybody ever told you that.'

'Also, find out what you can about the Hanovers, particularly Walter.'

Thanh knew his way around the various lists on the Internet, sources for financial data, criminal charges, political leanings and blood relations, as well as clubs and associations.

'OK.'

'Anybody call about the space?'

'Nobody we want to talk to,' Thanh said.

Lang was glad Thanh took care of the details. He would trust his friend with his life.

'Are you going home?' Thanh asked.

'In a little while,' Lang said. 'I need to talk to West. What are you doing here this early?'

'Like you, for me this isn't really early, it's just really late. I'll get us some coffee.'

Lang remembered the many years ago when he first met Thanh. The meeting was a result of an awkward misunderstanding. More awkward for Lang as it turned out. It was very funny for Thanh. Coffee was the peace offering then. Fortunately time and its mellowing effect allowed it to be funny for Lang as well. Even so, it remained one of their two secrets.

Lang got in touch with West, told him about the sounds of a motor scooter in the middle of the night.

'I take it the witness is highly impeachable,' West said.

'We should look at this as something that will lead to something else. Does your client have a scooter?'

'Didn't think to ask. He didn't say he did. Then again, as you are aware, he hasn't said much of anything. We still don't know who he is.'

'The family has hired an investigator,' Lang said. 'Carly Paladino.'

'Don't know her.'

'I checked. She worked for Vogel Security. Mostly civil law. She was senior investigator. Reported directly to Vogel.'

'That explains it,' West said. 'Noah, the cops are in a hurry.'

'It's the DA that's in a hurry.'

'Yes,' West said. 'They both are. The last thing they need is for this to drag out, top of the fold every day of the week reinforcing the notion that not only is the city experiencing record homicides, but they can't be solved and perpetrators can't be convicted.'

'And they're also getting pressure from the Hanovers,' Lang reminded him.

'All for swift justice when we have . . . nothing.'

Lang recounted his interview with the first Mrs Hanover and how her story of Olivia as Cinderella jived with that of Mrs Hanover's secretary.'

'With two wicked brothers?' West asked. 'What's next?'

'Maybe the two wicked brothers.'

'Be careful.'

'Chaz, on another topic altogether, do you know a Theodore Kozlov?'

'I don't. Should I?'

'No reason. Just thought if he'd come through the system you might know him.'

Lang clicked off the phone. For the first time in a long time he felt the pressure of guilt nibbling at his mind. Pressure wasn't new. But operating from guilt was rare these days. He was afraid the machine would swallow up young Daniel before they had a chance to make sure he got a fair shake and he wanted to know what might be impossible to know. In the second case, did he, Lang, play a supporting role in the death of Mrs Kozlov?

Black coffee for Lang. Latte for Thanh.

'I'm taking mine to go,' Lang said. 'Can I drop you somewhere?'

'No. Got a few more minutes here.'

Lang stopped at Eddie's Café – 'Breakfast All Day.' It was a basic little diner with a counter and booths in red leather on the corner of Fulton and

Divisadero. Lang grabbed a morning paper from the dispenser and had eggs and hash browns with his news.

The headline of the morning paper read: Murder Suspect a Mystery Man. The story was long with pokes at the DA and the police. The murder statistics that the paper quoted many times before appeared again as a sidebar to this story.

They were turning up the volume. He suspected the national press would be here soon. A society murder made for both high and low gossip. It was only a matter of time before the story became a *48 Hours Mystery*.

Carly didn't get the chance to call Pamela Hanover. Pamela called her first. The tone was friend-to-friend, almost warm.

'Hannah having her baby,' she said, 'what horrible timing. That sounds really insensitive, but you know what I mean. And Gary, he's so good with so much, but he's falling apart emotionally.'

'I'm sorry to hear that,' Carly said, not knowing what else to say. Obviously Pamela Hanover wanted sympathy. It was a set up for something else. Carly saw it coming.

'I'm really counting on you.'

And there it was. Pamela wanted several things. She wanted Carly to build a wall around her family to keep media and cops out. She wanted Carly to find out what the police were doing, what they knew, what the public defenders office knew.

'They have somebody out there questioning everybody,' Hanover said. 'Walter's first wife was visited by some PI asking about Walter's sons. She was very upset.'

Lang was very busy, Carly thought. Carly had thought him to be a little too laid-back. Maybe she was wrong.

'I know him. I'll keep an eye on him.' Carly smiled, aware of the double meaning.

Pamela Hanover wanted the media to stay away at least until the funeral was held.

Carly tried to explain that Pamela and anyone she hired had no real standing with the police, the DA or the public defenders. Among them there would be a certain amount of sharing of information. Disclosure of evidence was mandatory for prosecution and defense, but the Hanovers had no such legal claim.

'Go around them. Use our name. We are the victim's family. If we don't have legal rights, we certainly have moral ones. We can use the media to push for that.'

'Could come back to haunt you,' Carly said.

'What do you mean by that?'

'If there's damaging information with regard to your family.'

There was a long silence.

'Whose side are you on?'

'I work for you,' Carly said, trying to make the distinction without creating more anger. 'But if we push for all the information to be released by using the press to do it, there's nothing to prevent the press from revealing any suspicious activity on the part of family members. I'm trying to protect you as you requested.'

Another long silence.

'What kind of suspicious activity would that be?' Her tone had now returned to employer-employee. 'You think there's something we are hiding?'

'I'm being paid to protect you. We have to work for the best outcome, but be prepared for the worst. Olivia was killed in the middle of the night. No one has an alibi.'

'But they have the killer,' she said. 'What are you saying?'

'They don't have a witness. They don't have a motive, as far as I know. Maybe they have it wrapped up and maybe I'm being too cautious.'

'Find out,' Pamela Hanover said. 'Find out what they have.'

Carly decided to walk out on the ledge.

'You know, Mrs Hanover,' she said, 'you said it before. If the young man is charged . . .'

'If?' she said.

'If he's charged and it goes to trial, the defense will raise reasonable doubt. To do that they need to provide believable alternative scenarios. The likely candidates all live or work in your house.'

'I think you have your work cut out for you,' Pamela Hanover said coldly, and disconnected.

Thirteen

Lang's cell phone would have gone unanswered if Buddha hadn't used the sleeping detective's belly as a trampoline.

'I have voicemail, Buddha,' Lang said to his friend as he picked up the phone. It was West.

'I'm waking you up again,' West said.

'I was just resting.'

'Sleep was in your voice. Humans aren't nocturnal creatures, Noah.'

'Some are,' Lang said.

'Yes, that's true, isn't it? Our young friend Daniel appears to live in the night. He's a strange one. Still no fingerprint match. Got a call from the DA. The notebooks the police found in his crib weren't in English. They thought it was Chinese. It wasn't. It wasn't Japanese, or Korean or any other language for all they can figure out. They sent over copies as part of disclosure. It's either code or it's just gobbledegook.'

'I'd like to see it,' Lang said. 'If it's code, somebody can break it, right?'

'You are a code buster?'

'No. Not me. Just curious.'

'What's troubling is why would someone go to that much trouble?'

'Terrorist comes to mind,' Lang said. Though it was hard to imagine that the person known as 'Daniel' was really dangerous. The sad truth, though, was that it wouldn't be the first time an innocent, altruistic kid was used to deliver death. But why Olivia? She may have been rich, but she was hardly the poster child of spoiled rich kids.

'Maybe she figured it out,' West said. 'What he was doing, I mean.'

'Olivia? Whose side are you on?'

'We have to know all the possibilities so we can defend against them.'

'True. But what was he doing? In the absence of any real knowledge we could make up all sorts of things.'

Buddha, who had moved to the end of the bed, seemed to be waiting for Lang to end his call. Lang got up, went to the kitchen area, poured some dry food in a bowl as he chatted with West. He dumped out the water and ran fresh water into the bowl.

'It was Daniel's DNA. But that's not a surprise,' West said.

'You know the kid was definitely off the grid. He left no record except for some kind of note-taking that no one but him understands. He was moving through life without leaving a single footprint until this.'

'The phones did him in,' West said.

'Love did him in,' Lang said.

'You're a true romantic.'

'No. Think about it. He sacrificed his imperceptible existence, something he obviously valued – and still does – for her. What else did they share?'

'Good point,' West said. 'Maybe they shared a language.'

'Why don't I walk around his neighborhood? Also talk to the people in the building.'

'You did the building before, right?' West asked.

'But I might not have asked the right questions.'

'We need to find out if Daniel has or has had access to a scooter,' West said. 'You may have to talk to him.'

'What's his status?'

'The DA talks like they're going to charge him for murder, but they've got him on statutory rape. They're going to idle their engines until they're ready to go. But it doesn't look good.'

It didn't, Lang thought. The prosecution can put him with her very near the time of death. He had access to the house. He had sex with her. Both phones were found at his place. Why was that? He can't account for his time immediately after the time of death. No one knows anything about him, except that he kept some bizarre notes and refused to live a normal life.

'If the books turn out to be gibberish . . .' Lang said.

'Insanity rarely works.'

Carly was troubled. She knew that Mrs Hanover's priority was getting all of this behind her. But she thought that, at the very least, a mother would want to make sure the person who killed her daughter was the one who would be punished. Carly was also puzzled by Mr Hanover's apparent hands-off attitude. One would think that because Olivia was Pamela's daughter that he would have stepped in to support her. Wouldn't a big-time businessman want to protect his wife during these emotional times?

She called the assistant DA on the case and successfully set up a short meeting later in the afternoon. She called Vogel Security to check on their plans for the funeral and burial at Cypress Lawn Cemetery in Colma. Where else? she thought. There are more dead residents in Colma than live ones in San Francisco.

Vogel Security had it under control as Carly knew they would. There would be six operatives, dressed in black, with electronic earpieces. They would make sure the funeral went off without a hitch, that is without curiosity seekers and reporters gumming up the works.

She had time between now and the DA meeting to take another shot at Lang. Share was the message. After all, she would tell him, truth is truth. It's what everybody wants. She hoped that was true. She decided to do it in person.

Instead of Lang, she got Thanh, who this time looked very much a woman. Maybe she was. Just a little tomboyish the last time. This time Thanh's hair was swept back, and she had on a cashmere V-neck sweater and a delicate gold chain around her neck. Little gold earrings in each ear. A touch of color on her lips and over the eyes.

'He's out,' Thanh said, smiling. 'Are you reconsidering?'

'I haven't ruled it out,' she said. She was stretching the truth. 'But I really want to talk to Mr Lang about the case he's working on. The Olivia Hanover death.'

Thanh nodded. 'So sad.'

'I understand they've arrested someone,' Carly said, fishing.

'Is that right?'

'Are you involved in the investigation?'

'I work for Noah,' Thanh said in a kindly tone, 'but I'm not his spokesperson.'

Spokesperson, Carly thought. That didn't help. Why was she so curious about Thanh's gender? She told herself that it wasn't any of her business and what did it matter anyway? Carly respected Thanh's professionalism. If Thanh came with the office space, maybe she should reconsider. She could do with some help. More than she had allowed herself to think about.

At Vogel Security, she was covered by blanket liability insurance. Now she'd have to get her own. She would have to put together a website. No one made it these days without one. Hell, she thought, soon she'd have to get her own health insurance, probably not so easy for women approaching a certain age. It was scary. Billing, rent, collections. Staff did all these. Now, she was staff.

'I have a question,' Carly said. 'Who did your website?'

'I did,' Thanh said.

'And you handle billing, collections . . .?'

'Taxes, insurance . . .' Thanh nodded.

She hadn't yet put taxes on the list. Maybe she should just join another security or investigation firm. There was more here than she thought.

'. . . keep his motor running,' Thanh said.

'What?'

'His car. It's a rusty, temperamental, old thing.'

'You do that too?'

'I told him to buy a Honda, but he's a romantic. He wanted a Mercedes, so he has a banged up old Mercedes with 170,000 miles on it.'

Lang took the long way to the office, stopping first in the Tenderloin. He went to Daniel's building, knocked on doors. He showed those that answered and those he caught in the hallways the copy of the mugshot Lang got from West.

Most had seen him, but knew nothing about him. 'He kept to himself' was the common phrase suggesting he wasn't rude, but wasn't open to conversation.

He asked them if they'd ever seen him riding a scooter.

No one had.

Lang took a chance showing the kid's photo around out on the streets. He got nothing.

He went from the toughest neighborhoods nearer Market up Larkin Street to Little Saigon, an area that wasn't exactly gentrified, but showing signs of life from the influx of Vietnamese people setting up businesses.

Lang took the photo into a few of the restaurants. One waiter thought he might have come in a few times for take-out. But then he couldn't be sure. Lots of people come and go the guy said. While he was there Lang ordered a *banh mi*, a sandwich of sorts, his choice with chicken, fish sauce, chilies, pickled carrots, cilantro, daikon and a spiced mayonnaise. He consumed it as he walked through the small neighborhood that was growing quickly through the efforts of immigrant entrepreneurs.

Back at the office he found Stern and Rose. Stern was looking out of the window, his back to the door. Rose was lounging on the beat-up sofa, a smile on his face.

'They wanted to wait,' Thanh said. 'Must be paid by the hour.'

'I almost didn't recognize her,' Stern said, nodding toward Thanh.

'It's been what? Fifteen years?' Rose said.

'And the two of you still together.' Stern's tone was nasty.

Thanh's eyes rolled.

'You make a very nice couple, too,' Lang said, his glance taking in the two cops. 'Now tell me how long have you two been together?'

Stern looked unhappy. It was always difficult to tell if his insensitivity was an act.

'Twenty years,' Rose said.

'Silver anniversary, I'm impressed,' Lang said.

'Platinum.' Inspector Rose smiled. 'Or china. There's a big debate going on.'

Stern gave his partner a disgusted look.

'We'll have to catch dinner and a movie sometime, just the four of us,' Thanh said without looking up from the computer screen.

'So, thanks for dropping by,' Lang said. 'We'll give you a call.'

'Saw you on TV.' Stern wasn't leaving.

Lang didn't bite.

'What were you doing at Kozlov's place last night?'

'Was I?'

'Cameras, infrared,' Stern said. 'Sophisticated surveillance stuff, things you wouldn't know anything about.'

'That's more interesting than you know.'

'What were you doing there?' Stern did all the direct questions.

'I lost something. I went back to find it.'

'In the dark?' Stern asked.

'Well, you see, I lost it in the dark.'

'I like the way this boy thinks,' Rose said, grinning.

Stern didn't find it funny.

'Mrs Kozlov's death was ruled a suicide. What are you up to?'

'Did you think to look at his surveillance the night she died?' Lang asked.

'We did. No one came or went except you,' Stern said.

'Funny, isn't it?' Rose said. 'If you were to persist with some theory that it wasn't a suicide, but a murder and you actually convinced us of that, you'd be the only suspect.'

The truth of that remark hit him like a sledgehammer. Lang had given Kozlov credit for being smart, but this was even smarter. Lang was hired as an insurance policy to prove the woman had to have killed herself because a trained investigator was witness to her being the only one in the house. But it was more brilliant than that because if the investigator turned out to be a bad witness or if the medical examiner saw it as a suspicious death, then the tapes would prove that Lang was the only person who could have killed her.

'You don't see the humor in this?' Rose asked.

Stern stepped within inches of Lang and face-to-face said, 'Kozlov has made a formal complaint. You know what that means. If you put one foot on his property ever again you will be arrested for trespassing.' He stared into Lang's eyes. 'As a PI, you know that this warning sets that up, right?'

'You working for him now?' Lang asked.

'We are working for the safety and protection of all the fine citizens of this fair city,' Stern replied, loosening up now that the message had been delivered.

'You are a great American,' Rose said to Stern.

'And you are a great African–American.'

Rose shrugged and shook his head at his partner.

'You are an African–American, aren't you?' Stern asked with false concern.

Rose smiled. 'If I said no, I'd be in self-denial.'

'There you go,' Stern said. He looked bloated and triumphant.

'All's well that ends well,' Rose said as they went to the door. 'Cheers.'

Fourteen

'Nice friends you have,' Thanh said.

'Do you suppose they do that all day long?'

'Ms Paladino was here earlier. You're having a lot of visitors lately.'

'She say what she wanted?'

'She wanted information about your murder case. She also had questions about what I do here.'

'Hmmnn, either she wants to hire you away or is considering some sort of arrangement,' Lang said. 'Life is tough out there. You find anything out on Theodore Kozlov.'

'You should have checked him out before you took the job,' Thanh said.

'Because?'

'He plays for keeps.'

'And I don't?'

Lang hadn't meant to, but he touched on their common bond and their common regret.

'You do,' Thanh said sadly.

'I'm sorry.'

'Nothing to be sorry about,' Thanh said, but moved on. 'Mr Kozlov spent ten years in Sing Sing.'

'Why?'

'Murder.'

'Just ten years?'

'Intent to inflict bodily harm that led to the murder.' Thanh was reading it from the computer screen. 'A business partner slept with his wife.'

'I see. Not premeditated. Somebody just pissed him off. What does he do now?'

'You don't know any of this?' Thanh asked.

'I never met him,' Lang said. A phone call and a check. The check had his name on it. The check was good. 'A little sloppy, I know. You got a picture of him there?'

'No. I'll keep looking. Mr Kozlov is a registered lobbyist. I'll print out the information.'

'And Walter Hanover?' Lang asked, but his mind was still on Kozlov. Screwing around with this guy might not be in his best interest.

'That's next,' Thanh said.

'I'm going to go down to the Hall of Justice, talk to our client. Are we OK?' Lang wanted to make sure his accidental reference to what they both wanted to forget was forgiven.

'We are.'

The offices for the DA and ADAs were in a separate wing but on the same floor as the superior courts. The hall was a little brighter than the cold hall that led to the courtrooms. There was art on the walls of the long hallway that eventually led to a reception desk.

Carly waited only moments for Howard Dane, who wore a suit equally as dramatic as the one he wore when they met with the Hanovers. He made a show of things, bowing a little too chivalrously for her to follow him to his office, and gesturing a little too broadly for her to sit. Dane managed to turn what was a boring square space into something as garish as he was.

'I'm not sure there's anything more that you can tell me,' Carly said, sitting in one of the two guest chairs, 'but the Hanovers are understandably anxious about the case. I wanted to get a sense of where things are.'

Dane sat on the edge of his desk, looked her directly in the eye and smiled.

'I understand completely,' he said.

His degrees were on the wall. There were photographs of him with political and Hollywood celebrities. His nameplate was ornate and suggested the next step in his career might be something in the royal court.

He then reiterated most of what she already knew about the situation and about the young man called Daniel Lee – the phones, the security code, the lack of an alibi, the timing of his visit, the DNA. What was new were the notebooks filled with strange and so far undecipherable symbols and, he'd just learned, the possibility of some motorized vehicle having been heard around the time Olivia died.

'Are you charging him with the crime?'

'No. Not murder, yet.' He took a deep and dramatic breath. 'We believe we have the killer, Miss Paladino. But we don't have his name. We don't know where he is from. We don't have any idea where he might have gotten ketamine. We have no idea how he could have procured morphine and a needle to inject it. He has no known associates. We don't know how he earns his money. While we can charge a John Doe with a crime, there are too many unknowns and room for too many surprises.'

'Is your investigation leading you anywhere else?'

Dane looked uneasy. They both knew why she was asking the question. Were the police pursuing any notion that the Hanover family or staff had anything to do with the death? He stood up, turned his back, then turned back around again. His double-breasted suit fit him like a glove and most of his movements seemed sudden, jerky. She thought he might feel a little less tightly wound if he unbuttoned the jacket.

'We can't consider the case closed, but where to go? I don't know. Gratelli may have some thoughts. You remember him from the meeting?'

'Yes, do you think it's all right if I talk with the inspector?'

The assistant DA took that as an indication the meeting could be over. He grasped at the notion.

'Of course. Our thoughts and prayers are with Olivia's family and friends. We want this resolved,' he said, moving to the door. 'Quickly.'

Carly felt like she was just going through the motions, that she really wasn't earning her wages. All of that could have been handled in a ten-minute phone call. But she was making her presence known. She wasn't so much gathering facts as she was making the Hanovers' continuing and heightening concern with the case apparent. This wasn't investigation. This was public relations. That didn't make her happy.

With all her boredom at Vogel, they – and therefore she – expected the investigator to uncover the facts. What the client did with them was their business. With the Hanovers it was somehow different. Though it wasn't spoken, she had the distinct sense that she was to make sure all this ended quickly and well, whatever it took. And Carly didn't like it.

As he waited for the young man to be brought into the room, Lang thought about the kid's success in invisibility to the system. It was a skill Lang admired. To be, in some ways, a citizen of no country was to be in many ways free from all of its constraints. As a private eye, he was walking on the edge of the outside, but not the outside.

There were many times when Lang wished he were off the grid. When his wife left him, now some decades ago, all he could think of was moving to some cabin out in the middle of nowhere, living off the land, growing his own vegetables – though there wasn't an agricultural bone in his body – and let the world go by.

When he told a swollen-faced Daniel about this, the young man expressed no interest.

'Was it worse than it looks?' Lang asked about Daniel's face.

He nodded.

Lang would talk with West. The boy was too young, too small to be able to fend for himself in this kind of environment.

'Do you own a motor scooter?'

Daniel looked puzzled, but he didn't answer. Lang took that to mean he didn't.

'I don't mean to be an asshole, but if you don't help us help you, this is just going to get worse.'

Daniel looked at the floor.

'The other thing is that if they put you away for killing Olivia, whoever did it gets away with it.'

Daniel nodded solemnly.

'Do you know who did it?'

He shook his head.

'How do you earn your money? You pay the rent. You have to eat. How do you do that?'

Nothing. Was there no way into this kid? He wasn't being sullen, Lang decided. He was merely being secretive. Keeping his life to himself. Why wouldn't he? The last time he consented to be part of civil society, however slight and brief that participation was, put him here.

'Don't you want to help Olivia?' It was a cheap question, but Lang gave it a shot.

'She's beyond help, don't you think?'

'Did she take drugs?'

'No. No way.'

'Could she have killed herself?'

'At one time, maybe. She felt like she was an embarrassment to the family. There are things I can't talk about.'

'Those are the things we need to know.'

He shook his head again.

'You loved her.'

'We had something.' He seemed angry with himself for giving it away. 'It doesn't matter now. Nothing against you, but would you just go away.' His eyes suggested he meant it.

'It's OK to lose yourself. I believe that.' Lang looked around. 'Just don't lose yourself in here. Fight to get out of this fucking place. West and I will do what we can.'

Daniel shook his head in a way that said Lang had no idea.

'You can make calls,' Lang said before he left. 'Call me.'

So close to getting away, Lang thought. So close to just slipping out of sight. If he had killed her, he would have done just that, wouldn't he?

He couldn't get in to see Gratelli right away. He could see the detective through the blinds of a glassed-in office. It wasn't until the woman moved around he could see the woman was Carly Paladino.

He suspected she was lobbying for closure. He understood the dynamics.

The story was sifting upward into the national media. It wouldn't be long
before the ravenous feeding would begin, when their story would be bandied
about on every clueless talking heads and gossip show on television. These
buffoons would analyze the situation despite scant facts, and then analyze
the analysis.

He waited.

The conversation was brief. She looked surprised when she saw him.

'We're running into each other quite a bit,' Lang said.

'How about we talk?'

'I have to see Gratelli first.'

'I'll wait. I'll be out front on Bryant.'

Gratelli saw Lang approach. The cop had the look of a patient man giving
in to an unfortunate inevitability.

'What do we have to talk about?' Gratelli asked.

'Daniel. His eye is swollen. His lip is fat.'

Gratelli gave a weary nod.

'Trying to make him break by scaring the hell out of him, getting him
beat up?' Lang's anger came out a little stronger than he thought.

While Gratelli's glance wasn't macho, it was one of warning.

'It's a tough world,' Gratelli said. 'The honeymoon suite wasn't
available.'

'Did you see him?'

Gratelli didn't answer.

'I don't believe he did it.'

'It's a free country,' Gratelli said. 'Believe what you want.'

'You're right. It is a free country. Freedom of speech, freedom of the
press, right. That kind of free, you mean?'

Gratelli looked up, a slight grin on a face that looked like it couldn't.
'Yeah.'

'So I can let the world know what happens to a young suspect when he
is under police custody?'

'I'll tell the DA you might be giving interviews with the media about
our young prisoner. Anything else?'

'Thanks,' Lang said.

'None needed.'

Lang thought, though he couldn't be sure, that Gratelli was looking for
a way to help.

Carly saw Lang come out one of the glass doors on the face of the Hall
of Justice. She waved. He nodded and came down the concrete steps
toward her.

'Forces beyond our control seem to be bringing us together,' she said.

'Really. You were in a trance when you came to my office to question Thanh about the case?'

'In the park, remember? My coming to your office in the first place based on an ad? The other day here and then again today.'

'OK, fate. I forgot to count. How can I help you?' He hadn't shaken the anger about how young Daniel had been treated.

'First you could hide your condescension a little better.'

'I'm sorry,' he said with a smile. 'It was something else.'

'Tell me how we can work together on this.'

'As I told you before, my job is to dance with the guy who brought me.'

'We could settle all of this sooner,' Carly said.

'And I would imagine that Mr West will do whatever he can to free the young man. That includes having the time for all forms of investigation. That may mean some continuances, postponements and every attempt possible at dismissal of the current charges and any future ones. That seems to run at odds with the interests of your client.'

Carly felt herself grimace.

'Personally,' Lang went on, 'I don't want the kid railroaded to satisfy the agenda of some frightened politician or the comfort of some privileged family.'

She nodded. 'I don't either. But it helps no one if this turns out to be the next big reality show. Unless you're looking for your fifteen minutes of fame.'

'Your point?'

'Let's work together and let the chips fall where they may.'

'And I trust you because . . .'

'You're a romantic at heart,' she said, grinning. 'You believe in the innate goodness of human beings.'

People coming from both directions brushed them. He gently pulled her away farther from the steps.

'I don't.'

'How about this? I'm a romantic at heart and I believe in the innate goodness of human beings.'

'No, it doesn't work. I don't partner fools,' Lang said.

'How about "two heads are better than one"?'

'Depends on the heads.'

'I want to find out what happened just as much as you do. I have access to the house and everybody in it,' she said.

'Then what do you want with me?'

'You don't have access to the family. But you have the world outside the house,' she said.

'What about the Hanovers? You working in their best interests?'

'I asked Mrs Hanover if the most important thing wasn't finding and convicting the person who committed the crime.'

She did ask Mrs Hanover and Mrs Hanover did agree. But in Carly's mind, she said one thing, meant another.

Working with Lang made some sense. He could do things she couldn't under the constraints of her employment. But she could tell that Lang wasn't so sure the trade was even.

Fifteen

Lang used the afternoon to track down some political folks he knew in Sacramento or who had once worked there. Half a dozen consultants, staffers, and appointees came to mind – some he'd done work for and others that he'd investigated.

He couldn't find two of them. One didn't want to talk about Theodore Kozlov. The other two couldn't have been clearer, painting a picture of the tough guy behind a two-man lobbying team. The first was Emmett Lacey, a Milquetoast of a man, oozing with charm, platitudes, and promises, who helped state legislators and some national legislators raise funds. They would plan events, bundle donations, and send new clients and cooperative regular clients to exotic spots around the world.

Theodore Kozlov was the guy who threatened to do whatever he thought would work, perhaps short of physical threats, perhaps not. One of Lang's contacts suggested this was a kind of miniature mafia. Once you were in, it was very hard to get out.

'In life, Noah, there are some things you give a wide berth,' one of them said. 'This is one of them.'

Lang spent the rest of the night with Chinese food in containers, a new and supposedly final cut of the movie *Blade Runner* and enough Asahi Dry beer to get him through the movie and the night. He felt like he was sixteen again, and was grateful, at least for the moment, that he didn't have to explain this adolescent detour to anyone.

Buddha investigated each container, lingered over the spicier dishes and climbed on to the sofa. Clunky air taxis whirled through dangerous streets, and the reclining cat appeared to be interested in the old and decrepit future on screen.

*   *   *

One glass of wine with dinner. Carly was being good. She went to bed early, read until her heartbeat slowed and her eyelids grew heavy.

Her eyes opened before the next morning's light. It was Saturday. Sleep had been uneventful as far as she knew. And she felt rested. Unless there was an urgent need, she would take the day off. Coffee, orange juice, and a strangely good, toasted, flourless English muffin with butter.

When the light came it was good. Unlike previous mornings, the air was clear, the sun cast everything in silver. It was a perfect morning for a serious run. However, as she headed west to the ocean, what often happens happened. The fog had advanced or retreated as Fulton Street intersected with Stanyan. In this small city, the weather varied by neighborhood. Carly wouldn't let the disappointment prevent her from the run. She had already committed and continued, parking finally in the long lot by the beach.

She locked her car, set her iPod, packed her water bottle, and headed toward the large and ominously towering windmill and the beginning of Golden Gate Park. And off she went running the five or so miles back to Stanyan, then turning around and running back to the beach, keeping thoughts at bay, merely giving in to some rousing rhythm and blues.

Rose gardens, Japanese gardens, open fields, a carousel, waterfalls, a herd of buffalo, three bodies of water, homeless encampments, a couple of museums went by her as she ran the length of the park.

Back at the car, she put on a sweater and went down to the sand. The sky was gray, the ocean was gray, the sand was gray. Just different textures. There were a few humans and a couple of dogs, dots on the long landscape. There was a sense of desolation. She sat on a piece of driftwood and stared out. As always, the presence of water both calmed her and brought her into a real sense of being alive.

'What have I done?' she asked herself. There was no panic, nor any desire to seek a solution to her dilemma. She'd left her well-paying, stable job on a whim at the same time as her long-term, if not incredibly passionate, relationship had dissolved. She didn't miss the job, but she missed the security it provided, the order in her life. She missed Peter. She missed the comfort he gave her, the familiar smells, the teasing banter, the movies, dinners.

And where was she in life? Before too long having children wouldn't be a decision she'd have to make. Did she want to spend her life with someone? She thought she did. Was her heart broken? No, she told herself. You've had this discussion, she reminded herself. Give this new life a chance.

She smiled, got up, walked down the beach toward the dunes. She could barely make out the dark profile of a freighter cutting through the gray. Someone ahead had set a bonfire. There was laughter. Half a dozen twenty-somethings gathered around the flames, making the best of a dreary day. The smoke and the air were nearly indistinguishable. Seagulls screeched, making sure observers didn't forget there was a gray sky above the gray ocean. Dogs ran with abandon on the sand – free for a while from the walls of small apartments.

Carly wanted to feel a little bit of that freedom. She had it, didn't she? If so, when would she actually feel it?

The funeral service for Olivia Hanover was tomorrow. It had been set up. They were in the capable hands of folks at Vogel Security and the event planners Pamela Hanover hired.

It was sunny back at her place. Mr Nakamura puttered with the plants. He smiled and nodded as she passed. It was reassuring. In the comfort of her home, in her parents' home, things remained the same. She would be fine, she thought as she headed toward the shower. When she was done, she told herself, she would collapse on the voluptuous sofa with a blanket until something came along that was powerful enough to make her move.

Lang decided to walk. The early morning call was a surprise and he couldn't get back to sleep. It would take him maybe forty minutes to walk from his place in the Western Addition to Union Square. The walk would give him time to sort out what he was going to say to Theodore Kozlov and what his next steps ought to be in the Hanover murder case.

It was a little gray outside his place, but as he walked down the hill on Fulton, he could see the blue sky ahead. The sun bounced off the gold gilded dome of City Hall. He walked through Alamo Square, another park on the top of a hill, where people were tossing tennis balls for their Australian Ridgebacks. He detoured around city hall, cut through the park on the other side and walked between the Asian Art Museum and Main Library to get to UN Plaza.

Kozlov had been civil on the phone and wanted to meet right away. Lang told him to make it a public place and he could meet him at nine thirty. Kozlov agreed.

Lang walked through the plaza, the place where the original United Nations was located, now the site of a twice-weekly farmers' market and in early morning and late at night inhabited by pigeons and by people who have no place to live. He turned left on Market, the wide street that cuts through San Francisco diagonally. It was essentially the city's main street and offered very different scenes depending on where you were on it.

At the moment he was walking by cheap electronics stores, pawnbrokers, check-cashing operations, and sex shops. It was retail, he thought, where the hustle was less subtle.

He was currently following a striking, tall creature with glitter in her long black hair. She walked like she was on a runway – long, long legs emerging from a short, short denim skirt. Lang could barely keep up and he wanted to. Once he had enough of this strangely alluring show – he thought she was a little too much girl to be a girl – he watched the pedestrians coming from the other way as they got their first eyefuls. Wide-eyed and wide smiled. Then again, most people didn't seem phased. It was, after all, difficult to be outrageous in this city.

For Lang it remained one of those curiosities that can never be answered. What a strange God, he thought, to create man and woman and then confuse matters so well with such incredible and alluring shape-shifters. Thanh, a shape-shifter as well, was very different. Rather than flaunt the digression from accepted norms, Thanh digressed in a camouflaged, perhaps subversive way and seemed to relish embodying not one but a variety of intensities on the gender continuum.

Lang was finally released of her spell when the high stepper stepped off at Powell, where tourists lined up to get on the cable cars, where bracelet sellers and sidewalk performers competed with people carrying religious signs signaling doom, and a dozen or so tables were set up for avid chess players. Lang went back to thinking about this meeting. He'd simply level with Kozlov, he told himself. That was only fair and it might elicit some useful information. If Lang were barking up the wrong tree, he'd like to know it now, before his obsession grew stronger.

He sat at a small metal table just outside the little coffee shop next to Barney's and across from Macy's. He had a bread pudding brioche with his coffee, apparently having worked up an appetite with the long walk, which of course justified the calories.

'Are you Lang?' the man asked. Lang looked left to see a big man, well over six feet and well above 200 pounds. He wore an expensive suit that looked a little too fashionable for his face and build. He had a wooden toothpick in his mouth and it moved around as he spoke.

Lang started to stand up to shake hands, but Kozlov indicated he should remain sitting.

'Let me grab a cup. I'll be right back.'

It was 9.30 and Lang could see the retail clerks heading for work. Within blocks of each other are all the big-name retail stores – Bloomingdales, Nieman Marcus, Saks, Nordstrom, Versace, Armani, Gucci, Hermes, Louis Vuitton. The customers had yet to arrive, but the area was bustling with taxis, Brinks trucks, UPS delivery vans, and people rushing. Anybody from out of town, except those from New York, would be impressed by the big-city vibe.

Kozlov returned, turned the chair around, and straddled it. He sat with his back to the street, something Lang would never do. The man studiously opened the sugar packet. He had big hands. He had a big nose, a drinker's nose. A good head of hair and small eyes.

'My check no good?'

'Your check was fine.'

'You know, I checked you out.' He finally looked up. 'Before I hired you I made sure you were legit. You checked out.'

'I understand . . .'

'Wait a minute, Dashiell. When I'm crossed, I'm not a nice guy. You and me, we had a deal. I paid you for it as we agreed. You want something more, the only thing you're going to get is trouble – all kinds of trouble.'

Kozlov hadn't raised his voice, hadn't tried to stare Lang down. He spoke calmly and clearly.

'I'm not asking you for anything.'

'Then why are you pissing on my shoe, Mr Lang?'

Lang could only assume that one of the guys he called in Sacramento let Kozlov in on it.

'I think you killed your wife,' Lang said. 'And if you did, you already pissed on my loafers, Mr Kozlov.'

Kozlov shook his head. 'I'll be damned.' He laughed not with humor but with derision and when the laughter subsided he looked different. Lang wasn't sure if he was seeing repressed anger or repressed sadness.

'Why would I do that?'

'I don't know.'

'How did I do that? You were there. Did you see me?'

'I saw somebody leave.' Lang exaggerated the level of certainty he felt about what he'd seen or thought he'd seen.

'You didn't see who it was?'

'No.' He hoped he wasn't talking too much.

'Why would I hire you to watch my house and risk setting up an eye-witness?'

'Maybe you were just setting up an alibi.'

Kozlov's cell rang. It was loud enough to have alerted the National Guard and had a tune they could march to. He answered quickly and after a short conversation in Russian it was over. Kozlov was quiet. He looked down at his coffee, seemed to have gotten lost for a moment. He looked up.

'Why don't you work for me?'

'What?' Lang wasn't sure what he heard.

'Why don't I hire you to find the killer, if there is a killer?'

'I think you're the killer. You want to pay me to gather the evidence?'

'If I were the killer, I wouldn't do that.'

'You're not buying silence here,' Lang said.

'Wouldn't dream of it.'

'Anybody account for your whereabouts that night?'

'A blonde Amazon named Shareen.'

'And you were having your wife watched?'

'Hey, the world isn't fair. You figured that out already, right?'

Lang wasn't a prude. Adult humans, in his mind, were free to pursue any consenting relationship they wanted. But he didn't like deceit, the kind of deceit Kozlov practiced, one heavily mixed with a heavy dose of hypocrisy. Even so, it wasn't his business.

'You'll get your wish then,' Lang said. 'I'll see what I can find. You're out nothing. Not a bad deal.'

Lang could almost see Kozlov's mind working. He just couldn't tell what it was working on.

'Changed my mind. No deal,' Kozlov said coolly. 'Back off.'

Lang calmly took a sip of coffee.

'I'll let you know what I find out.'

'You have no idea who you're dealing with,' Kozlov said. It wasn't said in a panic. It wasn't a threatening look Kozlov had on his face. It was a knowing look, much more convincing than the religiously insane folks at Powell and Market who predicted the end of the world. But he did stand up and lean over the table to get his face close to Lang's. His huge body blotted out the sun.

'You look like a blowfish, Mr Kozlov.'

'Pretty apt, Mr Lang.' He stood back. 'Look, in my neighborhood back in the old country we did what we had to do. Not like you Americans. Not even like your gang bangers, you know, just shootin' from a car. We got up close and very personal. That's the way I grow up. Grew up.'

Kozlov slipped, gave away his accent and his sentence construction. Maybe he wanted Lang to understand this wasn't knock a guy down and you win kind of game.

Kozlov pointed his finger at Lang as one would a gun, raised his thumb as if were a hammer, and fired. Kozlov smiled, pulled the toothpick from his mouth, and using only one hand snapped it in half and tossed it aside.

Maybe I should have thought this through, Lang considered. There were guys who fought to the death over a card game or an insult. A real dogfight. Kozlov had already proved his seriousness, hadn't he? He'd done time for murdering his first wife's illicit lover. And Lang believed he'd killed his second wife, though Lang wasn't quite sure why. Had Lang bitten off more than he could chew? What was done was done, but Lang felt uneasy about it.

Lang sat there after Kozlov left and watched the increased traffic on the streets. Busy people – all of them it seemed – with at least a momentary goal. He moved to get more comfortable in his uncomfortable chair. He wasn't going anywhere. He was at that point in both investigations where he found himself directionless. Yet, he felt for all of them – the dead wife, the dead daughter, and the young, mysterious stranger accused of murder.

Sixteen

'You're not on the list,' said the man in the black suit, who was obviously part of security for the funeral service. He stood outside a large white tent, temporarily constructed on the rolling green landscape dotted with marble angels and lesser tombstones. Inside the tent, Lang could hear a light, polite rumble of conversation.

'I didn't know there was a list,' Lang said.

'Then it should be no surprise you aren't on it,' the man said, a little disrespectfully.

'You're new here,' Lang said. 'You have any idea who you're talking to?' This bluff rarely worked, but Lang trotted it out anyway. People were passing them by, a few noting that something wasn't going smoothly.

'I have no idea,' the man said.

'That's because you're new here.' Two could play that game. Lang started to move forward. The man's hand pressed against Lang's shoulder suggested he wasn't going to make it.

'Can I help?'

Lang turned to see Carly Paladino. She smiled.

'Crashing funerals. You must be desperate for a social life,' she whispered in his ear. 'Come on along.' She grabbed his hand, nodded toward the guard.

'Just desperate, Paladino,' Lang said. 'I don't really want to be here.'

'Why are you here?'

'See the players. The kids. The relatives. The friends.'

'Olivia?'

'I don't want to see Olivia,' Lang said.

'I know. I shouldn't have,' Carly said, her sense of fun suddenly gone. 'She looked so vulnerable . . . as if something bad could still get to her. You'll be discreet?'

'I won't embarrass you,' Lang said.

'OK, you're on your own.'

Carly went off to talk with a couple of men in black suits and Bluetooth phones in their ears. No photographers. Were they able to stop the media or merely fool them?

Lang was pretty sure the tall, dark-haired youth who acted as if he owned the place was the older brother, Evan. Thanh had printed out some pages from the *Chronicle* and *Gazette* that showed him partying with his fellow rich and famous friends. Evan spoke with a couple of other guys his age. Sitting on a chair was Jordan, Lang guessed. He was by himself and not happy. Walter Hanover was with a very old man, whom Lang imagined was Walter Senior. Pamela talked with a gathering of women, all looking rich in that quiet way the old rich often do. Walter's first wife, Katherine Hanover Wexford, approached her antisocial son. The attitude was clear. She was lecturing. He was listening. Not an ounce of defiance in his body language. In a few moments, he was up on his feet, moving around the crowd as if trying to find a way into a conversation with someone somewhere along the way. Instead he just floated around like a dead leaf in a swimming pool.

Lang pulled out the sheet of paper that Thanh had created from various Internet searches about the Hanover clan.

Noah, here are some notes on the Hanovers.

Pamela Hanover: *previously married to Timothy Hudson who was Olivia's father. Mr Hudson lives in Lake Tahoe and Tokyo. Hudson's family owned hotels, sold out to a major chain. Living on proceeds and investments. Previously Pamela was Pamela Grant, of Phoenix, Arizona. Middle-class upbringing. A brief stint in acting prior to her marriage to Mr Hudson, whom she met in Los Angeles. Minor roles in two films – both straight to DVD. She and her first husband lived in San Francisco until the divorce, after which he sold the family house.*

Walter Hanover Jr: *son of Walter Senior, who is still alive at 84 and running the family investment business. Senior is on boards of directors of international corporations, also a major figure in the city's social circles. Son is an investment banker. Family money. Walter Jr is successful in the eyes of his peers, but does not carry the weight of his father in terms of influence. Jr contributes to non-political nonprofits, usually arts and nature oriented. No scandal. No brushes with the law. Divorced Katherine, who later married Winston Wexford, to marry Pamela. Both wives are socially active and community minded. With Katherine, Walter had two sons, Evan and Jordan.*

Evan Hanover: *brushes with the law not listed, records sealed as a minor. As an adult, Evan has a DUI. Top grades. Various honors and clubs. Socially active, often photographed at fund-raising galas, usually with an attractive woman. Summers abroad. (I can be a broad in the summer as well.)*

Jordan Hanover: *a book of poetry and short stories published: Between a Rock and a Rock* – on becoming a diamond in the rough.

Timothy Hudson: *Olivia's father. Moneyed but not in the same league as the Hanovers. Home at Lake Tahoe. International traveler.*

Olivia Hanover: *personal accounts on MyFace, YouTube and other such sites.*

I can go into greater detail on some of this. Let me know what you want.

Thanh

Lang looked around, putting the brief bios with the faces. At one point, he found Carly and asked about a few of the folks. He was especially curious about the young guy who hovered around Pamela – the guy he saw with Paladino at the DA's office.

'Gary Gray, her private secretary,' Carly said. 'You know the phrase quid pro quo, right?'

'I owe you,' Lang said, noticing that Evan had deserted his friends for a young Asian woman. He was introducing himself, which meant he didn't know her or perhaps just didn't know her well. The wise-guy face he wore around his peers was gone. In its place was the look of a Sir Galahad – noble, brave, humble.

Lang didn't like him. But that would matter to no one but himself.

'Dinner?' he asked Carly.

'Information,' she said.

'They're not mutually exclusive.'

She smiled. Was he inviting her on a date?

She looked confused.

Did it sound too much like a come on, he wondered?

'Conversation in a relaxed environment.'

'Good. OK.' Her curiosity wasn't satisfied, but she was comfortable in the ambiguity.

'Evan seems to be hitting it off.' He nodded toward the couple.

'As I understand it, he has a thing for Asian women.'

'Is that permissible?'

'What do you mean?' she asked.

'In this rarefied atmosphere, is it breaking some kind of code?'

'There are few rules for dalliances, especially among the rich.'

'Is she rich?'

'She's here.'

'So am I.'

When Lang drove out of the cemetery and out of the town of Colma, he remembered the stories. For the most part no one has been buried in San Francisco since the 1940s. And in fact, the ones who were buried before that time were dug up and carted out to this place, six miles south of San Francisco. The necropolis, which also serves as the convergence of auto dealerships, is a town of 1,500 above-ground residents and 1.5 million residents below. Among the notables are William Randolph Hearst, Wyatt Earp, Joe DiMaggio and Henry Miller.

Now Olivia Hanover too, who will be even more easily forgotten than she was in her modest life.

Lang and Carly met in North Beach at six at a small corner restaurant far enough north on Columbus to avoid most tourists. It was an intimate place. This was good for conversation. But given that sunset wasn't until eight, the idea that the dinner could be construed as romantic was thankfully diminished.

Lang had never been to Italy. Even so he imagined there were many places like this – high ceiling, heavy drapery, dark oil paintings. Time didn't move here. The interior was cheerfully baroque – a look that might take on a more gothic look later when lit by candles.

Carly hoped the restaurant would live up to her past dinners. Not just because she recommended it, but also because she was hungry. She had skipped lunch, which wasn't smart. The tension of the day had taken its toll. She reminded herself to be careful with the wine. An empty stomach paired with the desire to obliterate the afternoon was a dangerous combination. She needed her wits about her.

'We're unfashionably early,' Carly said as they were taken the few feet from the door to the table by the window. She didn't care. She doubted if he did. It was something to say.

'In keeping with my lifestyle,' Lang said.

As they settled in, ordering wine and food, there was an odd nervousness in their conversation. Some false starts followed by awkward retreats.

Even Lang, usually matter-of-fact, had trouble finding the right tone or the right thing to say.

'You aren't from here originally,' Carly said.

'True. What gives it away?'

'I don't know. You seem Midwestern.'

'Right again. And you are a native San Franciscan.'

'Yes. What clue gave that away?'

'Only a native thinks that whether you're born here or not is the most important piece of information to get.'

'Oh?'

'San Francisco is a very class-oriented city,' Lang said.

'You're put off by that?'

'No, I find it funny. I mean it's so politically incorrect to think in terms of class and yet one of the country's most politically correct cities has this caste system in place. One's status is determined by how many generations you can claim residence. And if your family is rich on top of it, that's even better. But you could have a gazillion dollars –' Lang took a sip of his wine – 'and if you've just moved here from Dallas, forget it. I read the obituaries – maybe more than I should. Joe Blow was a fifth generation San Franciscan and oh, yes, before we forget, he won the Nobel Prize.'

She laughed. 'Guilty. We're a snobby group.' She acknowledged the arrival of the food. He was served a penne pasta with sausage, she a plate of sweet potato gnocchi. 'So why are you here?'

'I came here for one reason and I've stayed here for another.'

'Go on.'

'I came here because it was a wild, raucous city and I could get lost. I stay here because of the weather. Not too hot. Not too cold. Because there's a little bit of everything. Here we are in Italy. If I want, I can walk over to China. If you want to take a quick Mexican vacation, wander over to the Mission.'

'I like that part too.'

'What's your story?'

'You haven't told me that much of your own.'

'No, I haven't.'

'What about your helper?'

'Thanh?' Lang asked.

'Yes. Is Thanh a girl or a boy?'

'Thanh decides that every day.'

'I mean really.'

'I'm not sure what "really" means in this context,' Lang said, smiling.

'Biologically,' Carly said.

'That's up to Thanh to tell you. Not me.'

'You're loyal too.' Disappointed, she nonetheless nodded her approval.

'Thanh's my best friend. We have each other's back. Have for years.'

'I'm sorry. Too curious.'

'No, don't be sorry. Occupational hazard. Thanh's a puzzle. That's part of the charm. It's also intentional.'

'He keeps your car running,' Carly said.

'Yeah. And the computer fixed. Thanh gets around town on an old motorcycle. All beat up. All black, like the outfits, with a dull aluminum gas tank. Who knows how old it is. Or what brand it is. He keeps it running too. Thanh's a magician.'

'How did you meet?'

'Long story. I'll tell you sometime if we know each other for awhile.'

'Are you married?' Carly asked.

'Are you trying to find out if I'm gay?' Lang wasn't sure he wanted to answer. Because she looked like she'd just spilled a drink in his lap, he took pity. 'I'm hard-wired straight. Sometimes I think that's a handicap. As any good bisexual would tell you, I'm missing out on half the opportunities.'

'Sorry again. I'm just trying to make conversation.'

'I was married a long time ago. It was a bust.'

'She break your heart?'

'I probably broke hers. She thought I was a decent guy. I was a jerk. I needed to grow up.'

'Did you?'

'No, probably not. But I stopped subjecting nice girls to my jerky nature.'

'How about not-so-nice girls?'

'That might be different? How about marriage and Carly Paladino?' Lang asked, thankful that she had brought up the subject.

'No. Not married.'

'Girls or boys?' Lang asked, unsuccessfully trying to repress a grin.

'A couple of long-term relationships with guys that ran out of steam. You go out much?'

'When I'm not minding someone else's business, I tend to keep to myself.'

Before dinner was over, they not only covered in a shallow way Carly's life story and exchanged what they knew about the case. Carly was very interested in Daniel's coded notebooks and his ability to hide his identity. Carly, in exchange, provided more detail about the Hanover family and their staff, including information about Olivia.

Fundamentally, Lang disclosed nothing that wasn't already disclosed through Chastain West to the prosecution. For her, the more light shining on the case, the more help she could be to the Hanovers, having been assured however hesitantly that Mrs Hanover wasn't afraid of the truth.

The fog, as is its summer pattern, returned. Lang walked with her along Columbus Avenue, strangers passing, appearing from and disappearing into the heavy mist. A man, gaunt to the point of skeletal, and flesh as white as a porcelain sink, damp from the damp air, seemed to appear from nowhere. He was leaning against the outside wall of Puccini's coffee shop.

Surprised, Lang looked at him. Their eyes met. Something happened. It wasn't recognition. It wasn't an emotion. Maybe it was the wine. Maybe it was the weather. Whatever it was, Lang had the odd feeling that something wasn't right somewhere.

Seventeen

Buddha wasn't at the door. Whether it was a sixth sense – and Buddha seemed to possess something like it – or merely the sound of the key in the lock, the cat was always waiting at the door. Inside was dark. Not a surprise. He had left no lights on when he left earlier in the day. But something was amiss.

He clicked the light switch inside the door. Nothing happened. He ran his hand along the wall until he found the baseball bat he put there to discourage intruders and stepped in cautiously, stepping on things. He could only describe them as things, rubble under his feet. He stopped, waiting for his eyes to adjust. He could see the windows at the far end of the room and a very dim light seeped in. Still he could see nothing yet. Eyes were adjusting to the dark.

His heart was in his stomach. He was frightened for himself – hair on his body standing up – and sick about what might have happened to Buddha. He stepped back outside, pulled out his cell phone, punched in 911 on the little, lit numerals. As he spoke he moved toward his car half a block away and retrieved his flashlight. It was one of those large flashlights, used as much as a bludgeon as it was for light. Lang didn't usually carry a gun.

He arrived back at the door as a black and white pulled to a stop. No sound, but red and blue lights twirling.

'What's up?' the cop asked through the open window.

'Burglary, I think. No lights.'

'You hitting clean up?'

For a moment Lang didn't understand the question. Then he realized he was still holding the bat.

'You want me to put this down?'

'That's the idea,' the cop said, getting out of the car. His partner did the same from the other side.

Lang tossed it next to the door.

'I didn't know whether the guy was still inside.'

The cop, a young Latino, nodded. An even younger Asian female cop came up beside him. Times have certainly changed, Lang thought. For the better. He remembered when the cops were white – all white. But this was now a diverse city. He didn't know the exact percentages, but at least a third was Hispanic, nearly a third was Asian and the rest a blend of others.

They went inside with the flashlights. The place had been severely trashed. If whoever came in was looking for something, he masked curiosity with plain meanness.

'You break up with someone recently?' the female cop asked.

'A quarter of a century ago,' Lang said, still moving the beam of light around the room and up to the loft. 'I think she's over it by now.' That's when the shaft of light hit two big, golden eyes. Buddha, the intelligent being he was, had found a safe place.

Lang took in and exhaled a deep breath. The rest didn't really matter —the smashed, broken and bent. The idea of it, though, mattered a great deal. His home was his and his alone. He didn't like the idea that anyone had come inside, let alone without invitation. Lang found a lamp on the floor, plugged it in. It worked, casting an uneasy and strangely shadowed light over the debris.

The female officer had out her notebook, while Lang continued to look around, opening the bathroom door. The mirror was smashed.

'Your name?'

'Lang. Noah.'

'This is your place?'

'Yes.'

'You live here alone?'

'Pretty much.' He glanced up at Buddha, who sat on the edge of the loft and looked down, no doubt evaluating the situation.

'Your occupation?' she asked.

'Private investigator.'

'I see,' she said.

With the light on he could see more of the damage. His big screen TV, his stereo. Anything breakable was broken. The sofa was intact. For that he was grateful.

'Yeah, we all see,' Lang said.

'You have any idea who might have done this?'

'Maybe.'

'You called us out here, remember?' She didn't appreciate Lang being coy.

'I do.' His money was on Theodore Kozlov. The guy wasn't too pleased with their last conversation. But what bugged him was the fact that he was having dinner with Carly Paladino. Only she would have known he would be away and roughly how long he would be gone. She did step outside briefly to use her cell phone. 'I can't be sure, but a case with Theodore Kozlov didn't go well.'

Lang wanted it down officially. A police report would work fine. If the cops paid Kozlov a visit that would be even better. Priceless.

'This man, he threatened you?' she asked.

'Veiled threats at the very least. Worth a conversation, I think.'

She looked at Lang. Her expression showed she'd be the judge of that.

He hoped they would question Mr Kozlov, if nothing else, to let him know that this kind of threat wouldn't work. A tit for tat – kind of police visit for police visit. But vandalism in the Western Addition probably didn't count for as much as a similar breach in Sea Cliff or Pacific Heights.

The police didn't ask much more and they made no promises as they left. Lang didn't mention Carly. But the possibility was there and it was troubling. He didn't want to believe it. The thing was that being a private investigator has its hazards. One of them is that after a few years – much like a cop – you lose your ability to trust anybody, and for that matter, for them to trust you. You see too much. Just as civilians feel uncomfortable around the cops, they also feel uncomfortable around private investigators. The difference is the cops have other cops who share their world. PIs don't trust each other. It is the price they pay. It was the price he was paying with Carly Paladino.

The destruction of his little quarters could easily be a cover for a search. And if that was the case, then the Hanovers – and Carly Paladino – were as much suspects as Mr Kozlov. They wanted the case closed before it could gather any more media steam.

Lang wasn't given to self-pity. In the world at large, he had a pretty nice life. However, he did think it odd – as he sorted the debris into three piles: intact, destroyed and fixable – that the only two living beings he trusted were his gender-shifting friend Thanh and his often other-worldly cat, Buddha.

Carly had enjoyed the early evening meeting. Despite the fact that the two of them covered the sadness of Olivia's death, she couldn't deny that she'd enjoyed getting out of her flat for a less predictable evening. She was still evaluating Lang. The investigation field, especially the kind of street-level investigation that Lang practiced, was full of flakes and shady characters. Flaky or not, there was a little more electricity in Lang than in Peter.

She changed into her robe, poured a glass of wine that she promised herself she would make last the rest of the evening, and lit a fire. She put Norah Jones on the stereo. She brought her computer and blanket to the sofa and settled in. She again went to Olivia's personal listing. Had she missed anything?

This had become deeply personal. If it wasn't clear before, she had spent most of her life keeping everything at a comfortable distance. Her work was done remotely with names that meant nothing to her. Checking out this person for prior bad acts at the request of a corporation that was thinking about hiring him or her, investigating others to see if they had the assets they claimed to have before a firm invested in a new corporation, which is what she had done for Walter Hanover a few times.

These cases were easy. Facts spoke. She was never involved with the client personally nor the object of the investigation. Even her relationship with Peter was, by unspoken mutual consent, superficial. There were no heart-wrenching confessions, no teeth-grinding battles, no admissions of weakness or doubt or fear. No tears. Not much laughter. Not much anger. It was politely intimate, comfortably sexual. Pleasantly passionless. She didn't really miss him. She missed the idea of him.

At least work had changed. Yes, she had affected human lives. Someone doesn't get the job. Someone doesn't get the money or does. But until now her investigations were much like a pilot carrying smart bombs. They dropped from a great distance. They reigned down on unseeable victims. So abstract they didn't exist. Olivia was not unseeable. More and more she *existed* in Carly's mind. This was a whole different thing.

Carly went to the counter that divided the kitchen from the living room. She pushed the power button on the laptop and took it with her to the sofa where she could work in comfort.

She went through the lists of preferences and again clicked on the video.

What she saw changed everything.

It was grainy. The light was so low there was no color, only a pale gray face. Eyes closed, lips moving so slightly, they couldn't have uttered words, only sound. The eyes opened, then nearly closed. Even in the dim light, one could see pain. The screen went dark.

Carly was shaken. She held back her emotions. The obvious fact that Olivia couldn't have posted the video since it wasn't there earlier meant that someone else posted it. The murderer? At minimum, it was someone

who knew something more, something important. The scene was too
personal not to be connected in some way.

She tossed the computer to the foot of the sofa, retrieved her bag,
finding Lang's phone number. She punched them in.

'Yes,' came a frustrated voice.

'I'm sorry to bother you, but this is important.'

'Go ahead.'

'Someone posted a new video on Olivia's Z-Tube account.'

'What was it?'

'Of her dying, I think. They removed the earlier video and replaced it
with one of her nearly unconscious.'

'Maybe it can be tracked,' Lang said.

'I'll send you the link,' she said. 'Your email address?'

'Send it to the office. Someone smashed my home computer.'

'What?'

'While we were having dinner, some hood was at my place busting up
everything that could be busted.'

Carly didn't know what to say. She knew that she wasn't above suspicion. If the shoe were on the other foot, she would think the same thing.

'I'm sorry.'

'Did you tell anyone where we were going?'

Did she tell Nadia? Maybe. Still, how would that get to a perpetrator?

'No.' She understood why the question was asked, but she was hurt by
the implicit suspicion nonetheless.

'All right, I'm going down to the office. I'll talk to you later,' Lang said,
and flipped his phone shut. He needed to go to his office anyway to see if
it was spared the tornado treatment.

Lang's office was untouched. Actually, it was touched. It was cleaner. No
doubt Thanh had been in. The waste can revealed one lipstick-smudged
cigarette butt. Lang checked it. It was Thanh's brand – one of the three
smokes his friend smoked each day. At least those days when Thanh was in
touch with her feminine side. As a male, Thanh didn't smoke at all. She
was apparently in earlier to take care of some of her other business – about
which Lang knew little – and out again before Lang arrived. Fortunately
Lang didn't have to worry about Thanh.

Paranoia was a positive characteristic sometimes. As the computer came
to life and connected itself to the Internet, Lang still wasn't sure how to
figure out whether it was Carly or Kozlov who had trashed his home.
Kozlov let Lang know that before he'd been hired he was checked out.
Unless you were the kid incarcerated for the murder of Olivia, few people

get far enough off the grid to be truly anonymous. Anyone could have traced his power and light bill. Choosing Lang's home was a way Kozlov could let Lang know he was vulnerable and it was personal. Then again, was it another coincidence that Carly called him that evening after dinner – perhaps to get his reaction on the breach of his living quarters? Then again, dinner had been his idea.

Lang keyed in the code to get to his email. Another click and he saw the dozens of emails he had, most of them pharmaceutically regarding how embarrassing it must be to have a small penis. Carly's email was the most recent. He clicked. Nothing in the body of the message except the URL address of Olivia's video.

Lang clicked as instructed.

The response was quick. The screen popped back with a message. 'The video you requested is no longer available.'

Lang went back to the email, clicked again. Same message. He picked up the phone, punched in Carly's number.

'Carly Paladino,' she said.

'It's gone.'

'What's gone?'

'The video.'

'What? Wait.'

Lang took a deep breath, looked out of the dirty window. The lights on the street were fuzzy in the misty darkness and largely ineffectual.

'I don't know what happened,' Carly said.

'You're sure . . .'

'Of course I'm sure,' she said. 'Fuck. Sorry. Now the world is going to think I'm crazy.'

'The whole world, huh?'

'I left a voicemail for Gratelli telling him what I told you.'

'I don't think you're crazy,' Lang said. It wasn't crazy to make up some flimsy excuse to call him and get the lay of the land. That he didn't tell her.

'Thanks,' she said.

'Don't mention it.'

Lang's heart and mind were on different tracks. His mind couldn't dismiss Carly's possible complicity, a suspicion heightened by this recent event. How and why had the video disappeared – and so suddenly? But his heart had already judged Carly a decent human being. His heart landed squarely on Kozlov. It was the kind of thuggish behavior attributed to Kozlov by some who knew him.

He hoped the police would question him. Whether or not they do, Lang wasn't done pushing back. What was Kozlov's partner's name? Lacey.

Emmett Lacey. He sent Thanh an email to do a complete investigation of Lacey. What were they working on? In whose pocket were they at the moment? It seemed to him that Kozlov was more upset with the idea that someone was looking into his business – not the death of his wife. The business. Not a lover. Money.

So how might he take Lang looking into his business partner, reputedly the brains, Emmett Lacey?

Next, Lang called Chaz West. He filled the attorney in on the strange happenings with Olivia's videos. If Carly was right the second video must have been posted and removed after the young man was incarcerated. It could be convincing evidence that the boy didn't do the killing – or possibly there was an accomplice.

Lang asked Chaz about the journals that he'd nicknamed the 'codebook.' Lang could pick them up when he had the time, Chaz told him.

'I couldn't figure it out. Maybe you can, but I lay odds you don't.'

Lang looked around his office, toyed with the idea of staying there for the night, but thought again about Buddha. The intruder hadn't screwed up the bed. He'd go home.

He stopped at the Blue Jay Café for a blackened Snapper sandwich, fries and a beer. He wanted the bread pudding, but talked himself out of it. Vanity trumped gluttony. So much for one of the deadly sins. He still had a few others to contend with.

Eighteen

Carly Paladino thought she had probably lost Lang. Whatever trust she'd managed to build during their pleasant dinner was gone. The idea that the video was there only moments previous and then gone was mind-boggling to her. The idea that she should have decided to call Lang shortly after he'd discovered his home had been invaded and many of his belongings had been decimated during their dinner – it was all too much.

'Get a grip,' she told herself out loud. She was used to supporting other people, wanting to please other people, careful of their feelings. At Vogel Security, she had been a company girl, providing management with reliable management of day-to-day operations. She had had a high position, yes; but it had involved towing company line. She had rarely needed to challenge conventional thinking. With Peter, she had been comfort food, providing him safe emotional and physical harbor against the storms in his career. Though Peter wasn't especially demanding, she wasn't in the least. In both cases, she wanted acceptance, approval. She took note of how that had worked out for her. Had she learned nothing?

> *The sounds of prison at night — sounds some people make in the midst of dreams and nightmares — seemed like music haunted by despair and longing. Daniel Lee heard the notes, long notes. Each one he understood emotionally, allowing him to be able to isolate one soul from another. The moans and cries escaped through the cracks and slipped through the darkness like tendrils through the earth.*
>
> *He took the sounds in, individually and together. It created a sense of the place as if the place, too, were alive. When it was too much for him to bear, he escaped to his own place. Instead of outside, his was inside. It was a quiet place that, depending on where he chose to go, was full of constant wonder.*

Vincente Gratelli spent thirty-five years in the San Francisco Police Department, fifteen of them as Homicide Inspector. The less than fluid movement of his bony frame made it seem as if an arthritic puppeteer manipulated him. His pale face showed the skeleton beneath, and the bags under his eyes were dark and almost comically large. He had never been a looker, but had lived with his looks long enough to be beyond vanity.

He lost the love of his life five years ago to cancer. The children were off on their own. Two sons, one in Boston, one in Florence. He had lost his homicide inspector partner a few years ago to suicide, though that wasn't how it had been presented to the world. Gratelli was beyond mourning as he was beyond both shock and empathy. He accepted what had to be, and did his best to take care of those things that could be taken care of — like murder. And, generally, he was unfazed by what that meant day to day. Dealing with death had become almost clerical.

But he wasn't without intuition, and there was something that bugged him about the suspect in the Olivia Hanover murder.

He thought about that as he undressed to go to bed. The fog had come in late afternoon, cooling everything off. He wouldn't turn on the heat though. No need to heat the night. He slipped on his pajamas, stepped into his slippers, put an extra blanket on the bed and went into the kitchen to get a glass of water, which he put on the table by the bed. He went to the bathroom, absently checked the mirror to assure himself he was alive, then put the pills he had to take in the morning — a Prilosec for acid reflux, some calcium with vitamin D for his bones, and a multivitamin — into a small cup. This way he wouldn't forget.

Gratelli knew you couldn't tell a book by its cover or a murderer by his face or demeanor. Still, he couldn't bring himself to see Daniel Lee as a murderer. Everything led to the boy. And there was, in Gratelli's estimation, something not quite right about the boy. But murder?

These thoughts tumbled about in his mind as he made sure he continued his nightly ritual. Gratelli checked to make sure the apartment door was locked, turned off the lights in the living room, plucked his glasses from his suit jacket, picked up his book – *The Life and Times of Giuseppe Verdi* – and headed back into the bedroom. His wife thought the apartment was too small. Maybe then. Now it was too large.

In the bedroom, he undressed and climbed into bed, where he would read, until his eyelids became heavy, until he would convince himself that he would set his book to one side for just a moment.

He'd wake up in the middle of the night, usually around three. He'd put a the bookmark in his book, make his nightly trip to the bathroom, come back, take a sip of water, and turn off the light, and go back to sleep.

He often dreamed richly. This night, he was on a hilltop overlooking smaller rolling hills below. The clear sky was dark blue. Stars fell and frightened a puppy.

In the morning he had a bowl of Total and coffee and read the *Chronicle*. When he arrived at the office at 6.45 on Sunday morning, long before the few others who would make it in on this weekend day, he listened to his voicemail. At first he didn't understand what Carly Paladino was saying about these videos. Eventually, he pieced it together and realized that while it didn't clear young Daniel Lee, it put a hole in the wall of circumstantial evidence that damned him.

He'd talk to the tech support people, see if he could track down the person who removed one video and posted the other. He hadn't seen the video, but perhaps it had been done by someone trying to honor her in death. Perhaps it was the murderer. Based on Carly's description, either way, the work was done by someone who had intimate access to Olivia.

A little past eight, the cell phone beside her bed beeped Chopin. Carly Paladino tried to open her eyes, but her grasp of consciousness was tenuous at best. The other side tried to tug her back. Daylight won and she got the phone before Gratelli's gravelly voice was transferred to voicemail.

'I got your message,' Gratelli said. 'Sorry if I called too early.'

'It's all right. I needed to wake up. Things to do.'

'Would you send an email to one of our tech guys so he can check all this out? I'll get you the address.'

'I can.'

'What prompted you to check the site?'

'I wanted to make sure there wasn't anything I missed. And I was surprised that the original video was gone and more surprised at a new video had been posted on her page posthumously.'

'I understand. Do you have a pen and paper handy?'

'In a minute.' She went to the kitchen counter, found a Crate & Barrel catalog and a pencil. She wrote down the email address Gratelli gave her.

That was it. She put some coffee beans in the grinder and took a pitcher of filtered water from the refrigerator. It dawned on her that she had now told Noah Lang and the homicide inspector of her discovery, but had not told Pamela Hanover, who was paying for the information.

She checked the clock on the microwave. 8.17. Forgetting it was Sunday and that Pamela's secretary Gary, would not be there to screen the calls, Carly was surprised to hear the woman's voice.

'Something has come up,' Carly said. 'You have a moment?'

'No, I don't,' Hanover said. 'I'm sorry. I have a luncheon and I'm getting this together on my own. If you like, drop by the Magic Flute this afternoon – one thirty or two. Do you know where it is?'

'Yes, on Sacramento, right?'

'Yes. Drop by. I can steal a moment. Thank you.'

The connection was gone.

That was it. Carly hadn't actually agreed. But she didn't have to. There was no choice in the matter. That's how things were when dealing with the likes of the Hanovers.

A dozen or so women, maybe more, all about Pamela Hanover's age but looking ten years younger than they were, sat at a long table in the middle room of the restaurant. The first room was a cozy, traditional dining area, already full of Sunday brunchers. The middle space was a screened in porch overlooking the third, a large outdoor patio with umbrellas and heat lamps. The women ranged from attractive to beautiful. You used to be able to tell the well-heeled by their tans. Now it was just the glow of their spa-pampered flesh. The hair, the nails, the summer dresses were impeccable. Carly thought she recognized MaxMara, TSE, and Elie Tabaris. She remembered her mother's summer dresses, probably costing $19.99. These weren't her mother's dresses.

The restaurant itself sat on that section of Sacramento Street that had low-key shops. No neon allowed. No burrito shops. No Korean barbecue. Just some high-priced stores and a French laundry, where clients were encouraged to register before dropping off their soiled clothing.

The Magic Flute, known for its fine food, catered to the expensive

Presidio Heights neighborhood and, much like nearby Sociale, a lovely place hidden behind the storefronts at the end of a stone path, was essentially a neighborhood restaurant. Carly knew the Magic Flute, knew that families in Pacific Heights held their anniversaries, birthdays and bridal showers there on a regular basis.

Pamela's eyes followed the gaze of her fellow celebrants to catch Carly who stood just inside the doorway.

She smiled, whispered something to one of the women and came toward Carly. The two walked out in front of the restaurant, stood in the shade of one of the trees in front. She waited for Carly to speak.

'Sorry to interrupt, but I wanted to tell you about something odd in the investigation,' Carly said.

Pamela's look gave her permission to continue.

'It seems that Olivia had a page on a popular website for young people. She had her profile there and some photos . . .'

Pamela Hanover looked disturbed.

'All quite normal photographs. Many young girls – and boys – do this. You've probably heard of Facebook and YouTube. It's like that. She also had a short video up at the time of her death. I checked the video link again last night and the previous video was gone and a new video was there in its place. Slightly disturbing.'

'What kind of disturbing?'

'Just a few seconds showing Olivia out of it, as if near sleep or possibly on drugs.' The 'or possibly dying' Carly didn't mention.

Pamela Hanover was quiet.

'Can we take all this off the Internet?' she asked.

'The video is already gone. I'm sure we can find a way to take down the profile.'

'Good. Good work.' Pamela Hanover turned to go back inside.

'Mrs Hanover. It suggests something else.'

'What?'

'Whoever is messing with Olivia's page could have been involved in Olivia's death.'

Carly couldn't tell whether it was anger or sadness rising in Hanover's body. Something was shaking it.

'And the person the police have in custody?'

'We don't know what it means exactly. But Daniel Lee couldn't have switched the videos. It suggests that someone else was quite intimate with Olivia and had access to her.'

'Who's this "we"?'

'I've talked to the police,' Carly said, determined not to mention Lang.

'Before you talked with me?'

'Yes.'

'Well, perhaps they will pay you for your work from now on,' she said, turning to go back inside.

'Wait a minute.' Carly's voice penetrated the quiet street.

Stunned, Pamela Hanover turned back.

'If you hired me to make the crime go away, no matter what the consequences,' Carly said, 'you got the wrong person. If what you said just now was what you meant, then let's not leave my employment in question. I want an answer now. Are we working together on this or not?'

Mrs Hanover stood, frozen in place. Her face expressionless. She reminded Carly of photographs she'd seen of victims of atrocities. She was shutting down emotionally. She couldn't handle even this mild confrontation.

'I'm sorry,' Carly said, this time softly. 'We need to clear this up.'

Hanover appeared to nod. 'Let's talk tomorrow.' Her voice was weak and uncertain. 'It's all just too much, you know.'

They stared at each other for another moment.

'Please,' Pamela Hanover said.

Nineteen

Saturdays, Sundays, mornings, afternoons, evenings, nights – it didn't matter to Lang. His line of work demanded flexibility. It was what he loved and hated about the job. Unpredictability was guaranteed. He spent this morning getting rid of all that was no longer valuable in his violated domain. A former client, who ran a trash pick-up service, was convinced to come by and pick up the debris on short notice.

In the afternoon, with his living space having merely a sofa, bed, refrigerator and stove, Lang went to the office. Thanh, who regarded the normal schedules most mortals use for living with disrespect, was already there and had, out of boredom or duty, ran a whole report on Emmett Lacey, Kozlov's partner and, as Lang had confirmed from Thanh's work, the senior partner.

He also learned that Emmett Lacey, 63, was not nor had he ever been married. He had a degree in Law, an MBA in Business, and owned a lobbying firm, Lacey & Associates, for whom Kozlov was senior vice president. Lacey owned a condo in Sacramento, a vacation home in Maui, and a home in Presidio Heights, a neighborhood some considered part of Pacific Heights.

Known associates were high-end event planners, caterers, politicians, and San Francisco's moneyed or political movers and shakers. No doubt, Lang thought as he read the report, Lacey knew the Hanovers and Katherine Wexford. Lang quickly linked and then quickly unlinked the deaths of Mrs Kozlov and Olivia Hanover. The coincidence, even in this small big town, would be too much.

Lacey's wealth was in the low tens of millions, not in the hundreds of millions. He was a member of several private clubs which he attended, but he was rarely photographed at the important social galas, and often lunched at Le Central in what some good-humoredly called San Francisco's French Quarter – little more than a consulate, a lovely hotel and couple of fine French restaurants just south of the formal gates of Chinatown.

Lacey was highly visible to those that mattered, but not at all visible to those who watched those who mattered. He wasn't likely to come up in the gossip columns – and, Lang concluded – given the marginal legality of his activities this partial invisibility was highly desirable.

'This is good,' Lang said to Thanh, who was working on something else.

Thanh nodded. Seated at Lang's desk, where he usually sat when he was in, Thanh was androgynous today, having intended to be – or perhaps merely a result of indecision or indifference.

'You have fun last night?' Lang asked.

'I'm getting too old,' Thanh said. 'I go out. I stand. I have a drink. And it's loud and I don't care any more about all these people running around trying to fulfill their respective fantasies. I want to be home in bed watching an old movie.'

'It's finally set in, has it?'

Thanh smiled. 'But the libido isn't entirely dead.'

'No, I have a feeling that it torments our souls until the very last breath.'

He smiled too, but he was thinking of Carly Paladino.

'Something going on in your life?' Thanh asked.

'Sure, I would tell you . . . the Sphinx.'

'Mystery is the secret of my charm. What's up on your two cases?'

'Mysteries, both. But not very charming,' Lang said, still reading the report. 'Oh, that's interesting.'

Lacey's firm dealt almost solely with gambling, more particularly Indian gaming. This was big money. Getting, or for that matter losing, casino licenses was fraught with opportunities for fraud, bribery, and other forms of creative corruption all at the highest levels. It brought politicians and gangsters together, not that they've always been that far apart. Both shared a predilection for Byzantine plots and a desperate need for discretion in their activities.

'What you've done here –' Lang closed the file – 'is a big help with Kozlov. With the Hanovers, I need a better in with the family. I don't know how it could be anyone but someone inside the house who killed her.'

He realized that this suspicion was heightened by Carly's claim of a new but briefly posted video on a website. That too was suspicious. What was that about? He wanted to trust her. So far, that wasn't easy to do.

Carly Paladino met Pamela Hanover at eleven on Monday morning. Unlike past visits, Carly was led to the back garden. Hanover was already there, sitting on a yellow-cushioned chair at a Moroccan tiled table on a middle level of the three-tiered garden. The June morning was mild, warm. A slight breeze ruffled leaves and blooms. The spectacular view of the homes and Bay below was the only rival to the magnificent flora and fauna that surrounded them.

Hanover stood as Carly approached. Her facial expression, real or feigned, suggested vulnerability.

'Thank you for coming,' she said, nodding toward a chair at the table. 'After yesterday, I wouldn't blame you if you wanted nothing further to do with me.'

'You're under tremendous stress,' Carly said.

Hanover, wearing some expensive sweats, nodded. Carly thought she'd never seen someone so tense in such leisurely clothing. Hanover pushed aside a stack of notecards she had been writing, but remained quiet, acknowledging the approach of the housekeeper who carried a tray of croissants, butter and jam.

'Would you like coffee or tea?' Hanover asked Carly.

Thinking what formalities – and the need for a guide should she need to go to the bathroom – Paladino thanked them but declined. She really wanted one of those croissants, but willed her hands away from them.

'Tell Gary to come out here and pick up these invitations,' Hanover told the housekeeper.

'Yes, ma'am.'

'There is just so much to do, so much,' Hanover said.

The garden was on the north side of the house, a position best used for ferns and ivies. Yet further away from the nearly constant shade, sunlight had coaxed a number of plants to bloom brightly.

'Surely you can take time away . . .'

'No,' Hanover shook her head. 'There are responsibilities.'

'It's OK to grieve. It's important. No one will begrudge you that time, no one you should care about anyway.'

'You don't understand. This little gala will bring in at least three million dollars to help shelters for battered women. We haven't received the RSVPs we need. I can't just say "I'm too sad."'

'Can't someone else . . .?'

'Please, this isn't something we need to talk about right now.'

She seemed embarrassed and frustrated. Carly thought that the woman rarely showed one emotion, but always some complex blend as if her brain could never find just one feeling and the result was paralysis.

'I want to apologize,' Hanover continued, 'for behaving the way—'

'That's all right,' Carly said, interrupting.

'Please, this is hard enough. I want very much for the person who killed my daughter to be caught and punished. If I've sent a different message, I didn't intend to. However, I need for you to work for me . . . for us. I need for you to help insulate the Hanover family from any scandal, any hint of scandal, that could diminish our ability to fulfill our obligations. Someone has destroyed my daughter. Don't let them destroy the whole family. Our responsibilities do not stop because of this unfortunate . . . tragic . . . event.'

It was time for Carly to be straight with her. Though she wasn't a klutz when it came to dealing with people, public relations wasn't really high in her skill set.

Gary Gray arrived, taking the stack of notecards from the table.

'Get them over to Bobbie Markel so she can get them out today. We're already late. Also, these returns,' she said, pushing a small stack of returned invitations. 'Check out the addresses, get me their phone numbers so I can call them, and be sure to update their addresses.'

She seemed about to relax when another thought struck her.

'Make sure that Evan and Jordan attend,' she told him.

'I'll do my best,' he said, giving her a little warning smile and a shrug. He wasn't Superman, he seemed to say.

'I'll talk with their father,' she said. 'Just remind them to put it on their calendar.'

He nodded and left.

'Mrs Hanover, I'm not an insulator. I'm an investigator. I can't protect you from the facts, but I can provide you with them. If I'm not the person you want, that's fine. But before you decide let me tell you, since you've paid me for my services it is very possible that the murderer lives or works here.'

There was a long silence.

'You know what that means?'

Hanover stared blankly.

'It means that the police are not done with your family.'

'Go on,' she said.

'Daniel Lee may have killed her. He isn't ruled out. But if he did it, the video suggests that there might be someone else involved, someone who had access to her. Either way, I don't believe the police are done with their investigation of family and staff. And even if they are convinced they have the right person, the defense attorney isn't. And he has an investigator who, as you know, is determined to find someone else as a possible perpetrator to establish reasonable doubt. There you have it. Make of it what you will.'

Carly said all this in even, businesslike tones. No belligerence. However, she wasn't sure Pamela Hanover understood or even heard.

'I just want you to understand that,' Carly added.

Pamela Hanover took a deep, but interrupted breath, as one does sometimes after crying. Only she hadn't cried. Carly wondered if she had ever cried. But there were signs of strain. The outdoors seemed to do little to restore the woman's health. She was pale, drawn, exhausted. She also seemed brittle. So rigid, one of these little breezes could snap her.

On the way out, with her job still in limbo, Carly saw an invitation that had been dropped on the steps down, probably by Gray. She picked it up. It just had a signature, Pamela Hanover's, but no note. She put it in her bag. She wasn't sure why. Perhaps, because the Hanovers were so guarded, it was important to know anything she could about the family no matter how trivial it seemed.

The day for Lang was set. He'd called Amy Logan. She was the woman that Kozlov's wife met for lunch the day Lang trailed her. He had taken down the license plate of her Rover when he saw Mrs Kozlov lunch with her. He used his contact at SFPD to check the registration and learned it belonged to Howard Logan. Amy answered.

Initially Amy Logan wanted nothing to do with Lang. She was nervous, suspicious and not at all eager to get involved. When Lang told her the whole story, including his suspicion that Mrs Kozlov's death was not her choice, Amy expressed some interest, but refused to meet. Eventually, he convinced her to meet him in a public place. They would meet for lunch at Pizzeta. Lang knew of the place. It was out on the Avenues. And as the name implies, it specializes in pizza. That was just fine.

Before his meeting with Amy Logan though, Lang and West met again with Daniel Lee mid morning. The swelling in the kid's face had gone down, but he had the look of a Zombie – lifeless, drained of energy.

'You getting any sleep?' Lang asked.

Daniel Lee shook his head.

'Your notebooks?' Lang asked. 'I've been trying to read them. I can't make sense of them.'

Daniel remained quiet.

'Is this a real code? Or just gibberish.'

'Gibberish,' Daniel said with a hint of a smile that could have meant that he was pulling the wool over Lang's eyes. Maybe he was amused that anyone would spend time with his hobby, or he just found the word funny.

'You sure about that?' Lang asked.

Daniel nodded.

'There was a video on Olivia's online profile,' West said. 'Did you know that?'

Lee shook his head again.

'Well, there's something puzzling,' West said. 'After her death, the video disappeared and, more strangely, a new one appeared – this one apparently showing Olivia drifting off to sleep or drifting off to death. We're not sure.'

Daniel Lee's face remained the same.

'The police think you may have had an accomplice, someone close to you, who knows about all of this. Will they find this person?' West leaned forward, his eyes meeting Daniel's. But Daniel disengaged quickly, looking away, clearly demonstrating he wasn't about to answer.

Resigned, West sat back, took a deep breath.

'We have something we want to show you,' West said. He had loosened his tie a bit before going into the interview as a token sacrifice to the kid's distrust of suits. Now he stood up, slipped off his suit coat and placed it over the back of the chair, taking his time.

When he sat again, he slowly slid the eight-by-ten photograph across the table the prosecution had surrendered on discovery. It showed Olivia's body as it had been discovered in the brush on the northeastern slope of Lafayette Park.

Daniel Lee looked and then looked away.

'I showed this to a friend of mine,' West said. 'A forensic psychologist. He said that whoever put her there cared for the victim. Her position, on her side, head on her arms, as if asleep, was very respectful, perhaps even loving. She said that the killer either regretted Olivia's death or deeply regretted the necessity of Olivia's death.'

Daniel Lee did not respond.

'Daniel, you loved her,' West continued. 'You were intimate with her. You had sex with her with or without her consent. Did you take her against her will? Is that why you killed her?'

Lang knew that West was being prosecutorial because nothing else was working. He was getting nothing from the boy. Stone soup. But this time he got a response, if not any worthwhile information.

Lee's eyes flashed.

'I didn't kill her.'

'You were afraid that she would tell her parents and they would call the police,' West continued.

'Whose side are you on?' Lang asked Lee, his tone softer than the question itself.

Lee looked puzzled.

'If you didn't kill her, we believe that someone who knew her must have,' Lang said. 'You need to help us find that person. Maybe you know that person and you are protecting him?'

'I don't know what you're talking about. Just crazy. You're all crazy.'

'There's nobody else involved in this?'

'In what? Her death? I didn't do it. What else can I say? I don't know anybody. Olivia was the only person I knew. She's dead. It's all over.'

'If what you say is true,' Lang continued, 'you still need to help us find the killer.

'Think of Olivia,' West said.

Daniel gave him a bitter look.

'That's all I think about,' the young man said. 'You guys don't have to work that hard. It's not going to matter. Can I go now?'

Daniel was as unknowable as his journals.

Once Daniel was taken away, Lang suggested to West that the boy be put on suicide watch. He didn't like the 'it's not going to matter' remark.

Lang didn't care what people thought, but he liked the idea that he could move about the city largely unnoticed. For him that meant he dressed a little differently depending on what neighborhood he was going to. You didn't dress up to go to the Mission, but you might wear a blazer with your jeans if you lunched at Le Central. For a little restaurant out on the Avenues what he wore didn't matter a whole lot. This was good because he didn't like it when those kinds of things mattered.

Twenty

It was a pleasant early afternoon out on the Avenues – a neighborhood on the north side of Golden Gate Park called the Richmond. Richmond was home to the new, more suburban – if you could call anyplace in San Francisco suburban – Chinatown. It was also home to Russian immigrants, and a growing number of young up-and-comers. Pizzeta was a good-looking hole in the wall in a pleasant, and mostly residential, neighborhood on 23rd Avenue, just off California. Four tables out front, no more than four inside.

Amy Logan was there already. He recognized her and she seemed to sense that the man heading toward her table was Lang.

Slender. She was not quite a redhead. Short hair. Lightly freckled. She was fine boned and pretty in a dreamy way. Not like 'dreamy' man, but 'dreamy' as in other-worldly. Sensitive. She had a glass of white wine in front of her.

'Are we having lunch?' Lang asked. He hated sitting in a restaurant without ordering something.

'Go ahead,' she said. 'I've already ordered.'

He went inside, ordered a glass of red wine and the Margherita pizza. He got his wine right away and took it outside.

'Nice little place,' Lang said. 'I've heard about it. Never tried it.'

She nodded.

He noticed how slow her eyelids moved when she blinked. Dreamy. Fine nose. Clear blue eyes. Sensuous lips.

'How long did you know Mrs Kozlov?' Lang asked.

'I would like to know more, Mr Lang . . . you know . . . your interest in this. I didn't fully understand what you were saying on the phone.'

He hadn't said much – just that he wasn't sure Mrs Kozlov's death was a suicide and that he would like to learn more about her and her relationship with Mr Kozlov. He knew they were friends. There wasn't much to say, but he'd try.

'Mr Kozlov hired me because he believed his wife was having an affair,' Lang said.

She shook her head in disbelief.

'That's silly,' Mrs Logan said. 'The last person in the world . . .'

'I was outside her home in the car when the shot was fired. I'm not a hundred per cent sure, but I may have seen someone running from the home. Honestly, I'm feeling a little guilty that I might have been used to help cover up a murder. That's the whole story. Not much else to tell.'

Her eyes were large. Disbelieving in another way.

'You are telling me . . . ?'

'I'm only telling you what I suspect. I'm still trying to make sense of all this.'

She started to look down at her wine when her salad arrived. She smiled at the young woman who brought it.

'What kind of relationship did the two of them have?' Lang asked.

Mrs Logan nudged the purple and green lettuce leaves around on the plate with her fork.

'She was his property.'

'Go on.'

'She was treated like royalty on one hand. She wasn't expected to work, even to keep house. But she was on a short leash. She even had to sneak out to have lunch with me.'

'How long have you known her?'

'Since college. Best friends then.'

'Not so much now?'

'Not so much because we don't have a lot of time together. I was brides-maid at her wedding. She was his second wife and he seemed so romantic, so doting, so much in love.'

'Her family?' Lang asked.

'Gone now. Her mother died of cancer young. And after Lillia became Mrs Kozlov, her father retired to Mexico. She didn't want to burden him with her problems.'

'What did she tell you about Kozlov? Did he hurt her?'

'Not physically. She said he never struck her, but that once he put a gun in her mouth, saying that if she ever cheated on him, death would be his response.'

'Lillia,' Lang said, using her first name for the first time, 'didn't talk to the police or anyone about this?'

'She loved him,' Amy Logan said, sipping her wine. She still hadn't touched the salad. 'She said that no relationship was perfect.'

'No children?'

'No. He didn't want any.'

'Really? Seems as if a man with his ego would want to perpetuate it.'

'I think he didn't want to share her affection with children.' Finally she took a bite of her salad.

The pizza arrived. The thinnest crust Lang had ever seen. The whole slice was thinner than a cracker. It crunched as he bit into the first hot bite. It was maybe the best pizza he'd tasted. A sip of wine. He looked down the tree-lined street. The sun was soft and the breeze had no temper-ature. He was sitting with a beautiful woman. Not a bad line of work, he thought. Except of course, he wasn't getting paid for this gig.

'In the weeks or days before her death, did you see any change in her?'

'We only met once every couple of weeks. Maybe once a month. She found it hard to get out and I have a small business to run,' she said, and having reminded herself, she looked at her watch.

'Did she know much about his business?'

'No. If she did, we didn't talk about it.'

'What did you talk about?'

'Movies, books, clothes. The usual girlfriend things.' She looked at Lang as if measuring. 'No politics, no sports. Oh, she wanted a dog. She wanted an Irish Terrier.'

'So she wasn't any more or less nervous that last time you saw her than she was before.'

'No.'

'How well do you know Mr Kozlov?'

'Not very well. After the wedding, he began pushing people away from them, especially her friends.'

'Would she have confided in anyone else? Another friend? A lawyer? Hairdresser?'

'I don't know how she could have worked with a lawyer. He controlled the books. But you could check with Mikko's on Union. She had her hair and nails done there. She could go out to stay beautiful. But he'd call her there, not on her cell, but the salon's phone. Then he'd call her on the landline at home to make sure she went directly home.'

'Could she have killed herself?' Lang asked.

'I don't know. She didn't talk about it. If I had been that trapped and had no way out, I would have shot him.'

'That surprises me.'

'Looks can be deceiving, Mr Lang. She could have killed herself. She had been in that situation for five years.' She played with her salad, sipped her wine. 'Do you think he killed her?'

'Or had her killed, maybe. I don't know. That's the point. I need to know.' He didn't tell her that he needed to know because he didn't want to go through life as a possible accomplice. She could figure that out if she thought about it at all.

'You wanted me to bring a photograph?'

'Yes. Did you?'

She reached in her bag and pulled out a 5-by-7 photograph that showed Amy, Mrs Kozlov, and another woman.

'At a baby shower shortly after they were married.'

Lang thanked her. What he learned wasn't much more than what he'd heard and what he'd guessed during his brief association with the man. Kozlov was brutal and controlling.

Lang spent twenty minutes trying to find a parking space somewhere in the vicinity of Union Street. The area was one of a half dozen San

Francisco neighborhoods catering to expensive shops not far from Pacific Heights.

He found Mikko's and went in without calling first. He showed his identification to the receptionist and explained that he wanted to talk to the person who worked with Lillia Kozlov. It wasn't Mikko himself, apparently, but a stylist named Rachel. Rachel, it turned out, was in the middle of some critical operation on a client. Lang waited. The investment in time didn't pay off. Rachel said that Lillia was the kind of client who would rather ask questions than answer them.

'I'm afraid I did all the talking, sorry,' Rachel said. She was a stylish woman in her late thirties, Lang guessed. 'She was interested in my art and my life. She was teaching herself to paint, but said she still wasn't very good at it. She was so nice. I was so sorry to hear of her death.'

Lang returned to his de-teched home. No turntable. No CD player. No speakers. No television. No high definition DVD player – the very things that kept him off the streets. What would he do? Read a book? He did that. He laughed. That would be fine, but he'd become accustomed to cinema on his wall and reading with the sounds of jazz and blues in the background.

Without renter's insurance he would have to raise the funds himself, completely. It would be costly. He had no savings to speak of. Maybe this was what Kozlov had in mind. Instead of taking his vengeance out of Lang's hide, make him pay financially. As it stood now, Lang suffered a net financial loss. Kozlov's check wouldn't cover the big screen TV, let alone the rest of the destruction.

And the fact was that he was pretty sure now that it was Kozlov, or more likely, Kozlov's guy or guys. Paranoia had run its course and good sense set in. If Carly Paladino wanted the place searched, she came from a professional agency. She would know how to do it undetected. And what he was also sure of now, was that Kozlov had something to hide. Maybe he just didn't want anyone messing with what he did for a living. That seemed odd because it was Kozlov who brought it up. If it was murder he was hiding, he probably hired it done. By the same guy or guys who destroyed his abode? Lang was guessing yes.

And if that was true, then maybe there was a way to get to him through the hired help. Lang felt good. He believed he had a way in. A little probing might bring them out of the woodwork. He was pretty sure how to do that. He'd do a little poking at the guy who paid Kozlov – Emmett Lacey. And he'd do a little surveillance on Kozlov himself. He'd let the chips fall . . .

* * *

Carly wanted to catch him off guard. She didn't like doing it, but she didn't want Gary Gray girding up for her questions. This way she would get the truth or know that he was lying. She waited until she saw his car pull up – an hour later than she estimated based on knowing when he would leave the Hanovers. 'After seven, the house was theirs,' he said at one point.

Now it was 8.30 in the evening. The golden light disappeared just before sunset, replaced by the fog easily blanketing Gray's house in Diamond Heights – a nice neighborhood above the Castro, once Irish, then the free-love generation of gay men, and now giving way to the swarm of more conservative young marrieds with a varied gender mix.

She got out of her little Mini Cooper and went toward Gray who emerged from his Prius and retrieved two green canvas bags marked 'Whole Foods' from the rear.

As expected he was shocked to see her, but remained polite, inviting her inside. The fog brought a chill.

'Something wrong?' he asked, heading toward the side door of a small Victorian house.

'No. I have some questions. I'm sorry to intrude, but there's something troubling me about Olivia's death. So, I'm being selfish. I want to be able to sleep tonight.'

'I don't blame you,' he said. 'Come in.'

The door led into a spotless, well-equipped kitchen. A bowl of fruit on a counter that had stools and also held a double sink, which meant it could be used for dining and cooking.

'Gary, I hope you got the Japanese eggplant,' said the deep voice nearing the room. 'I forgot to mention it was the Japanese I wanted.'

The voice manifested itself in a tall, handsome black man with a little silver in his hair. Preceding him and headed toward Gary before she saw the stranger in their midst was a young Asian girl, maybe six. She stopped suddenly.

'I'm sorry everybody,' Gary Gray said, putting the bags on the counter. 'This is Carly Paladino. She is helping the Hanovers regarding Olivia.' He turned to Carly. 'This is my partner, Steven, and our daughter, Mia.'

'Nice to meet you,' Steven said.

The little girl smiled bashfully and moved backward until Steven caught her and held her.

'Nice to meet you too,' Carly said. 'I really am barging in. I should have called.'

'She's a private investigator and has some questions for me,' Gary said, holding up the eggplant for Steven's inspection. Steven nodded his approval.

If there was any real surprise in all this it was Carly who felt it the most. Somehow, she just hadn't connected Gary with a family. She was embarrassed that this should surprise her and more embarrassed because she knew they saw it all on her face.

'I'll play with Mia,' Steven said, 'while you two talk.' He smiled and nodded and started toward the door with Mia. He was charming. He stopped for a moment to say, 'Again, nice to meet you Ms Paladino.'

'Let me put these away,' Gary said, putting what needed to be refrigerated into the refrigerator. 'Would you like to stay for dinner?'

'Oh, no,' Carly said, almost too quickly. 'I've done enough damage for one evening.'

'Glass of wine at least. I have an open bottle of Pinot Grigio in here somewhere,' he said, rearranging the shelves in the refrigerator. 'Yesterday's. Should still be good.'

'Please. I'll be indebted to you through at least the next three reincarnations.'

He laughed, pulled out the bottle and leaving the rest of the groceries in the bag brought the bottle and two glasses to the counter.

'How can I help you?' Gary asked.

Twenty-One

Carly Paladino now understood why Gary Gray felt the way he did about Olivia – not just her death, but how she was ignored in life. He had his own daughter, on whom he obviously doted. He was a nice guy living the American dream of family and home. At least that's how he came across. And she believed him.

He had told her that he didn't like 'telling tales out of school,' before confiding a few more things about the Hanovers, particularly Pamela. He thought she was a 'control freak' who probably knew more about what went on in her household than she confessed. He couldn't tell if she knew about the midnight visitor, but couldn't imagine that she didn't know something.

Gary couldn't say for certain that Pamela Hanover was grieving over the loss, but he thought that she was certainly upset. She was always impatient, he told her. She always wanted unpleasant things to 'just go away.' But now her attention span was shorter. Her patience on a trip-wire, and her occasional wry humor now bitter. If he thought that this was anything more than adjusting to the tragedy – and that's what he thought it was – he would look for other work. But he wouldn't now. He wanted to give her time to recover, and help her get through this.

Carly rummaged through all that information as she fixed her dinner. It was late. It would be a light meal. She had a piece of halibut, some rice, and some snow peas. That would do it. She would have one more, just one more glass of wine. She had two at Gary's place. One of them she all but gulped down. Steven came in after a few minutes to start dinner and, Carly thought, to be there for Gary.

As she rummaged through the conversation, her mind also replayed the happy, warm scenes of Gary's home life.

'Maybe I should get a cat,' Carly said, looking around at her comfortable, but empty home. 'Now don't go getting all schmaltzy.'

Fish, she thought. Goldfish. She wasn't looking for high maintenance. Crawl before you walk, she told herself. She'd name them 'Cheap' and 'Tawdry.'

Her mind drifted back to another lonely girl. Olivia. If there was an inclination for Carly to feel sorry for herself, it was erased.

Sometimes, if he woke up especially early, Gratelli would go down a few blocks to Grant, a narrow, one-way street in his Italian neighborhood of North Beach and get coffee and a couple of eggs. He liked this old street early in the morning when it was still quiet and most of the shops were closed. Caffe Trieste, the coffee house of the old Beat Generation, always had an early crowd of coffee drinkers and you could sit outside, but they didn't have breakfast. So Gratelli would take his newspaper a little further up the narrow street.

Before leaving yesterday he'd contacted the jail to let them know that Daniel Lee might pose a suicide threat. Today he had to work through a dilemma. How much weight should he give to Carly Paladino's claim that she saw a video posted on Olivia's website after Olivia's death? The SFPD techies validated that there had been a take down, a put up, and another take down post-mortem. They could not, however, determine what it was.

Anybody on the job as long as Gratelli understood how things work – or don't work. One can't afford to offend rich, powerful families. However, if the police are perceived as being soft because of the suspect's ties to the rich and powerful, there would be serious problems as well. It was a tightrope to be walked by every civil servant involved.

He knew the powers that be wanted the whole thing over with quickly. There were no memos, no direct statements, but there were enough polite inquiries by various offices, including the mayor's and the governor's, to suggest that they didn't want this case to drag out. No fingerprints on the influence. Just some nuanced contact.

If he believed Carly he'd have to continue to poke at the wounds of the Hanover family.

He took a bite of jellied toast and sipped his coffee. And in his mind, he had this one resolved. He didn't want to retire, but he was old enough now that dismissal before retirement didn't matter. He could retire tomorrow. While he liked to think that didn't have all that much to do with his decision, since his decision was to do what was right, it took one tiny bit of pressure off.

Gratelli stood outside the diner. People arrived. Shops were opened – a mix of those there for decades and those who came and went as tastes changed, as trends blossomed and died, as old business families died off and entrepreneurs took chances. The thing he liked best was that there wasn't a McDonald's or Starbucks for as far as the eye could see.

Today, he would inform the prosecutor that he had some serious doubts about the guilt of Daniel Lee.

Morning came to Noah Lang after a long evening of nothing to do and an uneasy sleep. With no music and no movies, he had gone out to a bar and sat for a while before realizing he was just as bored there as he was at home. It took him too long to nod off and what sleep he felt was subject to fits and starts. He realized that he was angrier with Kozlov than he'd thought.

After his first cup of coffee and with Buddha staring at him, Lang punched in the numbers Thanh had given him for Kozlov's boss.

'Mr Lacey, this is Noah Lang.'

'I'm sorry, who?' came the puzzled voice of Emmett Lacey.

'Noah Lang. I'm an investigator. And I understand that you have . . .?'

'Wait a minute. Wait a minute, how did you get my number?'

'A number of people have your number. I understand you are a professional influencer, Mr Lacey. Talking people into things. And I understand you have some thugs working for you if talk doesn't get the job done.'

Click.

Lang called again. This time he got voicemail.

'This is Noah again. Just trying to get a cost estimate, you know if I wanted Mr Kozlov and his guys to break a few bones. How much is that an hour? Toodles. Oh, wait. By the way I might be calling a few of your clients to check references.'

He looked at Buddha.

'My work is done.' The call couldn't have pleased Lacey and it was quite likely as the senior partner, if not the boss, he would let the junior partner know of his displeasure. This would, no doubt, piss off the already pissed off Kozlov.

Lang, now that he'd poked the hornets' nest, showered, shaved, dressed and drove to his office. What he'd accomplished he wasn't exactly sure; but it felt good to strike back.

Lang, Thanh and Brinkman converged on the first floor of the office building.

'A boy today,' Brinkman said, shaking his head with melodramatic gloom. 'My exquisite Sasha, give an old man the goddess in your nature.'

'And you will give me your handsome youth in exchange?' Thanh said, taking off his riding helmet and tucking it under his arm.

'I would if I could. But the frog you see is the frog you get. Thing is, you have a choice.'

'I have many choices.' Thanh smiled at Brinkman. They often played games, teasing, flirting.

'Me, not so much.' Brinkman winked. 'Burial or cremation. That's about it.'

The three stepped into the elevator and stood silently as it climbed ever so slowly to the third floor. Lang took it only to be sociable. He preferred the steps. It was good exercise and the stairway didn't feed his claustrophobia.

Brinkman went right and headed toward his office, disappearing inside most likely to pass the day as he did most days, reading the paper and in an era of streaming videos listening to the radio – especially if there were a game on.

'Have a nice day,' Lang called out after him.

'Shut up,' Brinkman said before his door slammed shut.

When Thanh came back with coffee, Lang explained what happened to his home and how he retaliated by asking for more of the same, doing what Kozlov told him not to – meddling in his business.

'It could come here, Thanh,' Lang warned.

'We haven't had that kind of fun for a while.'

Lang knew Thanh wasn't easily scared. He had gone through more before he was sixteen than most people had in a lifetime.

Carly didn't know what to make of what transpired. Gratelli had called her to set up a time for new interviews with the Hanover family and staff. It was a courtesy on the part of the police, one that was taken as an affront by Pamela Hanover, who was also now convinced that Carly was not fulfilling her job responsibilities. It was the camel that broke the straw's back, it seemed to Carly. She called Gratelli back saying that he was now on his own, that she was off the case.

'Sorry to hear that,' Gratelli said.

'I'm not so sure I am. Good luck.'

Carly had two contradictory feelings – sadness that she had been dismissed from her first job without completing it satisfactorily and a great sense of relief that she was free to investigate the death of Olivia Hanover without prejudice. All this time she had this unpleasant feeling she was part of the conspiracy to minimize Olivia's worth as a human. With that in mind, she stopped in to see Lang in the afternoon.

'You're off the case and still working it?' Lang asked.

'Now, who would do a thing like that?' Thanh asked, not looking up from the computer.

'I'll help you,' Carly said to Lang. 'I want to know who killed her.'

'I still have a job to do,' Lang said. 'I work for the defense. My cause is slightly less noble than yours.'

She nodded.

'We both want the facts, don't we?' she asked, sitting on the arm of the sofa.

'You know better than that. Yeah, personally, I'd like to know what's going on. And I'm going to try to find out. But the way the justice system works, it would be unethical for me to divulge to anyone other than West the results of my investigation. You know as well as I do, the form of justice we practice is a process that at times seems to be at odds with the truth – adversarial argument not altruism. It's not that easy.'

'I know that,' she said, shaking her head.

'And if you are frustrated by it,' Lang asked, 'are you sure you want to be a private investigator.'

'Mildly frustrated.' She smiled. 'I've always done what's been asked of me. What I want now is Olivia's killer and I think that person is inside the Hanover household. Oh, and I *am* a private investigator.'

'Isn't it unethical for you to use information you derived while working for them against them?'

'Shame, shame,' Thanh said. 'She must be a monster.'

'There are gray areas,' Lang said, answering Thanh's sarcasm.

'I don't have any information currently,' she said, 'that isn't already known by everyone – the defense, the police, the prosecution. So I'm starting out even. And I'm not getting paid. Just an ordinary citizen trying to . . .' She thought about saying something sentimental about no one caring about Olivia and decided against it. 'Satisfy my curiosity.'

'She wants to do what's right,' Thanh said. 'You know about that, right?'

'I know, I know,' Lang said. 'Look Paladin . . .'

'Paladino. You can call me Carly.'

'Yes. I'll work with you where and when I can. Just remember, I might not tell you everything. All right?'

'I understand. Do you have a few minutes for us to talk about what we do know? Begin to narrow things down.'

'Sure,' Lang said.

Twenty-Two

Thanh volunteered to pick up sandwiches from the Whole Foods deli. He said he had some errands to run anyway.

'He works here full time?' Carly asked.

'No. Sometimes when he's here he's working for someone else. He has all sorts of jobs. I don't know half of them.' He realized this wasn't the kind of office environment she was used to. 'We're kind of informal around here.' Then to change the subject he added, 'So, where are we with our house full of suspects?'

She ruled out the housekeeper. That was about it. She explained her conversation with Mrs Hanover's secretary about how no one seemed to pay much attention to Olivia, and Olivia paid little attention to them.

'Motive?' Lang asked. 'If she was so inconsequential to all of them, why would anyone bother to kill her?'

'We didn't handle many murders at Vogel Security. I can figure some of this out, but what is your take on the subject? What makes a person kill?'

Lang sat back in his chair. The answer was fresh on his mind. Why did Kozlov kill his wife or have his wife killed?

'Anger. Money. Sex. Revenge. Jealousy. And there's insanity. Someone feels threatened or kills someone just because they want to see what it's like or to see if they can get away with it. Protect a secret.'

They hadn't made much headway by the time the sandwiches arrived. Putting their heads together had yielded nothing more than either of them had found singly. No one seemed to have enough of a motive to bother killing her. Was it possible that Walter had molested her? Could he have killed her? What about big brother Evan? She seemed little more than an irritation to him. And it was a big house. And neither Evan, the cold-hearted playboy, nor Jordan, the shy peacemaker, spent much time at home. They were away at school. Mom? Why? And the help? The house-keeper. It's not likely that she would bother with morphine and ketamine and a motor scooter. Then there was Gary. Motive? It wasn't likely that a guy who liked men – and Carly explained that Gary's lover was a man – would want to kill the young lady unless there was another motive.

'All right, let's look at the way she was killed and how her body was left,' Carly said.

'The person seemed to care for her.'

'And what we keep finding is that no one particularly cared for her, or at least about her.'

More discussion created more confusion. Carly bowed out mid after-noon. Thanh came and went as Lang decided to poke the beehive a little more, leaving messages at the offices of Kozlov's clients.

Lang ran into Brinkman in the bathroom, noticing the old detective stepping away from the urinal and heading toward the door. After being told to 'shut up' earlier, a mean, little jab was called for.

'You didn't wash your hands,' Lang said, just as Brinkman reached for the knob.

'Mr Lang, I washed my hands before I urinated because I didn't want to get my penis dirty. Think it through.'

Back in the office Lang's mind neglected to evaluate Brinkman's logic and allowed it to go back to the alleged suicide. If someone told Kozlov that Lang had an inquiring mind, then he would no doubt deliver a message that Lang wanted even more info – maybe which legislators Lacey favored and what other clients the two of them had.

Since he didn't know which of the five he called earlier had a direct line to Kozlov, he'd simply call them all again. When he was done with that he went online to look for electronics – flat-screen TVs, stereo systems.

It was dark outside before the thought struck him that a drink just might hit the spot. It was Thanh's departure that brought Lang out from under the hypnosis of the Internet and its many siren calls.

Running usually helped clear Carly's mind. And she needed to get a run in anyway just to keep the pounds at bay. It was work. She wasn't sure it cleared her mind at all. It wasn't fun. It wasn't inspirational. The mind rush never came. Still in her sweats she met Nadia at Peets Coffee on Fillmore. But her heart wasn't in to the light-hearted conversation that was the basis for their friendship.

Usually Nadia could cheer her up. Don't take yourself or life too seri-ously was the thread of Nadia's personality that often worked miracles when Carly's mood flatlined. But her mood wasn't flat, it was definitely down. Never in her life had she taken a case so personally. She remembered the moment in Bodega Bay, so struck by the beautiful and horrific in nature that she'd decided to embrace life. So this is what happens when you make that choice.

'This little girl,' Carly told Nadia, 'she . . .'

Carly glanced around the coffee shop. The customers, mostly young, sat inside and out chatting. Some lounged with their children, a few with their dogs, all seemingly content with the trajectory of their lives. This was a wealthy neighborhood. Not too many wants left unfulfilled. The Hanover kids could be sitting here with their friends.

'You were saying?' Nadia said.

'I don't know what I was saying,' she said, suddenly very tired, very sad.

'Yes, you do,' Nadia said. 'Don't start holding it all in. You do that. You did it with Peter. It's the way you are. You retreat. Prudence?' Nadia smiled.

'What?'

'Come out and play.'

'The person who killed Olivia cared for her,' Carly said. An overdose of morphine was the way doctors ended the suffering of terminally ill patients. 'The way she died says that the act was done with regret. That has to be the key. That's the tell.'

It was hard to tell if Nadia was puzzled or amused.

'Olivia said she was "a caged soul wanting its freedom,"' Carly said. She looked at her friend. 'But it's not that easy. I understand that all too well.'

'She wasn't freed,' Nadia said, sipping her latte, 'was she? She was killed.'

Carly nodded. 'Maybe just as she was about to be set free.'

She picked up a bottle of wine from the little wine shop next to the supermarket and by the time she got back to her flat it was drizzly and dark. That was just what she wanted. There was just a little too much light today.

Lang took the stairs. The stairway was darker than usual. A bulb must have gone out. His cell phone played out its strange tune and he stopped briefly to pull it from his jacket pocket.

'Couple of guys with bad hair cuts went into the building,' Thanh said. 'Another one is just outside, waiting.'

'Gotcha,' Lang whispered.

'You want me to call the police?'

'No, I want to talk with these guys. You see any guns?'

'No. One guy's got some kind of club or something. I'm coming up.'

'No. Watch the outside guy.'

Lang closed the phone and quietly retreated to the floor above.

He punched the button for the elevator. No sound. There was a whining sound when it was working. That meant it wasn't going to come. He went into his office, retrieved a roll of quarters from his desk, then went back out and farther down the hall, where he plucked the red fire extinguisher from the wall. He went back to the stairway.

Chances were that they were waiting for him on the steps leading to the landing. That would put them out of sight until it was too late for Lang to run back up the stairs.

He walked down normally, allowing his footsteps to be heard. Before he got to the landing, he pulled the pin from the extinguisher, which he held behind his back.

When he reached the bottom step, the one before the landing, he stopped. He became as quiet as he could. In the very near darkness he heard breathing not far away. He waited. Minutes, which seemed like hours, passed. He didn't move but his finger set to squeeze the extinguisher lever caressed the metal in anticipation.

Lang heard whispering, angry frustrated eastern European words. He waited. He sensed the exasperation just around the corner. The anger was in the air in that small stairwell.

A shadow lurched into view. Lang pressed the lever and white foam spewed. The man screamed, not out of pain, but out of shock. Lang stepped on to the landing, aiming the hose at him. The man shielded his eyes and continued forward, however his feet went out from under him, unable to navigate the now slippery steps. He careened against the wall and then down the steps while Lang swung the extinguisher at the remaining figure.

Lang followed the second body as the man tumbled down the steps, this one unconscious, coming to a rest halfway. He gave the first man, who was on his feet and angry, yelling, an uppercut which, with the force of a handful of coin, lifted him off the earth briefly before crumbling into a pile of bones and clothes.

Lang was out of the front door and on to the sidewalk of the narrow street. The third man, having been leaning against the wall of a building on the other side, started forward. He had an aluminum bat.

The sound of an engine cut through the quiet darkness. Lang knew it was Thanh's motorcycle. The revving stopped as the sound came toward the man. Thanh flashed on the lights. The man turned, ready to take on the cyclist. Thanh, in helmet and leather jacket held something in his right hand. The man, like a toreador, positioned himself for the attack. Just as the cycle closed in, there was a strange swoosh. An umbrella opened, obstructing the man's view of the cyclist. The umbrella itself would do little damage, but the shock of its sudden opening in the night knocked the would-be thug off his feet.

Thanh swung around to a stop. He was off the cycle and on his way to the man, stepping on the forearm of the man holding the bat. The man reached across his body to grab Thanh, Thanh kicked him in the head. The man relented with an outburst of what had to be curses. Thanh pressed the heel of his boot into the flesh until the man squealed and his fingers gave up the bat. Thanh picked it up.

'You move and I'm going to pretend I'm Barry Bonds.'

'Pretty handy with that umbrella, Miss Poppins,' Lang said, heading back toward the two in the building. He flicked open his phone and dialed Homicide.

'Kind of a Terminator–Mary Poppins combo, don't you think?' Thanh said.

'No one's dead,' Lang said into the phone, 'but pass on to Stern or Rose that a couple of Kozlov's men just tried to kill me. I have them here if they want them.'

After telling the police where he was, he moved the two unconscious men so that they lay side by side. He used their shoelaces to tie their hands behind their backs and to each other. He used the chubbier one's belt to bind all four feet together.

He went through their pockets to find wallets and identification. There wasn't much. No driver's licenses. No green cards or work permits. They were probably here illegally.

Lang did find something interesting. It was a small card that said in English 'Please take me to:'

That part was preprinted. Then in script, it gave an address on Valencia. This was the kind of thing that non-English speaking visitors had to guarantee they could get home. You showed this to the taxi driver.

Lang slipped the card into his pocket.

One of these guys, he thought, was the one who had destroyed his apartment. He suspected it was the one with the bat.

'Got a car key here,' Thanh said.

Lang went out. Thanh dangled a key with a black pad. Thanh pressed the pad and a black Cadillac flashed its lights and beeped. Lang tied up the third guy with shoestrings and belts. Thank God, he thought, these guys all wear running shoes.

The registration was in the glove compartment. DOA INC. The initials for Dead On Arrival. Either someone had a sense of humor or was dumb as a pound of peanuts. It was a Marin County address. An older registration was in the same little leather folder. Lang took the older one.

'Things to do now,' Lang said. He was happy.

Twenty-Three

Lang wanted to keep Thanh out of it. He sent the umbrella-toting motorcyclist on his way. Two beat cops arrived and took notes. They were suspicious of Lang's story, but there was no one else willing or able to talk, so that was the only story they heard. The bat-wielding attacker spoke a little English, but was nervous and uncooperative.

The fire department came first to administer aid to the fallen. Revived, ambulances took two of them away. The conscious one was handcuffed, but after a series of communications, neither Lang nor the conscious victim were allowed to leave.

It was no surprise that Inspector Stern showed up, no doubt slightly popped, and puffed by alcohol and bad humor. His evening was interrupted. If one of them had to show, Lang had prayed for Rose. Rose was less confrontational. Fortunately, Stern talked to the beat cops until Rose showed up.

'You want me to believe that you took out three thugs all by yourself?' Stern asked. He was practically spitting.

'I'm really sorry. I guess when people are trying to kill me I just don't know my own strength.'

Rose, who stood behind Stern and therefore out of Stern's view, mimed locking his mouth and throwing away the key.

'I'm in no mood . . .'

'These are Kozlov's guys. They smashed up my place and they were sent to smash me up.'

'You know that because?'

'I don't mean to taint all Russians, but the only Russian I've been involved with is Kozlov. It's not enough to convict, but it seems enough to investigate.'

'I'll determine what is and what isn't investigated,' Stern said.

'Your concern for Kozlov's interest is heart-warming.'

Rose shook his head, trying to tell Lang to cool it. It wasn't that he liked Lang so much as trying to avoid a scene.

'Seems to me you make enemies real easy,' Stern said.

'And you seem to make friends with lowlifes real easy.'

'We've got a car over here,' Rose said. 'We should take a look, right?'

'You take a look,' Stern said. 'Seems like we've got an attitude problem over here.' He stared at Lang. There was the cop stare, used to intimidate.

This went beyond that. The guy was ready to explode. And he wanted to. He wanted some reason to beat the crap out of Lang.

'Look,' Lang said, 'I'll stop being an asshole. I'm not trying to piss you off. I'm trying to find out why some woman died and I'm trying to stay alive while doing it.'

'You were warned to stay away from Kozlov.'

'I was told not to trespass. I'm not trespassing. He is. I never threatened him with bodily harm. He has. I suspect you'll find these guys are connected to him. If I'm wrong, I'll write "I'm sorry" on the blackboard a thousand times.'

Stern remained frozen. Lang hadn't disarmed the inspector's anger, but he seemed to have capped it. He didn't want to give Stern an excuse to beat the hell out of him. With the thugs, he was lucky – for now. Fighting with the cops was a no win. Stern's cell rang and he stepped away.

Lang went to Rose.

'You come down here to back up Stern?'

'I came down here to protect you and by protecting you I'm protecting Stern. He'd downed a few in front of his TV watching the As, and he doesn't like to be disturbed.'

'Overtime, Rose. You guys make more than the mayor.'

'Please don't tell him that. I'm trying to help.'

'What's with Stern and Kozlov?'

'Kozlov is a friend of the police department. He does favors. Not necessarily monetary, but he's helpful politically to the department when it comes to the mayor and the Board of Supervisors. Kozlov and his friend Emmett Lacey have connections all over the place. They know how to make friends and deal with their enemies. You're really not helping matters with your smart mouth, Lang.'

'I think it's in my DNA. I'll try. So how do I get a little justice here?' Lang asked.

'I'm not sure you can. I'll make sure these guys are turned over to ICE. But I wouldn't be surprised if they are released.'

'And there's more where they came from, right?'

Rose nodded, then put a finger to his lips as Stern returned.

'You know you broke a guy's jaw?' Stern said, shaking his head.

'Just defending myself,' Lang said. 'Is it all right if I leave, Inspector?' Lang asked Stern.

Stern looked at Rose. Rose shrugged.

'Get lost. And do us all a favor, stay lost.'

* * *

Early to bed and too early to rise was Carly's fate. She was wide awake at five and didn't want to face the slow emergence of day passively. She dressed in her running outfit and went off toward Lafayette Park. The steps were visible even in the drizzly darkness, but the rest of it seemed sullenly shrouded and forbidding.

She acknowledged this wasn't doing much for her mood. Why did she choose this route? Was she trying to punish herself? She ran up Sacramento, turned right on Laguna and right again on Washington. As she approached the last turn of the first lap, she realized she was near the spot where Olivia was found. The time and weather would be very much the same.

She stopped and walked a few feet into the brush. At night it might as well be a forest. Visibility was just a few feet.

It was quiet. Olivia and the person who brought her there to die – it was clear from the autopsy that she had not been moved post-mortem – were as alone in the universe as two people could be. Was Olivia conscious? Did she have a sense of what was happening? Did she die alone or was the killer by her side when she breathed her last breath?

No matter who we are, we make the final journey by ourselves. And more often than not, we have no control. At any moment, she thought, it could come – soundless, sightless dark. She wasn't scaring herself as much as depressing herself. She went off running. She'd run all the bad, sad stuff out of her system.

'Sorry to trouble you again,' Gratelli said at the front door at eight in the morning. Pamela Hanover, expecting him, answered the door. She looked out to see a crime scene truck parked outside and the officers who were with Gratelli.

She gave her quiet, subtle nod. No smile. She accepted the fact that he had to be there, but did not forgive him the intrusion.

He tried to give her a copy of the warrant, but she motioned toward a tall, attractive Hispanic woman who introduced herself as Mrs Hanover's attorney, Hannah Rodriguez.

Stern and Rose, and two uniformed officers, accompanied Gratelli. They would search everywhere. They were open to whatever they might find that would give them useful information. They were looking for Olivia's computer. That was pretty hopeless by now. A motor scooter would make the trip worthwhile.

Anyone with any sense would have gotten rid of the computer Olivia used knowing that a search warrant was issued. And this was the second one. But no one but Lang, the private investigator, knew about the motor scooter. Most likely it wouldn't have been discarded.

Stern sipped from a Starbucks cup as he went up the stairs with one of the uniforms. Rose and the other uniform searched the main floor. Gratelli asked to be shown the garage.

Outside the garage was a silver Prius. Inside was an old Austin Healey, a Range Rover and in the corner a pale blue scooter. It was a larger Vespa, but still a scooter and one likely to make the sound the private detective had told him about. There were no telltale marks of recent movement from its spot in the corner. There wouldn't be. The garage was immaculate – organized and dust free. There wasn't even the scent of oil or gas.

Gratelli went outside and asked the lab folks to wrap the cycle in plastic and take it in. Find anything that might be left on it.

Two hours later the officers reconvened in the driveway. They had, after much objection, taken all seven of the computers in the house. This included Walter Hanover's computer with all of its high-level financial information and business dealings.

Hannah Rodriguez immediately started making calls. Gratelli had no doubt she was going to the courts, to the mayor's office, to the police chief, to the district attorney.

It was a bold move, Gratelli realized, and perhaps a foolish one. But from what the police techies told him, all access to Olivia's profile page came from here. But that didn't mean that she wasn't using someone else's computer as her own, her stepfather's for example when he was asleep. Maybe she didn't have one of her own. All Gratelli knew was that all of the interaction with the website came from the network established on the telephone line at the residence.

Whether a member of the Hanover house killed her or not, this action was essential to getting the whole thing over with.

He tried to tell a panic-stricken Pamela Hanover, that this was the quickest way to cut to the truth. And that, perhaps, the truth would set them free. She wasn't buying it. Nor was her lawyer.

Lang slept in. Buddha had been patient. Instead of walking all over his keeper's body, he waited at the end of the bed. Lang opened his eyes to see the calm stare of his little brown cat.

'If you were – and maybe you are – the real Buddha,' Lang said, 'I have to tell you that last night I wandered completely off the eightfold path.' He noticed two things. Buddha stared at him unblinkingly for too long a time and that the knuckles on his left hand hurt. 'But then again I seem to have spent my life tripping pathless through the wilderness. It's just who I am.'

He slipped out of bed and, to cut the morning chill, into a robe before he fixed his mostly silent pal some breakfast and set coffee water boiling. The coffee-maker had been crushed along with the other electronic gadgets. He would make do with an old jar of freeze dried instant.

As the water heated, he called Thanh to see if he was all right. He was. He called Rose. At first, Rose wasn't in the mood to talk. But he did say, other than the one who was taken to the hospital, the attackers had been taken to jail. They would be arraigned this morning. They could be out by this afternoon.

'Thanks,' Lang said.

'Well . . .' Rose said, hemming and hawing, 'thanks for backing off on Stern last night. He wanted to blow and he's already on a short leash.'

'And he's not too fond of me.'

'You're a member of the human race. Don't take it personally. Listen, you still working on the Hanover girl thing?'

'Yeah.'

'I'm at their place. We're carting out computers and a scooter right now.'

'Smoking gun?'

'Not necessarily. But we're here looking for one. Be careful of the Russians.' Rose disconnected.

How often had Lang done something at night that he had cause to regret in the morning. He was pretty sure the war was far from over. It had probably just begun.

Lang unhappily sipped the instant coffee, vowing to go down the street for the real thing the moment his mind and body clicked in. He called Chastain B. West and said that they needed to talk with Daniel again. But could West get as much as he could from Gratelli on the status of their investigation? The attorney agreed to do that and set up a time for an afternoon meeting with the young suspect.

Having consumed all he could of the distasteful brew, Lang called Carly on his cell as he walked over to the coffee shop on Hayes and Central, praying there wasn't a line of latte drinkers ahead of him. The only thing he had against them is that the fancy coffee-making ritual took far too long.

'The police just executed a search warrant at your former employer's residence,' he told her when she answered.

'Good morning to you too,' she said.

'Apparently they left with all the family computers and a motor scooter.'

'Motor scooter?'

'I'll tell you about that over lunch.'

'Lunch?'

'You gotta eat. And I want a little more on the Hanover kids.'

Lang sat outside the coffee shop sipping good coffee and downing a blueberry muffin. That would do him until lunch. The morning sun was just about to penetrate the gray blanket. He could feel it burning through the light haze. It would be a warm day. He wondered if Kozlov had heard the news about the failed mission. He was pretty sure he would. He was also sure this wasn't over. Kozlov types didn't like to lose.

Twenty-Four

'Do you like Japanese?' Carly asked Lang. She cleaned the countertop in her kitchen as she spoke on the phone.

'People, cars?'

'Food.'

'All but the raw kind.'

'Perfect, I'll pick you up.'

It was settled. If he had an objection it was too late. She arrived in her little Mini Cooper.

'C'mon, get in,' she said, window down, car idling in the middle of the narrow street.

'Is there room for me and the clowns?'

She didn't say anything.

'OK, I got it. I'm the clown.'

As it turned out, this wasn't going to be local fare. They were headed out toward the Sunset district. The little place, Kitchen Kura, had maybe five tables, all covered with blue plastic. Plastic flowers, in a variety of colors, lined the window sills. Handmade signs touted the specials.

It was a picture menu and Lang had no problem picking out the fried chicken. He added a tofu dish for show. She went for the eggplant and some kind of fish, cooked. They shared a large bottle of Asahi beer.

Another characteristic Lang admired in a woman. Willing to have a beer now and then.

They chatted. About the scooter, finally, and what it suggested. And if the second video could be traced to the Hanover household how it put additional doubt that Daniel Lee was involved. If the scooter found in the Hanovers' garage could be linked to Olivia's death that would be another strong suggestion that it was a family affair.

They chatted. About the family, the personalities, and highly speculative motives. Neither of Olivia's fathers seemed to care enough to do something so drastic. Way too much risk for Walter unless she knew a deep, dark, secret. What would cause Jordan to kill her? Seemed even more unlikely. He was the peacemaker of the family. Unless there was some sort of unrequited love. Jealousy of Daniel Lee. Passion gone awry. And the older kid, Evan. She meant nothing to him. Maybe a thrill-seeking prank that went wrong?

Lang loved the food. Good, cheap and plentiful. He'd come back, he thought as they stepped outside.

Carly stopped. 'I think we're being stalked,' she said.

'Yeah?' Lang looked around casually. Saw a skinny guy half a block away leaning against a parked car smoking.

'I recognize the car,' she said. 'Not too many plain white Ford Victoria's around these days. Undercover cop?'

'Undercover Russian, most likely,' Lang said. 'What they lack in talent they make up in persistence. Let's go for a drive.'

Carly headed for the ocean. They weren't far away. It was straight west on Judah. The closer they were to the water, the more desolate the landscape. Faded stucco homes edged right up on the sidewalks as the street terraced down to the Pacific. The odd angle created the illusion of a giant wall of water ahead in suspended animation. At any moment it would break and sweep the neighborhood off the face of the earth. Global warming in overdrive.

'All this used to be sand dunes,' Carly said.

She found her way on to the Great Highway with the Russians in not so distant pursuit.

The two PIs parked in the lot that lined the beach. They got out to walk. It was a sunny day with a heavy cold, nasty wind. The beach was nearly empty. No wonder. The sand bit into their faces. Only a few kite-flyers braved the scene. One held on to a small kite with a colorful forty-foot tail. It was a master who held the string and choreographed a diving, swirling dragon. In the distance a surfer used a kite to propel his surfboard.

'No seagulls,' Carly said.

'Too rough,' Lang said, glancing around to see what the Russians were doing.

'You want me to lose them?'

'What? In your Mini Cooper?'

'Did you see *The Italian Job*?'

He smiled. 'I just hope I haven't put you in jeopardy. I didn't think they'd be back this quick.'

'Don't worry about it.'

'You can take care of yourself?'

'I can,' she said. 'You ever want kids?'

'You change subjects on a dime.'

'No, it's just that you're so calm. You'd make a great dad.'

They continued to walk, noticing that crows were braving the wind, sometimes just floating, and landing slowly, hovering and drifting down like British Harriers.

'I think I missed something big,' Lang said. 'But my adolescence lasted until mid-life crisis. So I kind of missed the window. And now I'm too old and too selfish.'

'Not really. You'd be old when the kid graduated college but not that old. I've probably been too selfish all along. But I think if I were Olivia's mother, I would want the person who did it punished. She seems to just want the problem to go away.'

'Repressing memories before they become memories.'

'What did you do to piss them off?'

'The Russians you're talking about?'

'Yes,' she said, and smiled.

'Just one Russian. These guys are just employees doing a job. In my mind, I am refusing to allow myself to be used as an alibi to murder.'

'In the Russian's mind?'

'I was hired to do a job. The job was done. I was paid. It was time for me to go away.'

'You're investigating the murder?'

'Now, since I was threatened, I'm investigating all kinds of criminal possibilities.'

The wind switched direction. The sand from the beach continued to sting their faces.

They turned and headed back.

'So, do you want me to lose them?'

Lang looked at his watch.

'No, but maybe you could drop me down at the jail. I'm going to talk with Daniel. I doubt if these guys will follow me inside. You mind?'

'No. Can I play with them?'

'Be my guest.'

West called Lang to say that he couldn't make it.

'Doesn't matter,' West said on the call. 'He's not telling me anything I need to know.'

It was true. Daniel Lee did nothing for his own defense – a blank slate of a past and journals full of gibberish. But Lang wanted to see the kid anyway. And he agreed that Carly could come along. Maybe a woman's presence would help. And she knew the players in the Hanover household better than Lang.

Lang was shocked at Daniel Lee's appearance. His jail garb seemed to have swallowed him and all of the life in the kid's face, particularly the eyes, seemed to have dissipated severely.

'Are they feeding you?'

Daniel nodded.

'Are you eating?'

He shrugged.

This is what it was, Lang was convinced: you imprison a free spirit, it dies. Lee was dying not in captivity but of captivity.

'This is Carly Paladino,' Lang said. 'She used to work for the Hanovers, but has since left them. She's a private investigator too and she's trying to figure out what really happened to Olivia.'

Carly smiled at Lee, whose eyes met her gaze, but he remained quiet.

'I know it's difficult for you to believe,' Lang continued, 'but we'd like to get you out of here. The good news is that the police are not just looking at you. You are the prime suspect, but there is some evidence that someone inside the Hanovers' home had something to do with this.'

With Lee's passive silence, it was difficult to know what Lee was thinking.

'Do you understand what I'm saying?'

'Yes,' Lee said, his voice full of the gravel that collects when so much time has passed without speaking.

'What we'd like to know,' Lang said, 'is more about the relationships Olivia had with her family.'

'I've told you,' Daniel said.

'What did Olivia tell you about them?' Carly asked. 'Can you remember exactly what she said?'

'Some.'

'About her stepfather?' Carly asked.

'She never talked about him. He never came up.' The words came with an angry abruptness that was surprising.

'Mrs Hanover?'

'She said her mother was very disappointed in her, that she wasn't holding up her end as a Hanover. I don't know exactly what that meant, except that she was supposed to be more social and more interested in things she wasn't interested in. There was some big dance she was supposed to perform in or something. And she refused.'

'Anything else?'

'Her mother had started to ignore her like the rest of the family.'

'Did she like anyone?'

'She liked that guy who worked there.'

'Gary Gray'

'Him. Yes. He was the only one she could talk to, but he was only there during the day and he was busy most of the time with her mother's affairs.'

'What about the brothers?'

'The older brother constantly harassed her.'

'Harassed? Physically?'

'No. Words. Hateful, sarcastic, anything to make her feel small and stupid.'

'What about the younger brother?'

'Depended on who was around, she said.'

'What do you mean?' Carly asked.

'Well if the older brother was around, then the younger brother didn't pay any attention to her. If they were alone together, he treated her all right. He'd sometimes try to coach her on how to act.'

'Sounds like Olivia was the poor relation living right there in the house,' Lang said.

Daniel nodded.

'Anything else you can think of, Daniel?' Carly asked. 'Anything.'

'Not really.'

'There was morphine in Olivia's system. And ketamine. Could she have gotten hold of this stuff?' Lang asked.

'We didn't do drugs. We didn't drink.'

'Do you have any idea if anyone in the house had access to that kind of stuff?'

'Never heard Olivia talking about drugs. Her brothers drank. No drugs in the house except for the pills her mother took to feel better.'

'What were they, do you know?' Carly asked.

'No. You know, we didn't talk about her family all that much. It wasn't pleasant.' He seemed to drift off for a moment. 'It really wasn't.' He seemed to come back. 'We talked about other things.'

'What other things?'

'We were going off together, get away from everything and everyone. That was the only way to protect her.'

'From what?' Lang asked.

'I'm sorry. I promised,' he said. 'I promised.'

'You don't have to . . .' Carly said softly, but Daniel Lee shrugged and shut down.

As they walked out in the hallway, Carly said that Lee didn't look well.

'He may not make it,' Lang said.

'One innocent death isn't enough, I guess,' she said. 'Can I give you a lift?'

'No.'Lang smiled. 'You go out the front to your car. I'll go out the back and walk to the office. It's not that far. It probably won't make any difference to the goon squad out there, but it might screw with their heads.'

As Noah Lang put the key in the lock of his office door, Barry Brinkman appeared in the hallway carrying what looked to be a .38.

'Going hunting?' Lang asked.

'Thought they were coming back.'

'Who?'

'A couple of ruffians,' Brinkman said, lowering the pistol. 'They were trying to pick your lock.'

'Russian ruffians?'

'Sounded like it. You piss off the Russians too?'

'Not the entire country, Barry.'

'Someone's always trying to kill you.'

'No one's tried to kill me in a long time.'

'Then it's about time,' Brinkman said.

'You call the police?'

'No.'

'Because they would want to know what you're doing with a firearm?'

'That maybe. But what would that have accomplished. The guys would have gone . . .'

'You could shoot them.'

Brinkman lifted the gun. 'Doesn't work. No firing pin. As I was saying, the thugs would be gone and I'd have to fill out all those reports.'

'And you don't have time for that?' Lang asked.

'You want me siding with the Russians? You're pissing me off too.'

'You going to shoot me?'

'Putting a firing pin in here is not a problem.'

Twenty-Five

The phone call came as a complete surprise. Carly was sautéing a crab cake and slicing tomatoes for a light dinner. As she moved about the kitchen with the non-taxing tasks at hand she allowed her mind to move from a sense of freedom and approval of it to a mix of sadness and insecurity that came from giving up on solid, steady employment and losing a long-time lover.

It was the latter on the phone.

'Hi, Carly,' he said.

'Peter?' she asked, despite knowing it was. She pulled the small pan off the stove and the crab cake from the pan.

'Yes. Am I interrupting anything?'

'Ah . . . no . . . no . . .' She grabbed her wine and went to the back deck. The sun was beginning to set, but with only a southern view, she saw the slices of pink in the blue sky not the actual setting. Below her Mr Nakamura's fine garden looked elegant and serene.

'How are you doing?'

'Fine. You know. Interesting. I left Vogel Security.'

'Really?' He sounded genuinely surprised. 'Where did you go?'

'Out on my own,' she said, mustering a little more cheer than she felt. 'A little review of my life and . . . and . . . here I am. Free. Ready to take on any adventure.'

'I don't know what to say.'

'Congratulations would be in order,' she said, trying to put fun and laughter in her voice. She wondered if she succeeded.

'OK,' he said. 'Congratulations.'

'Thank you, sweet of you to say.' Keep it light. Keep it light, she told herself.

'On your own? I mean you are setting up your own business?'

'Yes. My own office as an investigator. Time to leave the nest before I'm too old to fly.'

She thought about thanking him, telling him he was part of the reason, but didn't know why she would say that. Did she want him to share in the blame if she failed? Did she want to let him off the hook by suggesting that his leaving was actually good for her? She didn't know what she thought about all of that.

'How are you doing? Are you all settled in Seattle?'

'I found a nice place. A view of the skyline. A little too "cool and crazy guy" for someone like me.'

'You're cool.'

'You're kind. I miss you,' he said.

Carly didn't know what to say. She didn't want to go there. And she thought it was a little unfair in a call out of the blue.

After a long pause, he continued. 'Some things are better left unsaid, I guess.'

'Peter. We had a good time. We treated each other well. We didn't break any promises to each other.'

'Because we never made them.'

'No one was wronged. Maybe we're both a little disappointed, but . . .'

'You're moving on.'

'I am. You OK?' she asked.

'Yeah. You?'

'I'm going to make it,' she said.

'I know you will,' he said.

'And so will you.'

'Maybe after awhile, you could come up and . . .'

'You never know.'

'Good talking with you,' he said.

'You too.'

There it was. Final. Really final. She sipped her wine, looked up at the changing sky. Was she hungry now? She was. She finished heating the crab cake and took her dinner and half-bottle of wine out to the deck. She watched the day begin to shut down.

Lang was more careful now as he went into the hallway or out on the street. He carried the roll of quarters in his jacket pocket and was consciously aware of his surroundings out in public. At that moment he checked the rear-view mirror as he drove to Valencia near Market Street.

The area was evolving. Further down Valencia was also somewhat rundown, but the street saw the growth of trendy restaurants and it – and the Mission District in general – had become the heart of the new and young bohemians. The whole street was being gentrified. Nearer market, though, there were few galleries and restaurants scattered among seedy dives and hotels. The address he found on one of the assailants gave a Valencia address near Market and before the night was strung out too far, Lang wanted to check it out – let the goons know he knew how to find them too.

He found the address and because there were only a scattering of businesses, mostly closed now, there was a place to park. The hotel, a four-story building of no particular style of architecture, advertised in somewhat ancient signage that rooms were available by week or month. Standard in these kinds of places, there was a desk clerk, or a more accurate description, gate keeper – someone to keep tenants from subletting their rooms to an unlimited number of folks and keeping the place from veering off into chaos when the bars closed.

An unhappy man sat at the desk, which was behind wrought-iron bars. He looked up and took a measure of the detective.

'I'm looking for some Russians.'

'You try Russia? I hear they got plenty over there.'

'I think I caught your act in Reno. This room better for you?'

'You got a funny way of asking for a favor. And I'm guessing it's a favor you want.'

'Is this better?' Lang slipped a twenty between the bars.

'Getting that way.'

Lang noticed the nicotine-stained fingers. 'No, it's better. Take my word for it.'

'What do you want?'

'Are they here?'

'No. Only two of them came back this morning. And they went out, probably to eat.'

'They're all in the same room?'

'Yeah.'

'I want to put something in the room.'

'Put something in?' the guy asked with a smirk.

'A present.'

Lang wouldn't tell him what kind of present.

'I can't leave the desk right now,' the guy said. 'Leave the present with me and I'll tell them you dropped it off.'

'OK,' Lang said. He found a fifty in his wallet and waved it at the guy. 'Change your mind? This is all I got. I want this to be a surprise. What do you think?'

'Make it quick,' the man said. 'I don't know when they're coming back.'

The man at the desk gave him a number on the third floor and a pass key. Lang didn't bother to see if the elevator worked. It looked like a death trap to him.

Inside the room was a mess. Clothes, potato-chip bags, empty bottles. Lang pulled a picture from behind his jacket. In it was the photograph of Mrs Lillia Kozlov that Amy Logan had given him during their lunch. Thanh had scanned it in to the computer, Photoshopped out the others in the photo and enhanced the remaining image of a smiling though now quite dead Mrs Kozlov. Thanh had also inscribed the words 'Love, Lillia Kozlov. See you soon' at the bottom.

Lang cleared a place on the bureau and set the photo down after wiping it free of any prints that could tie it back to him. He hoped one of them could read English. Then again, if they took it to Kozlov to read all the better.

Lang took a moment to look through the debris, hoping to find a name or some other indication of who the guys were and any other connections that might pop up. There was a notebook. But it was all in Russian.

He laughed. It might as well have been in Daniel Lee's code. But there was a phone number and he copied that down – not knowing who it belonged to. Could be the guy's mother, though Lang hoped it would be a little more helpful.

He also found a luggage tag on one of the bags: Yuri Nikitin. Lang wrote the name down. He gave the place one last look and got out of there.

'What do you know about all of this?' Lang asked the guy at the desk.

'Nothing.'

'Good, these are dangerous guys.'

'Now you tell me.'

'If they ask, tell them a very pale, mysterious woman asked about them.'

'You're the mysterious woman? That's what you're telling me?'

Lang nodded. 'Why not? I promise you it will take the sting out of it.'

There was a great burrito place just a few blocks down on Valencia. Buddha liked burritos.

The cold summer night forced Carly Paladino inside. After shutting the double doors to the deck, she turned on a few lights. She cleaned up in the kitchen. There were two things she did every day to keep from sinking into chaos. The previous night's dishes were always done the previous night. And she would make the bed before leaving the house.

Even in the light, though, she couldn't dispel the feeling that she was adrift, looking for land.

It was 3 a.m. when she fell on the sofa exhausted. Two fat rolls of Viva paper towels were gone. Her hands were dry and red, but her flat was spotless, dustless, and microbe free. She took a few deep breaths and realized that the same empty feeling that drove her obsessions was still there. The only thing that she could say of it all was that she was finally exhausted. And now perhaps she could sleep.

Twenty-Six

Carly was up before first light. She had slept well. Dreamt well. A visit from her mother assuring her that all was the way it was meant to be smoothed the rough edges of consciousness. It wasn't sad, it was what the mood was during her mother's visit. Calming. Wise.

Carly had plans for the day – at least for the morning. And it paid off. Calculating when Anna Mendoza would have to leave her outer Mission home to get to Pacific Heights before seven, Carly set out when morning light was just a sliver on the horizon. She had to get to the Hanover house-keeper before she boarded the bus. She knew the woman rode the Divisadero bus and lived near 30th and Mission Street. That meant she would be boarding there. It was a little iffy, but it was a good gamble.

The fog was still in evidence on the downslope of Pacific Heights when Carly left her flat. The Mission, in its own climate just a few miles away, was sunny and warming up.

Despite the fact that there were dozens of middle-aged Hispanic women waiting for the bus to sweep them off to various wealthy neighborhoods to clean homes and take care of babies, Carly found her stunned prey.

Reluctantly, the housekeeper and her bags were inside the little car and Carly had begun the trek back to Pacific Heights.

'I don't know anything, Miss Paladino,' Mendoza said. She still looked frightened. 'None of this, you know, is my business. I mind my business. That is my job.' She spoke with a thick accent, but she had no problems understanding what Carly wanted.

'You walk through the house,' Carly said, 'and their lives go on. Anger, arguments, plans for the day, complaints, laughter.'

'There is not so much laughter,' Mendoza said.

'Not now, of course.'

'No, never. I can tell you this is not a happy family. But that's all I can tell you.'

'Do they dislike each other?'

'I have never seen nothing like it. When I grow up, we shout and yell and hug and laugh. This is like everyone is in a library.'

'Did you see Mrs Hanover with Olivia?'

'Why do you ask these questions? The police have a boy, right?'

Mrs Mendoza held her bags to her as if someone might reach in and take them.

'Yes. But there are some questions. There are some inconsistencies.'

They rode in silence for a few blocks, Carly trying to find the best way back. Going out was going against most of the traffic. Coming back in, a driver fought bicycles, cars, trucks and all sorts of busses for the right to pass.

'There's a missing computer, Mrs Mendoza. Do you have any idea where it might be?'

Mendoza shook her head.

'Did you ever see anyone riding the scooter out in the garage?'

She shook her head.

More quiet.

'She used to ride it to play tennis down near the Embarcadero, but she doesn't play down there any more.'

'She?'

'Mrs Hanover. She still plays tennis. Three times a week.'

'She's very fit,' Carly said. 'She's quite a woman.'

'She works out every morning. Early. Sometimes, they tell me, it is still dark. She doesn't need very much sleep.'

'I asked you about how Olivia got along with her mother. Did they get along?'

Mendoza took a deep breath.

'I told you it was all so quiet, so polite, but you could feel the tension sometimes. So much stress. Mrs Hanover had to take care of her mother. Lung cancer. So very sad. Poor Mrs Hanover, she seemed so embarrassed to have her poor mother there and for her to be so needy. You can say that for Mrs Hanover though, she cared for her.'

'She died?'

'Yes. In the house just a few months ago.'

'Did the boys ever ride the scooter?'

'So many questions, Miss Paladino. I feel this is not good. You should ask Mrs Hanover. You work for her, right?'

'Not any more.'

Darkness fell across Mendoza's face.

'Please,' Carly said. 'This is for Olivia. What can you tell me about the Hanover boys? Did either of them ride the scooter?'

'I don't know. I don't watch them when they leave. They both have cars. Maybe a few years ago. I don't see anything lately. I have things to do in the house.' She was quiet, but did not take her eyes off Carly.

'What?'

'I am worried about my job. I can't afford to lose it.'

'I'll drop you off where the bus drops you, Mrs Mendoza. I won't mention anything about our discussion. And what did you tell me after all?'

Mendoza nodded wearily.

'About the boy. What do you know? What did you see?'

'The stranger?'

'The young man Olivia had over late at night.'

'I hear about him once or twice. I heard Mrs Hanover ask Jordan if the boy used drugs.'

'Really?'

Mendoza nodded.

'And Jordan replied?'

'I couldn't hear what he said. But he shook his head. You're right, Miss Paladino, sometimes I am just a hat rack.' She smiled.

'Any other references to the young man?'

'No, but I saw him a few times . . .'

'I thought you said you didn't see him?'

'On video tape. From the security cameras.'

'I didn't see any security cameras.'

'No, you wouldn't. They were taken out before you came to work for her.'

'When?'

'A week before. Maybe. Something like that.' ·

For Lang, the morning didn't start off all that good. Out of coffee – still. Funny, he thought, how it didn't just magically appear after he took note of its goneness the morning before. He had too much on his mind. But now, here he was, no familiar morning TV show in the background as he got ready. He'd only tune in for the news and the weather. He seldom gave into the saccharin trivia that took 50 minutes of each hour.

After chatting with Buddha and putting down fresh water and the feline's favorite dry morsels, Lang was off to the coffee shop a few blocks away. As he walked his brain funneled a few moments of Carly Paladino into his consciousness. He ought to call her. Saying what, he didn't know. But he ought to call her.

Then the Russian boys intruded on his thoughts as he waited behind lagging latte drinkers. What would they do when they saw the photograph? He didn't think they'd laugh. No sense of humor.

What he hoped was that the Russian boys would be freaked. He hoped they would register their feelings with Kozlov and get him all upset. Lang smiled thinking about it.

Then there was Daniel Lee. He would contact West, maybe Inspector Gratelli. Something needed to break. Soon. There was the scooter. What had they done about it? How could he gain access to the family? In that mansion, he was convinced, were all the answers.

The day continued to be uncommon. Just inside his office door, Lang found Thanh, in an apparent feminine mood, at the computer. And behind him, outside, in the window staring in was Barry Brinkman, smoking a cigar. He was standing on the fire escape.

Lang waved at him.

'Don't encourage him, please,' Thanh said.

Brinkman smiled, waved his cigar.

'You might find it interesting to know that Lillia Kozlov was part Native American.'

It had never occurred to Lang to do a background check on the wife. But it made complete sense.

'Go on.'

'She was part of a tribe attempting to get federal recognition as a legitimate tribe and she was, according to the tribal website, the leader in that effort.'

'Was she a leader in trying to get the tribe a casino?'

'Doesn't say,' Thanh said. 'My guess is that this was a step-at-a-time operation.'

'First make the tribe official and then move on to a casino – or not,' Lang said. 'I'll be damned.'

'Most likely,' Thanh said, smiling. 'You said that there was no evidence of an affair. Then why would Kozlov want her dead?'

'Right.'

'Am I good?' Thanh asked.

'The greatest.'

'Can you get that lunatic off the veranda?'

'I'll try.'

Later that afternoon, Lang made his phone calls. The first was to Amy Logan. She confirmed that Lillia Kozlov had ancestors who were Native Americans and that she romanticized the notion to the extent of taking courses in Native American studies at the university and was in fact an activist for their causes.

'She continued to do that after she married Kozlov?' Lang asked.

'I think it went underground.'

'Underground?'

'She didn't attend any activities, but she was active on the Internet.'

'She talk to you about this?'

'Not so much,' Logan said. 'I was, am I suppose, a complete WASP. I just know she felt strongly about how the American Indians were treated by government.'

'Past tense?'

'Present,' Logan said.

'Can you tell me more about that?'

'I'm sorry. I wasn't allowed into aspects of her life. She didn't talk about her husband or about her involvement in politics. I got pieces of them. A sense of them.'

'So you're not sure what specifically upset her about the way the Indians are treated?'

'Right.'

Switching gears, Lang called West. He went directly to voicemail. He called Gratelli. The inspector was out or not answering his phone. Lang left word. He leaned back in his chair, wishing that Thanh was still there to do some research on Bay Area Indian tribes. While his knowledge of California history was at best sketchy, he knew there were folks here before the Spaniards came. The Ohlone, for example. He'd seen a turn-off to Ohlone land on Highway 101 going north, but had never stopped.

The notion that Kozlov was involved with Indian gaming was not lost on Lang. Neither was the fact that another of Kozlov's shoes had yet to drop.

Twenty-Seven

How had the fact that the Hanovers removed their video security system just days before Olivia's death been overlooked? She would let Gratelli and Lang know. But first she wanted to find out a little more.

Having many of her Vogel Security files on her personal laptop had enabled her to do work at home at any hour. It also came in handy now. She knew who the major video security firms were. There was a fairly short list of those who had the most discreet products and who would also be trusted to do that kind of work for the landed gentry.

Within an hour, she had a Galaxy Home Security executive on the phone.

'We heard that the Hanovers had used your system,' Carly said, 'but then we heard they had had them removed. I'm just trying to find out if there are problems with the system.'

Don Singer knew Carly, but not well enough to know she no longer worked for Vogel Security. She didn't correct his assumption. Galaxy would be eager to have Vogel's recommendations and not at all eager to have their services called into question.

'Nothing was wrong, Carly,' Singer said. 'They said that they were uncomfortable having their guests on tape and, I think, they didn't like the idea that they would be recorded. It's a privacy matter. They called and had it removed. I'm sure if you called them, they would confirm the fact the system worked. They still have our alarm program.'

'Who are "they"?'

'What do you mean?'

'You said "they" called. Was it Walter or Pamela?'

'I'd have to check.'

'Could you?'

'I can call you back. I've got your number.'

He would have had her number at Vogel. She had to move quickly.

'Could you check now? I'll hold.'

She walked out to the deck. The fog retreated hours ago, but the clear air was chilly. Mr Nakamura was trimming the hedges that ran along the privacy fence. The idea of a Japanese gardener was so stereotypical, she thought. But he wasn't a gardener by profession. He was a musician, retired from the San Francisco Symphony.

He and his family were rounded up and put in camps during World War Two. He was only five at the time. They were US citizens but it didn't matter, her mother had told her one day.

'Using the logic that their ancestors came from a country at war with the US,' Mother Paladino said, 'they should have locked us up too. Mussolini was as bad.'

The family lost everything while they were away, but they came back and were successful. So was Mr Nakamura. He seemed remarkably at peace with the world.

Carly could see into the adjacent yards – all well kept. The light was silver as it usually was early in the day. It would turn gold in the afternoon. A black cat roamed through the ferns in one of the yards, coming in and out of view as he stalked his potential prey. Ferns waved in the breeze. She thought of Lang and her clumsy comment about men and cats.

'A Gary Gray called,' Don said. 'He works for them, I believe. Handles day-to-day business.'

Carly thanked him and flipped her phone shut. She was perplexed. She and Gary had talked a few times. He seemed to genuinely care for Olivia and deeply regret her death. Why wouldn't he have volunteered that information? Surely he knew it was pertinent. And who told him to have the cameras removed?

Gratelli, who took the morning off to check in with his doctor, settled into his desk and checked his voicemail. He had stopped downstairs to pick up the report on the scooter. Lang had called inquiring and Gratelli had the answer in the folder. The question was whether or not he should tell Lang. It should go to the DA's office.

Gratelli dialed the number Lang left.

'The way this works,' Gratelli said, 'is that Lee's attorney needs to check with the DA, who will have that information soon.'

'You can't tell me anything?' Lang asked.

'It would be wrong of me to tell you that there was DNA on the scooter that matches Olivia's. It's against policy and I could get in a lot of trouble.'

'Thanks,' Lang said.

'Don't thank me.'

'DNA? How?'

'Did I say DNA?' Gratelli asked.

'All right,' Lang said. 'Catch you later.'

Gratelli wouldn't tell him more. But it appeared that some skin from Olivia's bare leg scraped against an area of the cycle. The defense attorney would try to say that this proves it was a member of the family. And Gratelli was beginning to move in that direction himself. But it was possible that Daniel Lee had appropriated the bike to take Olivia to the park and then returned it. That scenario just didn't seem right.

He leaned back in his chair. The doctor had given him a clean bill of health.

'Inspector, you're going to live to be a hundred,' the young doctor told him after the examination.

Gratelli shook his head. How unfair. His beautiful, purposeful wife gone and he, not all that interested in living, would live a long, long time.

The phone rang. It was Carly Paladino.

Lang called Amy Logan and found out that Lillia's maiden name was Evencio. On a hunch, he googled Lillia Evencio and found several references. Most referenced a website devoted to San Francisco Bay Area Indian tribes.

It didn't take long to understand that Lillia Kozlov wasn't just a housewife, doing housewifely things. She was an activist and, under her maiden name, a primary force in rights for Native Americans. While she was 'spiritually opposed' to the creation of gaming casinos, in lieu of the United States living up to its treaties, the tribes had the right to do what they wanted on their own land.

He'd have to think about this. Lang sent Thanh an email asking him to find out what he could about Lillia Kozlov and Lillia Evencio.

The knock on the door startled him and he didn't have time to respond when it burst open. Carly came in.

Lang smiled, composed his thinking. Lillia Kozlov was put aside for the moment.

'Inspector Gratelli said you know something about a scooter,' Carly said, dropping her bag on the sofa.

'Come in,' Lang said.

'Thank you. I have.'

'Olivia was more than likely transported to Lafayette Park on the back of a scooter.'

He waited for her to digest the fact.

'Points to the family,' she said. 'Maybe.'

'"Maybe" is right.' He had passed along the information to Chastain West, who felt it was helpful in tearing down the wall of circumstantial evidence, but by no means destroyed it. Daniel Lee was still on the hook.

Lang leaned back in his chair, glad to take a break from the intensity of his search for Lillia's lineage.

She sat on the arm of the sofa.

'You always seem so . . . la . . .'

'Laid back?'

'I was going to say lackadaisical.'

'Nice word. Nobody uses "lackadaisical" any more. It's kind of an old word.'

'Thank you.'

'Insincerity is the sincerest form of hostility.'

'I'll quote you if I ever write a book. Now you gave me something. I'll give you something. About a week before Olivia's death, security video cameras were removed from the Hanover premises. All of them.'

The phone rang.

'I have to get this. Just be a moment,' Lang said, picking up the receiver. It was a board member of the foundation that ran Lillia's activist group. The name was Margaret Davis. She was willing to talk, but not on the phone. Could they meet for lunch tomorrow?

'Where and when?'

'Greens at Fort Mason. You know it?'

'Yes,' Lang said. 'It had been a long time since he'd been out there, but he knew the center and the restaurant.'

'Noon?'

'Noon is fine,' Lang said. He put the receiver back on its ancient hook and wrote himself a Post-it. He faced Carly. 'On whose orders?' Lang picked up on the previous conversation.

'Her secretary's. But I haven't talked with him about it yet.'

'Seems stupid.'

'It wasn't discussed with the police or with me or, I suspect, with the defense. I got it from the housekeeper.'

'Good work,' Lang said.

'Still, it's dumb, I agree.'

'You want to grab a bite to eat?'

'Thanks, but not this evening,' she said, not sure why. She had nothing to do. And they could talk about the case.

'You like eating alone?'

'Who says I'm eating alone?'

'Who says you're not?'

'You still have your stalker?'

'Stalkers. I really pissed them off this time. You afraid?'

Dinner was a modest but sloppy affair. Memphis Minnie's is located on lower Haight Street, the part of Haight that the tourists don't know about, the part of Haight Street that hosts bars with tough, sad-faced clients with careless hair cuts, people not likely impressed by sartorial splendor. It's where the local grocery is O'Looneys and one of the most interesting places to get cocktails is Molotov's. It was one of the tougher, straighter neighborhoods. And one senses that the overthrow of the government could begin on a local bar stool.

Lang thought the Russian thugs should feel right at home if they were following him.

And now Carly and Lang were standing at the counter at the loud and busy Barbecue Joint and Smokehouse at Lang's suggestion. They had to order and had to choose from such non-nouvelle California cuisine as slow-smoked beef brisket, pulled pork sandwiches, or catfish – with collard greens, vinegar slaw and stone ground corn muffins as possible sides and sweet potato pie as dessert.

'Ohlone,' Lang said over the din of eager eaters once they were seated. 'What do you know about them?'

'Ohlone? My first thought was Ohlone with Gorgonzola sauce, but you mean the Indians. From my California history courses, I remember they were probably the first humans in the Bay Area, where they thrived for a long time, hunting and fishing. Then the Europeans came, decided they weren't living right and proceed to enslave them and give them deadly diseases to nearly wipe them out. The usual.'

'We Europeans are a nasty lot,' Lang said.

'Well, Mr Lang, you don't have to dig all that deep into any culture to find tragic behavior. Look at Olivia. What harm could she have done to anyone?'

Lang nodded, put a little butter on his cornbread.

'Why are you interested in the Ohlone?'

'Trying to figure out what Native American activists might want these days?'

'Casinos,' Carly said with a hint of sadness in her voice.

Lang nodded.

'What else have they got?'

She shrugged. 'I don't have a side here. I don't know. You working on something with the Ohlone?'

He told her the story.

'So you've made this Mrs Kozlov your mission?'

'For the most part I don't have missions. I say let the native people hunt and fish and go naked if they want. But I don't like other people using me for something other than what they say they're using me for. I'm not fond of being deceived.'

'I'll keep that in mind.'

Twenty-Eight

Lang, who had taken the long walk to his office earlier, rode in Carly's miniature car to the Lower Haight. After the early dinner, he walked her to her car before setting out by foot for his little place in the Western Addition – not all that far away.

Their talk yielded little beyond what they already knew. Carly would question Gary Gray about the removal of the cameras and Lang would brief West on the strange goings on in the Hanover household. The truth was that Lang was more focused on the Kozlov death, perhaps because his own survival was involved. He felt a little guilty. He didn't want to short-change Daniel Lee, but that whole affair was less in his hands. He didn't know what else to do at the moment.

The sun was still out – in his face, in fact, as he walked west. Walking in the neighborhoods where there were mostly just homes – Victorians, Edwardians and a scattering of usually ugly botched remodels – one saw a few folks. There were bicyclists, retirees out for a stroll, some on their way to take care of business, some walking their dogs. But it wasn't crowded.

When the guy came out of a doorway right in front of him, Lang didn't know what to think. The backlight blinded him to any specific features, but he was pretty sure there was a knife in the man's hand.

Maybe because the light was so harsh behind the assailant, Lang could see the long dark arm swinging around and the gleam of silver at its end. Lang could hear the swoosh as he ducked the slicing arm. He fell backward as the man lunged for him.

'Lang,' came a voice behind him. 'Yo!'

The attacker froze for a second, then took off like a flash.

'Wait.'

Lang turned back to see Rose and Stern coming toward him. Rose had taken off after the stranger, while Stern half-heartedly jogged toward Lang.

'What's with your friend?' Stern asked, coming closer.

'You mean the guy with the knife?' Lang asked. 'One of Kozlov's boys.'

'Nah, this area can be dangerous sometimes. Mugging more than likely,' Stern said. 'Good thing we came along.'

'Lucky guy,' Rose said, returning without a body in tow.

Funny thing about luck, Lang thought. When people survive earthquakes and tornados, their homes lost, loved ones dead or injured, people say how lucky they are.

'Yeah, well, thanks. You might want to give Kozlov a call. Then again, you don't care much about that.'

'On the contrary,' Stern said, uncharacteristically cheerful. 'We care a lot about Kozlov.'

'His wife was murdered,' Lang said. 'Do you care?'

'We agree. She was murdered,' Rose said. 'We've seen the light.'

'And Kozlov said you were the guy who killed her.' Stern's smile was not a pleasure to see.

'What?'

'You were there. You were inside the house,' Stern continued.

'What?'

'There's more,' Rose said. 'She had bruising sex before her death, the autopsy revealed.'

'And you have this flimsy story of maybe seeing somebody leaving the scene. Kozlov said he never believed that his wife would end her life. She had too much to live for.'

Lang felt his stomach dip. While Lang was pissed at being used as an alibi, Kozlov was raising the stakes even more, making Lang the perpetrator. This guy was good or had hired Karl Rove as an advisor. Kozlov should work in politics. Oh, that's right, he did. And Lang was being triangulated. Lang, the chief accuser, became the accused. If that didn't work, then Kozlov's thugs would kill him and make it look like a mugging. Game over. Kozlov takes a bow.

Lang told himself to stay calm. Carly seemed to like his laid-back, lackadaisical attitude, didn't she? He told himself if he got mad, he'd lose. He'd at least not think straight. But he couldn't help wondering if he hadn't bitten off more than he could chew.

'You got anything to say?' Stern asked, enjoying himself.

'The guy is playing you, Stern. There's a part of me that hopes that you know that. Otherwise you're just too dumb to exist. And I don't want to think that about you.'

'There's no law against having an opinion,' Stern said. 'Let's have a little chat downtown. How about that?'

'I don't think so.'

'We think so, don't we, Rose?'

'We seem to be of one mind. I'm not sure whose mind it is. I had hoped it was my mind. But one mind, nonetheless. And a mind is a terrible thing to waste.'

'That means we go downtown, Lang,' Stern said.

'Am I under arrest?'

'Could be. Attacking a pedestrian. Assault and battery. I personally witnessed it.'

Lang was only a few doors from his abode, but he wasn't going to make it. Rose patted him down before he was seated in the back of a big, black Crown Victoria. He was allowed to keep his belongings. The two cops sat up front.

Halfway to the Hall of Justice, Lang felt the phone wiggle in his pants. He looked at the screen. Thanh.

'Lang,' he said after flipping open the phone.

'I have some information on Lillia Kozlov.'

'That's great. Listen, something's come up.'

Stern, who wasn't driving, looked back and smiled.

Lang lowered his voice, but not that far. He wanted the two cops to hear him, but he didn't want them to think he was intentionally including them on the call.

'Listen,' Lang continued, 'I want you to call Tony at the station. Tell him I've got breaking news.'

'Who's Tony? Oh . . .' Thanh said.

Out of the corner of his eye, Lang noticed that Stern and Rose were paying attention. He smiled at them, pretended to cup the receiving end for privacy and wondered if they could see the light bulb hovering over his head.

'Seems as if the police now believe that the Kozlov suicide is actually a homicide. If you call now, he can get that on the eleven o'clock news tonight and that means it will be in the papers in the morning.'

Rose stopped the car.

'Wait, wait, wait . . .' Stern said, getting out of the car and opening the rear door. He slid in.

'Come on . . .'

'Hold on?' Lang said to Thanh. 'What?'

'Don't do that.'

'You've got me for murder, right? I mean, you're questioning me about the murder. The public has a right to know. Maybe I'm dangerous. Shouldn't they know that? And shouldn't they know what a wonderful job you two guys have done?'

Stern's face puffed and turned red.

'Make up your mind,' Lang said. 'You ready for all that?'

Stern glared at him.

'If you'll excuse me, I'll get out here,' Lang said, nudging Stern toward the door.

'A lot of bridges are burning behind you,' Stern said.

'Doesn't matter. They're all over troubled water. Isn't that right, Rose?'

Even if Rose sympathized with Lang, it was doubtful he would do anything to piss off Stern. He stayed quiet.

Lang waved bye as he walked away from the big old sedan.

It wasn't lost on him that after an assassin was foiled only by police seeking to make him a murderer, his walking back home could be more of an adventure than he was prepared to take.

'Taxi!' he called out once he made it to Market Street.

The telephone call with Gary Gray didn't happen. Gray's partner refused to connect her.

'I'm sorry,' he said, 'Gary signed a confidential clause in his employment agreement and he is worried about how far he's gone already. He doesn't want to speak to you.'

Carly had nowhere to go but the bathtub. It was her primary escape. And each time she soaked, she thanked her mother for tearing down the utility room to extend the bath. The huge tub and the scented water were part of the bliss. Peggy Lee singing about disappointment and a lightly chilled glass of wine contributed to her welcomed melancholy as well.

For a moment she chided herself for feeling such a petty and, at first glance, selfish emotion. But just for a moment. Next the feeling seemed right, a small sampling of something far more meaningful. This too drifted away.

When her cell phone played its own tune, Paladino thought that maybe Gary Gray had changed his mind. It was hard to believe, after their previous conversations, that he was suddenly willing to abandon the affection he felt for Olivia.

But it wasn't Gary Gray. It was Noah Lang.

'You find out anything?' he asked.

'I'm fine, thanks for asking,' she said. She didn't know why, but she was suddenly cheered.

'Now that the pleasantries are out of the way,' Lang said, 'your boy have anything interesting to say?'

'No more comment,' Carly said. 'I think after the police search, the

Hanovers are circling the wagons. I'm guessing Pamela's attorney reminded the young secretary that he had signed a confidentiality agreement.'

'Makes sense.'

'I'm not sure he'd have answers even if we could ask the questions. I am certainly without answers.' She began a little internal debate about saying goodbye or staying in a tub of water that was starting to cool down. He'd hear if she ran more hot water.

'I have answers. All sorts of them. Just don't know what questions they go to.'

'Tell me,' she said. She took a sip of wine.

'Blue. The Tip of Antarctica. April the fifth, 1965. Monkey. Albumen. Should I go on?'

'No. But you can tell me something. Tell me what you do at the end of the day that brings you pleasure. Smart ass or obscene answers disqualified.'

'Until the Russians bombed my home, eating a few crab cakes, having a glass of beer and watching a movie – maybe *Blade Runner* or some old black and white movie with William Powell or Humphrey Bogart.'

'Those two couldn't be farther apart.'

He also liked Robert Mitchum and David Niven, but telling her that would only confuse matters further.

'What can I say? I'm a complex guy.'

'You make your own crab cakes?'

'I do. Mostly I make fish cakes. I like things like that, where you mix things up together. I make chicken patties or, I suppose if I made them in little balls, croquettes. But I make patties.'

'Fascinating. You should think about writing your memoirs.'

'You asked.'

'Your idea of fun is not a night about town?'

'No. Used to. Now I'm completely boring. And, because the Russians broke my toys, bored.'

She started to say 'me too' but she decided not to.

'And you?' he asked.

'A hot bath and a glass of wine do the trick.'

'But at the moment, the water is getting cold?' Lang asked.

'What?'

'You heard me. You don't think I can tell? There is an extremely hollow sound to your phone, save the Peggy Lee in the background. And she's echoing a bit, which means hard surfaces. A tiled place. And occasionally, there was the sound of water, a wisp of a sound, probably when you move your hand.'

'I'm going to have to get a less sensitive phone,' she said. 'I gotta go.'
'Hey, I can't see you.'
'Bye.'

'Well, let's review,' Lang said to Buddha. Buddha seemed interested. 'So far, in my attempt to prove that Mr Kozlov had something to do with Mrs Kozlov's death, I have managed to provoke him and his henchmen into trying to kill me. No evidence. Just tremendously bad feeling, wouldn't you say? If you could say, I mean. And on the Olivia Hanover front, we keep finding things that suggest that someone in that house was instrumental in her death, but those same discoveries don't exactly rule out our young client, Daniel Lee.'

Lang walked around the quiet, all too empty room. Buddha, perched on the back of the sofa, didn't follow, but continued to look Lang's way.

'Do go on, you say? Well there's not much more to tell. We'll have to see if there was really a conflict in Lillia's view of Native American relations and her husband's.'

He looked back at Buddha.

'Thank you,' he said. He picked up his cell phone and called Chastain West. After briefing him on the Hanovers' timely elimination of video security, he moved to his other, unofficial, case and asked if there was a way to find out if Lillia, using her married or Native American name, filed any court cases.

'Divorce?'

'Maybe. Maybe civil on some other matter, or an injunction possibly.'

'I can try. By the way, they're going to indict Daniel Lee.'

'What? The scooter. What about the scooter?'

'As you suggested. He could have been the driver. I think the Hanovers upped the pressure on the city to get this over with.'

'Damn.'

Apparently the new Hanover strategy was to get tough. Putting pressure on city officials while gagging the staff had the feel of a coordinated political campaign. Should anyone expect less? One of the powers of the wealthy is to buy the best of whatever it is you want, including politicians.

On the other hand, Lang understood this: Daniel could have done it. It was just that Lang didn't want him to have done it. He wanted Daniel to be a wanderer, a free soul, not a freak murderer. What he wanted, of course, meant nothing in the whole scheme of things.

Twenty-Nine

For Lang, the morning was full of information. Thanh had discovered quite a bit about Lillia's alternate personality. She was executive director for a second nonprofit that was organized to convince Native Americans that they 'had been fooled again by the white man.'

The organization pleaded with visitors to support a movement in which Native Americans would create businesses that took the lead in the green movement, using their land, whatever riches they'd gained from gambling, and their natural connection to nature to overcome global warming and other environmental destruction.

Mrs Kozlov, aka Lillia Evencio, was, in effect, supporting her husband's goal to prevent Indians from owning casinos. Intentionally or not, she was helping Las Vegas interests. This ran counter to Lang's belief that maybe she wasn't killed out of some deranged jealousy but because her efforts, her passion ran counter to her husband's business interests.

The information on the website was interesting, much more political than the one from the foundation. The words suggested that while Native Americans were now, for the first time, participating in American capitalism, the downside was that Native Americans were now, for the first time, participating in American capitalism. It was just another trick like peace treaties and new happy hunting grounds.

Thanh, a handsome and stylish young man this morning wearing jeans, white shirt and blazer, had picked up some beignets from the little place in the Tenderloin, knowing that Lang had a weakness for almost anything from New Orleans. Thanh, who regularly noticed if Lang gained a few ounces, and chided him for it, also regularly tempted him with all sorts of things that would fatten him up.

But coffee and beignets? For Lang, as he grew older, life was increasingly about food.

Thanh smiled as Lang bit into one and the powdered sugar exploded all over his suit.

'You're a cruel man,' Lang said to him.

'Perverse to the core. How's your new girlfriend?'

Lang shrugged. 'People's lives cross and then they uncross. At the moment, Carly Paladino and I are crossing. Don't make too much of it.'

By mid morning, Chaz West had called. He found nothing useful. There were no lawsuits by Lillia Kozlov or Lillia Evencio and none against Mr Kozlov or the firm he worked for. Nothing pending.

He asked if Lang had had any luck deciphering Daniel Lee's code.

'Daniel told me it was gibberish. Maybe it is. Maybe the kid's as crazy as a loon.'

'Not according to the doctors. Antisocial maybe, they said. But then, so are you.'

She was aware that some might think that what she was doing was morbid. It wasn't. Her mind, after the run and now sitting in Lafayette Park, was clear.

Last night she cleared out all the cobwebs of melancholy in a long, hot soak. Afterward she found herself in some wild combination of aerobics and dance with music in front of a mirror. It was frantic, perhaps a little hysteric, but wonderfully exhausting. Afterward she slept the sleep of the dead.

This morning, Carly Paladino was ready to think about someone else. Olivia. And now thinking of her with lessening sentimentality. Down to business. It was time to get down to business.

Whoever left Olivia here, she thought, loved her. She had seen the photograph. It was respectful. The location, short of floating on a petal-ridden raft in a quiet pond, was almost romantic. Carly had talked only briefly to the young man under arrest, so she had no real take on him, but the gentle resting place seemed to rule out a few in the Hanover family. She could not imagine Walter or his eldest son bothering with these kinds of details.

There was no science in this, of course. There was no way these conclusions constituted evidence. However, for her, it narrowed the field. She now had a list: Pamela Hanover, Jordan Hanover, Gary Gray, and the young man.

The cooler than body temperature air combined with a layer of sweat from the run gave her a chill. She decided to move on. She walked back to her flat, asking herself what possible motivation would any of these folks have to kill a young, vulnerable teen. That was the next job on the list.

Greens wouldn't have been Lang's choice for restaurants. He was, after all, a meat eater and Greens was, after all, one of the world's most noted vegetarian restaurants.

Mrs Margaret Davis, who he recognized in the lobby because she wore a feather brooch as she said she would, seemed averse to discussing the business they came there to discuss. As with many older, refined ladies, there was a certain protocol. Light chit-chat first. Pleasantries. Weather, always unpredictable in a city with a dozen or more microclimates, was the first. New restaurants, always a lively topic in a city where a certain chef is more important than the outcome of the Giants' last baseball game, came second.

She did not know, it seemed, that Lang did not possess the means to sample the exquisite places to dine and make comparisons. Even being at Greens was a few pay grades above his norm, though he would have to admit halfway through the entrée that the mesquite grilled mushroom brochettes with pumpkin seed brown rice made him forget about meat and for a moment forget about the conversation.

Sitting by the window at the Fort Mason Center restaurant, watching the small boats in the Marina bob up and down and with the correctly venerated Golden Gate Bridge in the background made him forget he was a lowly PI who would soon mentally count the bills in his wallet so he could get out of the place.

'So,' she said, as the plates were removed, and there was at least half of a bottle of wine left to go, 'let's talk about Lillia.' She smiled.

'The first picture I had of Lillia was as a housewife under the thumb of an oppressive husband. That she kept the house nice, did the shopping, and didn't have much of a life of her own.'

Lang waited to be corrected.

'She didn't talk about her private life,' Davis said. 'She came out here every Thursday morning for a meeting with the foundation staff and she spent those same Thursday afternoons working with the spin-off group.'

'Spin off?' Lang's stake-outs began after a Thursday and ended tragically before the next.

'The first was a foundation, primarily interested in raising funds and then funding programs that helped various Bay Area Native American groups achieve their goals. The second was an activist group that she started that would fight against what she called the "spiritual burglary of the tribal soul." She was smart, serious, and didn't seem to be the mousy housewife type.'

The way Margaret Davis said 'mousy' suggested she believed that women were meant to get involved.

'Gambling was one of the burglaries.'

'Yes. Drinking and gambling. These were troubling for her.' Davis looked troubled. 'I wasn't all that supportive of her efforts in this second venture she was undertaking.'

'Why?'

'The jury was . . . is . . . still out on the efficacy of her goals.' Again, she looked as if she was struggling with words, or possibly thoughts. 'What right do we have telling a group of people, who in the past were denied both their own way of life and the American dream, that we were against the only avenue they seemed to have to support their families, their community.'

'Lillia had other thoughts.'

'Yes. There had to be a better way, she thought. It was noble. She believed that the Native American history of working with nature was a tie in to what is happening everywhere. They could not only be the symbol of it, but also the prime mover.'

'Her husband didn't want there to be Indian gambling either. That was his job as a lobbyist for Las Vegas gambling interests – to keep the tribes out of the casino business. Was she supporting his efforts, maybe?'

'I wouldn't like to think she was working *sub rosa*,' she said, taking a sip of her wine and letting the view from the window distract her. 'I believed her. I believe her. You obviously believe that there was something queer about her death.'

Lang nodded, noting that only the old generation still used that word to mean odd. And she was quite old.

'You didn't know Mr Kozlov?'

'Kozlov?' she asked, drawn eyebrows rising.

'You knew her as Evencio?'

'Yes, that wasn't her name?'

'That was an ancestral name,' Lang said, feeling a little full of it saying the word 'ancestral.' It was also clear Lillia was keeping her worlds apart.

'She was,' Davis said, 'going to tell me something. We were going to meet here the morning that turned out to be the day after her death. It seemed important, but it's lost now.'

'You have no idea?'

'No.'

Outside, Lang said his goodbyes. She had picked up the tab and when he'd objected she'd given him a kind but curt piece of her mind.

'Just because you're male doesn't mean you pick up the check,' she'd said. 'You must learn that. Did you enjoy your lunch?'

'Very much. With you paying the bill for some really great vegetarian food, I just might come over to your world.'

She'd smiled. 'You're welcome.'

Lang took a walk before getting in his old, beat-up Mercedes. Fort Mason Center was quintessential San Francisco. An old military base turned into a home for nonprofits. The old piers were used for big events and the smaller buildings, some of them elegant, some of them earthy. Many of the other buildings housed small nonprofits, organizations that worked to ban nuclear weapons, teach art and music, save rivers, and provide recreation for youth at risk.

He walked around one of the piers, looking out over the bay as pelicans flew near him – in formation – so near him that he could see the texture of their feathers. A cormorant fished in the water between piers. A seal popped up out of the water and then disappeared again. Sausalito and Tiburon were on the far side of the choppy water. To his right the gray, jagged rock of Alcatraz seemed hard and sullen. In between a few sailboats braved a fast and swirling wind. He was reminded that the world could be spectacularly beautiful and deeply, darkly ugly – and that only place or a moment in time separated them.

The Russian stood there – in the center of Lang's office – with a gun in one hand and a picture frame in the other. Carly noticed that Thanh, who was a stylish young man today, tried not to look at the guy whose rantings bounced unintelligibly against the walls. He stared at the computer screen. As a survivor on the streets, Thanh knew better than to engage a madman.

'I can come back,' Carly said, slowly moving from the center of the office toward the door.

The Russian jerked his face toward her, scowled, shouted, waved the photograph. The only word Carly understood was the word 'Lang' which had figured in his earlier yelping.

'I don't know her,' Carly said about the woman in the photograph. She shook her head, raised her hands. It was the universal 'nothing-I-can-do-to-help-you look.' There was nothing they could do. He wanted answers to questions no one there could understand.

'Lillia Kozlov,' Thanh said.

Carly thought Thanh was incredibly calm.

The intruder understood. Nodded.

The office door swung open again. Another Russian. He yelled at his countryman. The man's body language indicated that he wanted his friend to leave with him. While Carly could not understand the words, it was clear the second man was pleading.

This seemed to excite the mad Russian more. He waved his gun, lurched toward Thanh, screaming, then turned back to Carly. The second man continued to talk, pleading one moment, demanding the next. The gunman looked around crazily, waving the photograph.

Obviously the guy wasn't trying to find out who the woman in the photo was, but something else.

As threatening and dramatic as the mad Russian was, he lost his audience.

All eyes were on the window. On the fire escape, Barry Brinkman stared in with eyes-wide confusion. The gunman, finally tracking the new object of the room's attention, raised his pistol and fired at the man on the fire escape, and raced over, following the path of the bullet, to the window.

Thanh stood, wrapped the string from the Venetian blinds around the gun hand of the Russian, and pulled, raising the hand straight up. The gun went off again, this time sending a bullet into the ceiling. The Russian's feet were still on the floor, but his body was stretched far enough that he wouldn't be able to get in any force in a kick or even a punch with his free hand. Thanh pulled a knife, held it under the man's chin.

The second man pulled out his own knife and started toward Thanh. Carly whacked him in the Adam's apple with her elbow. She thanked Vogel Security for requiring its investigative staff to take a series of courses in self-defense. As the stunned man gasped for breath, she took the knife from him, put a foot behind his legs, and brought him down easy. She didn't want to hurt him any more than she already had. Except for a sputtering, coughing partner, the event looked like a fine piece of modern dance.

'The thing is,' Brinkman said, coming into the room and looking at the strange scene, 'almost getting killed makes you feel alive.' He had a gun in his hand and a smile on his face.

Thirty

Lang recognized the two Russians, nodded in their direction as a form of 'hello.'

'You came late to your own party,' Carly said.

'As usual, the fun part is all over,' he said. 'It is nice of you, though, to bring gifts, all tied up and all.'

The small office was full – the two assailants, bound at the wrists and ankles, sat on the floor; Brinkman smoking his cigar and nipping at a bottle of bourbon; Carly perched on the corner of Lang's desk; and Thanh sitting at the computer as if nothing out of the ordinary had happened.

Brinkman held up his bottle in an offering to Lang, who gave the man an encouraging nod.

'Better not let the landlord catch you with the cigar, Barry,' Lang said.

'He'll be too busy screaming at you about the bullet hole in your window and another one in the ceiling,' Brinkman said as he poured some of the bourbon into Lang's coffee cup.

'Either of you speak English?' Lang asked the captives.

No nods of yes or no, but one of them looked away.

'This one does,' Lang said, pointing to the Russian who came to retrieve his friend.

'One of them definitely doesn't,' Carly said, 'and the other one might, but might not be able to at the moment.'

Lang looked perplexed.

'Carly is a gentle thug. You are definitely going to like her,' Thanh said. 'She elbowed him to the throat and then set him down gently on the floor as if he were a piece of delicate china. Next thing we know Dirty Barry here comes in and creates a sense of order.'

Lang's cell sounded. It was West.

'The DA has turned over some information from the search of the Hanovers' house,' West said. 'I don't see a smoking gun anywhere, but maybe you want to take a look.'

'I do,' Lang said. 'As soon as I dispose of some rowdy Russians, I'll drop by.' He flipped the phone shut, then looked at the guys on the floor. 'What do we do with you? You keep coming back.'

'When you get rats or cockroaches, you can't just ask them to leave,' Brinkman said. 'You have to exterminate them.' He looked around the room. 'I know where there is a big old furnace. Pfffft. Gone forever.'

Lang picked up the photograph. He set it on the desk facing out so the Russians could see it. He smiled.

The Russian who could only speak Russian tried to speak through his gag. Whatever he was saying it was in hysteric tones. The other, calmer and fed up with his pal, just shook his head.

'You want to talk to us?' Lang asked him.

He shook his head.

Lang dropped down on his haunches, pulled the gag from the calmer Russian's mouth. 'Look, I don't like you or hate you. I don't care if you live or die. But the thing is you are posing a serious threat to my existence. The police won't keep you locked up. Your boss says you have to keep trying to kill me until you succeed. What options do I have? Think about a solution.'

'He would kill us,' the man said. The accent was heavy, but he did understand the question.

'What if the man went away? You know. Permanently.'

'You can't do it,' the Russian said. Lang couldn't understand what he said next.

'What?'

'He said this man knows too many important people,' Carly said.

'Nothing will happen to him,' the Russian continued.

'Your friend is afraid too?' Lang asked.

'More afraid. He's afraid of his own shadow.'

'Of Mrs Kozlov's shadow?'

The Russian nodded.

'Which one of you killed her?'

The Russian looked away.

'You want to get a bite to eat?' Lang asked Carly as he stood up.

'What about these guys?'

'What about 'em? Brinkman will take care of them, won't you, Barry?'

'Yeah. I know a guy deals in organs,' Brinkman said. 'Kidneys, livers. These guys are worth a fortune in spare parts.'

'Brains aren't much use though, but there's money in eyeballs,' Thanh said. 'They're young, relatively healthy.'

'What's left goes to the furnace,' Brinkman said. 'We'll keep them here until nightfall, then my guys'll come over to pick them up. It's not going to be easy, we got to keep them alive until we can get them to the clinic.'

'Do we have to wait for our money?' Thanh asked.

'We sell wholesale like you buy a cow. The clinic takes care of the rest, you know T-bone, sirloin, hamburger.'

'What are you in the mood for?' Lang continued his conversation with Carly. 'There's a great Burmese restaurant on Clement.'

'Wait,' the Russian said. 'I don't know. Don't be crazy. Let me think. OK?'

'Let's move them in the back room,' Lang said, 'then we'll take off.'

The space was empty since Lang moved all his personal stuff to his apartment and in preparation for someone to share the office. It wasn't all that appealing, but the windowless space was perfect for incarceration.

'This is kidnapping,' the Russian said.

'Oh, it's much worse than kidnapping,' Lang said as he and Thanh pulled the young man into the room. Brinkman and Carly did the same with the other.

'Don't worry they have stuff to kill the pain, it won't be so bad,' Brinkman said. 'I mean they're not cruel by nature.'

Both men were gagged and left in the dark.

In the hallway, the four of them discussed a plan that might expedite information, maybe a confession.

Lang drove this time and they stopped at Chastain West's law office in the Civic Center, which was near the new and imposing courthouse that held civil cases. As unlikely as it was for an attorney to handle both civil and criminal matters, West also defended the poor and powerless in civil law suits brought against them by the rich and powerful.

Lang made the introductions.

'Came over to the light?' West asked Carly.

'I'm not taking sides in this one. Just want the facts.'

West looked at Lang.

'The facts are the light,' Lang said.

'You've been watching science fiction again,' West said. 'Noble though. Something said in the *Star Wars* movie.'

'Thanks for trying to help,' Carly said.

West didn't have much. He had the report on the scooter, which revealed there was some DNA there. They were running it. They indicated what was found on the family computers. Basically nothing that would implicate anyone. Olivia had no doubt had her own and it was missing.

As Lang finished reading each page, he passed it to her.

'Did you see the list of pharmaceuticals in Pamela Hanover's bathroom?' Carly asked.

'Something jump out at you?' West asked.

'She takes Prozac, which is not uncommon, but unless they wrote this down wrong, the prescription date was back in March – and there were half a dozen pills in the bottle.'

'So?' Lang asked. 'She decided she didn't need them any more.'

'Her housekeeper said she took care of her dying mother at the house,' Carly said. 'She died in March. Then there was Olivia. How was Pamela coping?'

'Maybe she just pushed her way through it,' Lang said.

'Or she found another way to medicate for her pain, her anxiety.'

'Where are you going?'

'Long shot,' Carly said. 'Ketamine has been used as an antidepressant.'

'What?' West asked, getting interested.

'I don't know if the Medical Association is endorsing it for use in the treatment of depression and anxiety, but there are those at least experimenting with it. A low dose of ketamine, some say, provides a quick and long-lasting fix to dark moods. It's not just a "Special K" trip at the club.'

'How do you know all this?'

'A friend.'

'A friend?' Lang asked.

By the time they were ready to eat, there was a line in front of Burma Star, a particularly popular restaurant on a street full of restaurants, mostly Chinese and Vietnamese. Lang and Carly stood out on the street as the chilly fog drifted in. The summer's long day was turning into a short and nearly wintry night.

'Summer in San Francisco, can't beat it,' she said, smiling.

'I think we had at least three seasons today.'

'Do you never eat at home?' Carly asked.

'Used to. I've got to learn to eat without watching something on television. This way, I can watch people.'

'You really scared the bejesus out of those guys. You give any thought to the Geneva Convention?'

'I couldn't make it. I had a dentist's appointment.'

'Cruel and inhuman. This is torture.'

'I don't know if either of those guys killed Mrs Kozlov, but I know they tried to kill me. Twice, not counting this little visit. I don't plan on killing them, or hurting them, physically.'

'What's with the photo?'

'It was a gamble. I was hoping one of the crew was a little superstitious, make him nervous. It worked.'

'This Brinkman fellow has an evil mind.'

Lang nodded, smiling.

'He doesn't have anything else to think about. Evil? Imaginative would be my description. You believe in evil?'

She nodded. 'You?'

'I think some people get so screwed up they need to be separated from the herd. Even that can be a tough decision sometimes. The rules aren't clear as far as I'm concerned.'

Finally, inside the restaurant Carly felt warm space engulfed in aromatic smells. The nice thing about getting chilled is taking the chill off. On the menu, curry, ginger, basil, and garlic dominated the menu. The trouble wouldn't be finding something she liked, it would be the trouble choosing.

After today, she couldn't complain about not living a more exciting life.

Thanh went butch for the evening, even wearing a baseball cap. His hair was tucked up inside. He stood outside the office door, chatting with Lang and Carly.

'Where did you get the white jacket?' Lang asked him.

'The restaurant. Restaurant, medical clinic. Same thing.' He grinned. 'I even have a hypodermic and a gurney. The gurney is inside.'

'You are very resourceful,' Lang said. 'And where did that come from?'

'It came from Brinkman's office. It's part of the desk his secretary used, when he had one. A little narrow and wood, but I doubt if these guys are thinking all that clear. Put a sheet over it and it looks pretty good.'

'Speak Vietnamese to them,' Lang said.

'They don't speak . . . oh . . . OK.'

'Adds to the insecurity. Crazy guy they can't communicate with is taking them away.'

'I take back what I said about Brinkman,' Carly said. 'You have quite an imagination as well.'

'I'll speak Vietnamese to you sometimes.'

'You don't speak Vietnamese,' Thanh told Lang.

'I know, but they won't know. Just don't laugh, OK?'

As they went into the office, Thanh started to flip on the light.

'No lights. Let's go in with a flashlight. We have one, right.'

'You should direct horror movies,' Carly whispered.

'Low-budget horror movies,' Lang whispered back.

Thirty-One

It wasn't a particularly talented improv group who went into the darkened room. The flashlight created sharp shafts of light and bizarre shadows. Carly watched, thinking that this was a far cry from the sophisticated investigations of Vogel Security. It was more like *Night of the Living Dead*.

She watched as Lang made sure the two Russians had quick glimpses of the gurney, of a disguised Thanh brandishing a hypodermic needle and the photograph of the late Mrs Kozlov. What am I doing here? Carly thought. Have I gone completely out of my mind?

The Russian who had been in a state of metaphysical anxiety when he arrived was now unbearably hysterical. The saner of the two was also now less than centered. Hours in the dark and some measure of sensory deprivation had increased their anxiety, making the theater presented to them believable. Thanh babbled something in Vietnamese and Lang responded in mock Vietnamese with a touch of impatience. Thanh picked up the tone and yelled back. For all anyone knew, he could have been ordering roast beef and mashed potatoes, but it sounded like a serious disagreement.

'What's going on?' asked the more reasonable of the two captives.

'Oh, don't get me started,' Lang said. 'The clinic doesn't want to put you guys out completely. He wants to save some of the anesthesia for the surgery. I don't know why . . .'

'What?' the Russian asked.

'Don't worry. These guys take out a kidney just like that.' Lang snapped his fingers. 'So the severe pain won't last that long. Then all it will be is a little achy.'

'You can't do this? This is America.'

'C'mon, you know how the black market works. You Russians are masters. And you are ideal candidates. You are here illegally. No one even knows you're here – except for Kozlov. We called him and he said he doesn't know you.'

The English-speaking Russian said something in Russian and Carly thought it probably wasn't a kind thing. He spoke to his partner and the partner was crazed.

'Wait, wait,' the Russian said. 'Can we talk?'

'About what?' Lang asked. 'The weather? Current events?'

'You know.'

'I know the only thing I'm interested in is finding out about Mrs Kozlov's death. You want to talk about that?'

'Yes.'

Thanh, makeshift medical orderly, vanished and reappeared thirty minutes later in seductive feminine garb. She brought with her a video recorder. The two Russians sat in the bright lights of the office. The spiritually haunted Russian sat in the corner, curled into himself, probably having private night-mares – maybe believing that the ghost of Mrs Kozlov would travel with him to the other side once his organs were harvested. The English speaker sat at Lang's desk. He answered questions.

Lang asked Carly to pose the questions he had written down. It would add a little credibility to the interview, though it wasn't likely that the 'confession' would hold up in court anyway. Lang's goals were to find out why the murder happened and elicit enough information to upset Kozlov and embarrass the police into an investigation. The voice of a disinterested person would add a patina of professionalism.

Carly didn't agree easily. Kidnapping, however justified it might appear to be to the average person, was still illegal. But in the end she couldn't tear herself away from what was going on.

Thanh set up the scene, putting a sheet over the window so that the background was anonymous. Thanh put the camera on a tripod and arranged the lighting so that the man's features would be harshly clear. The lens was set so that the Russian's face nearly filled the frame.

Carly sat behind the camera so that when the man answered her, he'd be looking into the lens. Straightforward and honest. She read from a lined, yellow notepad.

Carly: 'What is your name?'

Yuri: 'Yuri.'

Carly: 'Last name?'

Yuri: 'No.'

Carly: 'Where are you from?'

Yuri: 'Chernyakhovsk, then Moscow.'

Carly: 'Where are you living now?'

Yuri: 'This city. San Francisco.'

Carly: 'Are you legal?'

Yuri: 'No.'

Carly: 'Do you have a job?'

Yuri: 'Sometimes.'

Carly: 'Can you explain a little more?'

Yuri: 'I work for Mr Kozlov.'

Carly: 'His full name please?'

Lang was happy. She knew what she was doing. She might even do it better than he would.

Yuri: 'Theo.'

Carly: 'Theodore, you mean?'

Yuri: 'Yes.'

Yuri swallowed. It was as if he was swallowing a small mouse. It was dawning on him that he was trading one very serious threat for another. He looked at his friend who was as fetally positioned as he could on a chair.

Carly: 'What did you do for him?'

Yuri: 'I drove him.'

Carly: 'Is that all?'

Yuri: 'Sometimes other jobs.'

Carly: 'What other jobs?'

Yuri: 'Deliveries.'

Carly: 'Other Russian immigrants worked for Mr Kozlov. Right?'

Yuri: 'Yes.'

Carly: 'How many?'

Yuri: 'Three.'

Carly: 'And they were all drivers?'

Yuri took a deep breath. He looked down.

Carly: 'You all worked together sometimes?'

Yuri: 'Yes.'

Carly: 'And you did illegal things for him?'

Yuri: 'We did what he told us to do.'

Carly: 'Did he tell you to trash the apartment of a private investigator? Noah Lang?'

Yuri nodded.

Carly: 'Did he tell you to ambush Mr Lang at his office?'

Yuri nodded.

Carly: 'Did he tell you to kill his wife, Lillia Kozlov?'

Yuri seemed to freeze. He looked forward, but his eyes glazed over.

Carly: 'Yuri?'

He clicked back into the real world.

Carly: 'Did he tell you or anyone you know to kill Mrs Kozlov?'

Yuri nodded. He took another deep breath. He knew that he could not go back. The line had been crossed. In that moment of dazed silence he had to be contemplating, perhaps again, the gamble that the confession would be less painful than keeping the secret.

Carly: 'Is that a yes?'

Yuri: 'Yes.'

Carly: 'Please tell us how it happened.'

What followed was the Russian's fumbling attempt at not saying what he knew he had to say. He, Yuri, did not kill Mrs Kozlov. It was the frightened one.

Yuri: 'He sees the photograph, he is frightened. A dog scared of his own fart. Could not stop him.'

He, Yuri, was not involved in the discussions, but he did drive his friend, Dimitri, to the house and he did wait in a parking lot way down the beach. And, yes, it was instigated by Mr Kozlov.

Lang was amazed. The young Russian, if Yuri was to be believed, was not too frightened to kill someone, but easily frightened by the portent of her ghost.

Carly: 'Why did Mr Kozlov want his wife killed?'

Yuri shrugged and shook his head.

Yuri: 'Mr Kozlov does not discuss such things as why this or why that. He tells us to do things. We do them.'

Carly: 'Or what?'

Yuri: 'What do you mean?'

Carly: 'If you didn't do what he asked, what would happen to you?'

Lang was impressed. Carly wasn't just reading the script, she understood what was needed to get where they needed to go.

Yuri shook his head as if to ask her what she thought the outcome would be.

Yuri: 'We go back to Russia.'

Carly: 'Is that so bad?'

Yuri: 'For us, yes. And worse, we have family. We do not have a choice.'

It was clear to Lang that Kozlov was at least as bad as he thought. He was, in fact, a gangster, willing to use any means necessary to achieve his goals. Kozlov had these guys by the balls. No doubt these guys were thugs to begin with. But murder? Lang almost felt sorry for them.

But all of this posed a couple of new questions. The obvious was that they still hadn't gotten the 'why.' What was the motive? The second was not so obvious. Was Kozlov all that tough without his enforcers? There would be a day of reckoning on this matter. Lang would find out.

They paused the camera and set up Dimitri. Yuri asked the questions, basically designed for the young tough to confess. The difficulty was that there was no way to know what he said since no one besides the two of them spoke Russian. But Lang made it clear that a translator would view the tapes and confirm the confession before the two of them were off the medical hook.

Dimitri was shown the photograph again, on camera, and his eyes widened and he chattered away as Yuri just shook his head. If Dimitri hadn't reacted to the photograph none of this would be happening now. Lang counted his blessings. The photograph was just a wild idea. He was just throwing it against the wall, hoping something would come of it.

A Carly contact, who spoke Russian, confirmed Dimitri's answers indicated that he killed Mrs Kozlov. There was nothing else to do but let both of them go. They left relieved and frightened, then Yuri looking back as he started out the door. What have you done to me? That's what the look seemed to say. While they escaped the plucking of vital organs, there were other dangers only slightly less lurid. If not the police, there was Kozlov.

'You guys want to catch a drink somewhere?' Lang asked his co-conspirators.

Thanh gave them a Mona Lisa smile and declined.

Brinkman had gone home before the horror theater began.

'Why not?' Carly said. Sleep would not come easily and a mild depressant wasn't a bad idea. She was pretty wound up. When was the last time she was involved in something so bizarre?

'What now?' she asked him as they went out into the narrow street.

'I call Kozlov, tell him that some of his boys are probably on their way to Mexico City and that I have some interesting video I'm thinking about putting on YouTube.'

'You like pulling his chain,' she said.

'I do. I really do.'

'So what did you think of our little theater troupe?' Lang asked her.

'The more I think of it, I have a sense of Marx Brothers meet Fellini.'

Lang nodded his approval.

'You've captured our whole gestalt.'

'Gestalt?' She laughed.

'It's a psychological term,' he said.

'I know,' she said, shaking her head.

He didn't let her see him smile.

'Thank you for helping out tonight,' Lang said as they waited for their drinks at the bar.

'You do a lot of this kind of thing?' she asked.

'Drinking at a bar or the community theater thing?'

'Theater.'

'Not a lot. Frankly, I don't get a lot of murders. Now I have two. How about you? How different is this from your stuffy office at Vogel?'

'You answered your own question. I'm not sure I'm cut out for this. When are you going to call this Kozlov fellow?'

'In the morning. Stretch it out a little. Give the guys a little time to get out of town.'

He ordered a beer called Dogfish because it was called 'Dogfish' and she a Ramos Gin Fizz, because it was her mother's favorite drink. The Alembic, a crowded, dark little bar tucked almost anonymously on Upper Haight, was full of cool people drinking retro cocktails. When she took her first sip, she nearly swooned. No wonder her mother liked it.

'Supposed to have those kinds of drinks for breakfast, but I doubt if you'll get arrested.'

She smiled. 'Kind of a New Orleans feel to the place. The drink is really, really good.'

'This ketamine thing is interesting,' Lang said.

'She also took care of her dying mother. Cancer. Cancer equals pain. In my experience, the terminally ill are often prescribed a morphine drip and Mrs Hanover was the primary caregiver.'

'Maybe the mom died before she had used up her prescription?'

'It's not much, but . . . it's something.'

'How would she get the ketamine?'

'A friendly doctor, a friendly friend.'

'Kind of a young person's drug. Maybe one of the kids?'

'Mmmnnnnn,' Carly said, sipping her drink. 'Speaking of drugs.'

'They do good work here.'

'We need to do some good work,' she said, getting serious again.

Thirty-Two

Buddha was by the door when Lang got back, but after a look headed toward the kitchen. Lang was late. Buddha was slightly pissed. It was the way the cat turned that gave his mood away.

'I'm sure impatience is covered somewhere in your teachings, Buddha,' Lang told him as he dutifully fixed a mix of wet and dry food that the cat had come to prefer. 'And you probably should be a vegetarian. It's not as bad as you think.'

Out of the kitchen, Lang looked at the blank wall. He had to get a television. What was he to do? Read? OK, OK, he told himself. There were a few unread books up in the loft. First, though, he decided to be a little more prepared for Kozlov's revenge. Maybe tonight.

Lang climbed the ladder to the loft, reached into the pillowcase, unzipped the pillow and reached between the soft foam for his Walther 9mm. It was the compact version, the P99c – kind of ugly, but light and small. Easily concealed. He didn't have a license. Guns and San Francisco went together like any two countries in the Middle East. Sometimes he was surprised the city let its police carry firearms.

He opened a book he'd had a while. It was a book about Bangkok. A guy dies in a car full of snakes. Well, he thought, just what I need. Buddha appeared, as he often did, suddenly, as if he could materialize and dematerialize at will. He would lie at the edge of the loft, looking down on his world. Lang often felt as if Buddha was guarding him. The truth was, probably, that Buddha was guarding himself.

It was nice, wasn't it, he asked himself, to be out with an attractive woman like Carly? Just social. Just pleasant business. He wondered if he was fooling himself. Over the years, he'd fooled himself more often than he cared to admit.

Carly was still reeling when she got back to her flat. Nothing had pushed her out of her safe and comfortable world so much as the events of the day. In the course of one day, she had had her life seriously threatened, after which she'd had a lovely dinner punctuated with new and exotic tastes. Next she'd participated in a loony, surreal charade, after which she'd lounged in a bar she would have never thought to patronize sipping a Ramos Gin Fizz.

And the thing of it was: it was good. It was like that moment in Bodega Bay. She felt alive. What had she been doing all those years? Now, when she had probably already passed the equator of her existence, she was out in it. Really out in it.

She poured herself another glass of wine and went out on to the deck. It was cold and she could see part of the garden below. But she knew there was an extraordinary world out there beyond the fog. The world was waiting to be discovered. So was she, it seemed.

It happened nearly every night now. Gratelli believed that it was just part of the aging process – waking up in the middle of the night, usually between three and four. He knew he wouldn't be able to get back to sleep. Maybe he needed less now, but he didn't like facing these dark, empty hours alone. He'd coped with his wife's departure some years ago by keeping himself busy.

However, in the sober, sober night, he could not see anything to do. His mind refused to let him read. Listening to music was worse. It hurried his trip to unpleasant places. Television helped a little. It was mind numbing. It was almost like sleep.

Carly's call earlier in the day was troubling. Though it wasn't likely that this had awakened him or kept him awake. He'd had worse cases. He still wasn't convinced either, he reminded himself, that he saw the capability of murder on Daniel Lee's face. Yet both possibilities were not so far-fetched. His gut feelings were just that and along with the loss of sleep he could be losing the intuition informed by decades dealing with bad deaths.

He looked out of the living-room window. He could only see directly below, the rest of the neighborhood no longer visible. Perhaps it wasn't there any more. His laugh turned into a cough. His thoughts were increasingly metaphysical as the prospect of his own death came nearer and nearer.

The city was quiet now. San Francisco, unlike many big cities, went to bed early.

His thoughts turned to practical matters.

The Assistant District Attorney was ready to indict Daniel Lee. He wasn't going to like what Gratelli would tell him later in the morning. The rush to judgment was a result of the pressure to solve cases. Statistically the city wasn't doing so well in the murder department. Homicides were up. Solved cases were down. Even so, Gratelli worried about making a big deal about solving the Olivia Hanover murder when two private eyes were working hard to prove otherwise – and he, himself, wasn't convinced.

Gratelli fixed coffee, put English muffins in the toaster. The morning *Chronicle* wouldn't arrive for a couple of hours. He sat in his big chair in front of the small TV, trying to be patient, sipping his coffee and eating the muffins with orange marmalade and waiting for the day to begin.

It was rare that Lang felt any real anxiety. But he knew he was about to play the endgame with Theodore Kozlov. When he awoke – and it was early – he was wide awake. He climbed down the ladder and went to the bathroom. He put fresh water in Buddha's bowl.

He slipped on his jeans, an abused cashmere sweater and his battered black leather K-Swiss shoes.

'Be right back.'

Outside it was summer, the kind of summer most people expect summer to be, not the kind of summer that San Franciscans usually experienced. It was warm and warming and sunny. Pretty nice.

He walked the couple of blocks to the coffee shop, ordered an apple turnover and a large cup of coffee. Nothing fancy. People were already tapping away at laptops and reading the morning paper.

He went to the corner grocery across the street and picked up a *Chronicle* and returned home. He went out to the back, sat on the folding chair at the old and rusting metal table, drank his coffee and checked the paper for word – of anything.

Once his turnover was consumed and half the coffee gone, he set the small tape recorder on the table and flipped open his phone. He punched in the number for Kozlov.

'Hey, Theo,' Lang said to the groggy voice.

'You make one mistake after another,' Kozlov said.

'Kozlov, you speak Russian?' He pressed the play key and put the phone down next to the speaker. Hysterical Russian punctuated the morning calm. Lang had no idea what was being said, but a translator had assured him that the guy had admitted to killing Olivia.

After a few moments Lang could hear a shouting Kozlov, though it sounded tinny and from a great distance. Lang picked up the phone.

'I've got it in English from Yuri too.'

Kozlov disconnected.

Lang leaned his head back, let the warm sun hit his face. Buddha hopped up on the table, found his place in the sun as well.

'This is the beginning of the end,' Lang told him. 'I just wish I knew what that meant.'

Carly lurched forward. She wasn't sure if it had been a dream that caused her to jump from sleep with such suddenness. She thought it might be that her unconscious sent her the message that she was sleeping the day

away. Her subterranean brain still worked for Vogel Security. She had no
reason to hurry today. She had no office to go to. No real work to do.

Other than her obsession with Olivia's death, what did she have to think
about? She had no path to follow to find resolution. She had done all that
she knew how to do. She swung her body around and put her feet over
the edge of the bed. Sun streamed in the window. Cold fronts battled with
warm fronts, she thought. One of the fronts won – she wasn't sure which
one – and they would have a rare sunny June day.

Carly grabbed a glass of orange juice, slipped on her running gear and
went out in the strangely calm mid-morning air. She ran what was becoming
her regular route, up the north side of Lafayette Park on Washington Street.
She didn't circle the park, but slowed as she passed the area where Olivia
was found. Continuing down the hill she crossed Fillmore, people sipping
coffee in the sun, dogs obediently waiting. Ahead was Alta Plaza, another
park, a larger park. She ran up the steep stairs, past the tennis courts and
the children's playground and continued to run. She ran as if she wasn't
going to stop.

But she did stop, eventually, and walked, exhausted, home.

She went to the kitchen, put the coffee in the grinder, pressed the button
for the number of seconds she knew to yield the right grind for her Krups
coffee maker. As the coffee brewed, she plucked a small canister of yogurt
from the refrigerator and grabbed a little plastic container of blueberries.

She mixed the blueberries and the yogurt and wandered out to the back
deck. Indeed, there was no trace of last night's fog. Clear as a bell. She
hoped her mind would soon be the same.

Lang came into the office, Buddha riding on his shoulders.

'You've got a strange looking parrot,' Thanh said.

Lang called Thanh earlier to see if Buddha could stay with him for a few
days until the threats were gone.

'Aye, matey,' Lang replied.

'Sometimes he's a cat, sometimes a bird, sometimes a monkey,' Thanh
said as Lang leaned down so the brown cat could jump to the sofa.

'Kind of like you,' Lang said.

'We're a lot alike. You think he rides on your shoulder because he loves
you. It's actually because he doesn't want to get his feet dirty.'

'Wouldn't surprise me. He's smarter than I am. Anyway you take Buddha
wherever it is you live.'

Thanh smiled. Mona Lisa again. Most of Thanh's life was a mystery.
Lang knew the rough road that brought him to the US, but not much after.
Strange bird, he thought. What would he do without the shape-shifter?

Buddha hopped on the desk where Thanh worked to observe for a while. The two got along well.

Lang tried to reach Stern and Rose, but they were out. He left a portion of the English version of the confession on Stern's voicemail. It would have been smarter to leave it on Rose's voicemail, but Lang was in an antagonistic mood. He wanted Stern to face facts about his friend or face the dilemma of trying to overlook Kozlov's illegal acts.

Now, what would he do? Wait. There was plenty of waiting in his profession. He tried to move his thoughts to the Hanovers. He called Gratelli. Gratelli was too busy to talk long, but he said they were indicting Daniel Lee this afternoon. It was a formality. There would be no testimony. Nothing for him to do. West no doubt already knew and didn't include Lang because there was nothing Lang could do.

Lang didn't like it. He called Carly.

Carly didn't like it either. She knew that once the system got started, it was hard to stop. The police wanted the case solved and the pressure of all these murder cases lessened. The DA wanted the pressure from powerful influences to stop and they wanted a conviction. That's how the department proved its worth and that's how individual district attorneys made their careers.

'I'll figure out something,' she said. She didn't know what. 'How are you and the Russians?'

'Waiting for the other shoe to drop,' Lang said. 'Probably made out of lead.'

'You talk to the police?'

'I'm expecting visitors. Not sure who is going to get here first.'

She wanted to ask him if she could help. But that might be insulting. She didn't know him well enough to know if she should challenge his manhood or if, in fact, this would be a challenge.

'Let me know if I can help.'

'Help me with the Hanovers. The murderer lives in Pacific Heights. That's your neighborhood, right?'

'Geographically,' she said. 'I'm not really in the club.'

'Do I detect a sudden class awareness?' Lang was having fun.

'I've never denied the class system, Mr Lang.' She called him Mr Lang on purpose and with emphasis. 'I merely suggested that if you suddenly became worth a billion or two, you'd be a little suspect of new friends.'

'Got it. The rich are just like you and me, except that they have all these extra burdens to bear. Finding a new gardener when one quits, paying the staff, keeping up a couple of homes. It's tough.'

She laughed.

'Will she see you?' Lang asked.

'Pamela?'

'Yeah.'

'I don't know. Maybe. Just seeing isn't enough. One question she decides is intrusive and I'm out on my ear.'

'The kids give us anything?'

'I've thought about that. Getting to them. They have no more reason to cooperate than their mother.'

'Stepmother,' Lang said.

'Stepmother. Maybe I can get to them.'

She did. She had an idea. She searched her bag and found the envelope.

'I have an invitation to a fund-raiser on tomorrow night,' she said. 'I can't go because they know me, but maybe you could attend?'

'Me? At a high-end party?'

'You're a PI. Assume an identity. You've done that before, I bet.'

'I have. An insurance salesman, a utility inspector. Not a Rockefeller or a Getty. Anyway, they have a list, and I'm sure I'm not on it.'

'You'll find a way.' She was enjoying herself, thinking about the anti-aristocrat among the aristocrats. She'd like to go just to see it. 'The thing is this is a fund-raiser, not a private gala for one of their own. They expect and hope for a certain number of curiosity seekers. Just say you were on the list and that you RSVP'd. They'll let you in. They want the money.'

'I have to give them money?'

'Just imply that you already have. They're not usually that organized.'

'Hmmpf,' Lang managed.

'It's your chance. Everything you need to know is right here,' she said, handing him the invitation.

Thirty-Three

By mid-afternoon, Thanh, who had gone out for lunch, hadn't returned. He went wherever it was he went and would come back when he came back. It was that kind of arrangement. So, aside from Lang, the office was empty when Rose and Stern came in. Lang wasn't sure who would contact him first – the so-called good guys or the genuine bad guys. Now he knew.

Buddha saw the door open and jumped to the desk next to Lang.

'I don't like cats,' Stern said.

'Don't feel bad. You didn't hurt Buddha's feelings. He doesn't like cops either.'

'He talk to you, does he, Lang?'

'He thinks cats can talk,' Lang said to Buddha, who looked at Lang and then back to Stern.

'You don't give up,' Stern said, who was now moving into the reason they dropped by.

'Murder,' Lang said. 'Kozlov's boys say they did it. It's what they call a "confession" in the justice system. You might want to look that up.'

'Where are they?' Rose asked.

'Probably on their way to Iscrewedupistan.'

'You picking on Russians?' Stern asked.

'Discrimination,' Rose said. 'Tsk, tsk.'

'I like *Dr Zhivago*. Dostoevsky. David Duchovny.'

Stern looked perplexed.

'Like we said before,' Stern said, 'you ain't out of the woods. He's selling the idea you knocked her up and then knocked her off.' Stern raised an I-gotcha eyebrow.

'Why would I do that?'

'Why would he?'

'Wait a minute. When is it you guys do something on this? I give you a confession. Now you want me to arrest them, prosecute them and find them guilty. I mean you guys got to do something here.'

'Seriously, Lang, we need a "why" on this,' Rose said. 'He suspected his wife was having an affair. You were hired to find out. And you hadn't made your report. So why wouldn't he wait to find out if she was cheating?'

'I'm working on that,' Lang said. 'Meanwhile, inspectors, I think these guys are telling you what happened, if not why.'

'Is that right?' Stern said.

'Look, the first time these guys ransacked my place, leaving no piece of electronics unbroken. The second time they came here to my office to, at minimum, beat the hell out of me. Then one of them tries to take me out on the street in the middle of the afternoon – oh, that's right, you were there. And then they came back here and confess. Now, it seems to me, if I can give you all this info you might want to contribute something to this little murder investigation.'

'Seems to you, is that what you're saying? Seems to you? What seems to you is of no fucking interest to me,' Stern said.

Rose rolled his eyes.

'OK,' Lang said. 'I'll just do it myself. I think I'll put the English confession on YouTube and then, as they say, "alert the media." I'll send the Russian version to the Russian embassy with a little note explaining what it's all about. I can cc the mayor's information office and the DA.'

'One day, you're going to wake up and find yourself dead,' Stern said.

'Yogi Berra couldn't have said it better.' Lang looked at Rose. 'You live with this?'

Rose nodded.

'Every day?'

'It's possible,' Rose said. 'Out of body experience. You wake up one morning, your body is below you down on the bed, and you're looking down at your dead self. Could happen.' He shrugged, walked toward the door. 'Look. Hold off a day.'

'I could be murdered in the interim,' Lang said.

'Yeah,' Stern said, 'but that will help your case.'

'Every once in awhile, he makes sense,' Rose said, smiling.

Carly Paladino stood at the intimidating front door of the Hanovers' home. She had no hat, but if she had one it would now be in her hand.

The housekeeper opened the door, saw Carly and lowered her eyes.

'Please wait.' The door closed.

When the door opened again a few minutes later, it was Gary Gray. He was not surprised. He had been forewarned and given the time that elapsed, was prepared.

'What are you doing here?' His tone wasn't antagonistic, but a little cold.

'I'd like to see Pamela,' Carly said.

'She's not available.'

'It's important. She's going to want to know what's happening before it appears in the media.'

'Just a moment,' Gray said.

Carly had uttered the magic word: media.

Pamela Hanover was in the kitchen, a large room, plenty of windows open to a gray day. She was cutting the ends off white long-stemmed French tulips. She resembled them, dressed in white, flesh pale, face without make-up. Elegant. Fragile.

'What is it you wish to tell me?' she asked.

Carly noticed that the young secretary had disappeared. The two of them were alone, but Pamela continued her work, ignoring Carly.

'You probably know they're indicting Daniel Lee for your daughter's murder. Maybe as we speak.'

'Yes,' Hanover said softly.

'The defense is going to try to paint you as the murderer, Mrs Hanover.'

There was no shock. Hanover placed the freshly cut ends of the tulips in the cut crystal vase, and began arranging them.

'They believe that you had access to the morphine from you mother's illness and that you may have also had the ketamine as part of an experimental treatment of your depression and anxiety attacks.'

Hanover looked up, but her face betrayed no emotion.

'Why are you telling me all this?'

'Because I thought you ought to know.'

'You're not on the payroll any more, Ms Paladino. Why are you bothering with all this?'

'If there's something you're hiding, it will be found out sooner, or, worse, at the trial. It would be doubly bad if you were to allow an innocent young man to be convicted of a crime he didn't commit.'

'You're not answering my question,' Hanover said in even tones. 'Why are *you* bothering with all this?'

'So that things can be straightened out. I don't have to be paid for trying to . . .'

Hanover, vase in hand, walked away. Over her shoulder, she said without feeling and, Carly thought, without sincerity, 'Thank you for trying to help, but you're not part of this any more.'

Thanh came back late and apologized. He didn't offer an excuse nor was he asked to provide one. But Lang stayed around to make sure Buddha would be taken care of. From there, on this long summer day when the California light stayed on until eight, Lang found a place to park on Clement in the new Chinatown, and had dim sum.

As he had before, he noticed that the Chinese clientele were given a different menu. He knew that it wasn't a matter of language, but a matter of offering. There were items the Chinese assumed most Caucasians wouldn't eat and in Lang's case they were absolutely correct. He knew it was only a matter of cultural bias, but he suspected he'd never get around to eating duck tongue and chicken feet.

He'd chosen well – partial to dumplings with his beer – and by the time he left, the late trending darkness was on its way. He crossed the street and wandered down to Sixth Avenue to wander around Green Apple Books. There were two slightly ramshackle Green Apple stores on Clement – a multi-story bookstore that sold new books on the main floor and used books on the second. One could spend hours wandering among the stacks upstairs and on some days Lang did. There was a second store, which had magazines, DVDs and CDs, as well as used books.

He wanted something to read until he got his own little movie theater set up at his place. There were a number of high-quality, reduced-cost new books at the back of the first floor. They were remainders of some of the best books published in the last year or so. Living at an annual income that would be fine in most Midwestern cities, he was at poverty wages in the City by the Bay. A really good, virgin book at less than five dollars made this his favorite aisle.

Still, it took him awhile to pick up a couple of modern 'classics.' Now, he'd have to do the parking spot search all over again in his own neighborhood, usually cruising until someone's departure coincided with his timely proximity. He found a spot a block away on Lyon.

In the darkness, it wasn't so dark. The moon was full and hovering in such a way that the street was lit as an impressionist might paint it. The trees gave off soft, ghostlike shadows. Lang was hyper-aware of his environment, not just for its beauty. There was the constant threat of retribution. Even if Dimitri and Yuri fled, there was Kozlov and the third Russian.

Lang came to his door. He pulled the keys from his pocket. As he glanced down to find the lock, he noticed a toothpick, snapped into an L-shape, on the ground by the door. Kozlov and maybe some of his friends had been there, or were still there. Maybe they had knocked and getting no answer, had left. Or they may have attached an explosive device to the door. Or they may be waiting inside so that Kozlov could witness Lang's death up close and personal. Lang couldn't blame him. Kozlov had had trouble relying on his employees to get the job done. But the question was obvious. Now what would he do?

The Foreign Cinema is more restaurant than cinema – a fun, upscale restaurant on a stretch of Mission that was considered by some as dangerous as it was trendy. Drive-bys somehow coexisted with energetic youth seeking the hottest nightspots. On the other side of the Foreign Cinema's double doors were a couple of dining areas, one outside, where at dusk movies are shown on a large bare wall.

Carly and Nadia met at the bar, located at the far end of the inside dining room. They had dinner outside while it was still light and, as night descended, moved next door to Medjool's sky terrace – a rooftop bar.

Nadia was curious about Carly's life now that she was out on her own, curious about this Noah Lang she had heard mentioned more than once, curious about the murder case and the semi-famous, super-rich family involved in it. It was one of those rare conversations in which Nadia was willing to listen.

'What I guess I didn't know . . .' Carly began, but halted.

'What?'

'I don't know if I want to get into it,' she said.

'You can't get into it with me? Who can you talk to?'

'I know,' Carly said, but still she debated it.

She noticed the big, full moon. Maybe that was why her emotions seemed to want to run out of control.

'You know I don't miss Peter,' she said. This wasn't the heart of what she was going to say. It was peripheral.

'Go on,' Nadia said.

'I miss the idea of Peter,' she said. 'I liked him. I was sorry he moved away. But he didn't break my heart.'

'Good,' Nadia said.

'I'm not so sure that's good,' Carly said. 'I didn't realize that I kept everyone, everything, at a distance.'

'Me?' Nadia asked.

'Yes. I'm having trouble now talking about it, even with you.'

Nadia smiled. 'Oh, please. I tell you everything . . . my deepest, darkest secrets.'

'Since my trip to Bodega, I seem to be wriggling out of a shell or out of one shell into another and out of it . . . and . . . I don't know. And when you let things in – like Olivia . . .'

'The dead girl.'

'Yes. When you let life in, you get caressed and then you get slapped. It's . . . I mean, with Peter . . . comfort. No teeth gnashing, stomach churning. Nothing soaring, spirit lifting. No storms, only breezes.' Carly laughed. 'There was no life. And at work, I did the job, you know. I did a good, professional job, coloring within the lines, keeping our distance from our clients and from each other.'

'The case is getting to you. It will pass.'

'I don't know that I want it to pass,' Carly said. 'Then again, maybe I do.'

She took a sip of her gin and tonic.

'I thought it was you,' the man said.

'Michael,' Carly said as her old friend leaned down to kiss her cheek.

'Hi, Carly, Nadia. I have been very bad.'

'You've not called me back,' Carly said.

'I know. I ran into Nadia and she told me about all these life-changing experiences. I'm sorry. I've been so busy . . .'

A handsome blond guy came up and smiled.

'And this is Blair,' Michael said.

'Hi, Blair.' Carly stood. Nadia didn't.

'This is my best friend Carly and this is Nadia,' Michael said to his friend.

'And this is the reason you've been so busy,' Nadia said.

Michael smiled. 'And work. Nadia told me you were working for the Hanovers. We're catering tomorrow night's affair.'

'Will you be there?'

'I put in eighty hours a week as it is. I have a catering manager. She's got it under control. You'll be there. I understand you're Pamela's right hand.'

'No more. Long story. Can we talk?'

'Yes, Miss Rivers,' Michael said.

The two of them went to the edge of the roof. For Carly it was good to be with her long-lost friend and she let him know she understood. For Michael, work *and* a boyfriend was unheard of. Ambition was yielding to living a little. She understood that better now than she would have before. They chatted some more, keeping it light, before the two guys bid farewell.

Even so, it was another of those relationships where 'keeping it light,' was the glue that held it together.

'So this Noah guy?' Nadia prodded, but directing it to a less serious level than before.

'Interesting guy. He's not afraid of living . . . or dying for that matter, it seems.'

'You're smiling,' Nadia said.

'Am I? I wonder why.'

Carly got up, walked back to the edge of the roof, looked out over the intersection four storeys below – people walking, people in cars going places, neon lights flashing, lights in windows in the distance.

Nadia came up behind her.

'You are taking risks now,' she said. 'Do you regret leaving your safe little job?'

'No. But I'm scared.'

'As long as I've known you, you've never been scared.'

That made sense. She would never have admitted to herself, let alone anyone else, that she felt something so deep as fear.

'I'm not sure what I'm afraid of.'

That was true.

Thirty-Four

What to do. Call the police? Call Thanh for backup? Instead, standing outside his own home, he pulled out his cell phone, punched in the speed dial for Kozlov, put his ear to the door. He could hear the ring. Lang went back half a block.

'Kozlov,' the voice said. 'Is that you, Lang?'

Bad thing about cell phones, they ID the caller. The good thing is that no one knows where you're calling from. Lang could have been calling from Beijing.

'Yeah, how's it goin'?'

'You're a dead man.'

'Nah. Everybody knows you did it now. We know when, where, how, but we don't know why. That's it. Don't need to know, probably. But I'd like to know. Pretty wife. Devoted to a good cause . . .'

'You look pretty good for it, Lang. Your witnesses? Where are they?' Lang didn't answer. Kozlov continued, manufacturing a carefree voice. 'You know, maybe we should get together.'

'Talk about old times? Our little coffee together downtown? That was fun.'

'Talk about how you're going down. Where are you?'

'Sacramento, talking to some of your friends.'

The phone went dead.

In a few seconds Lang heard the hardware on the door make its sound. He stepped back up the street and into a stairway. He hoped Kozlov wasn't coming his way. But he had no way of knowing. The guy was probably armed. Lang wasn't. He hit all four of the buzzers into the building.

One answered.

'It's me,' Lang said. He heard Russian out on the street as he was buzzed inside. He stood at the base of a long stairway.

He peered back through the door in time to see the burly Kozlov and another guy, whose mouth was wired – probably shut. That meant Kozlov was doing the talking and, Lang hoped, that it was the last member of Kozlov's staff who was doing the listening. Then again, both of them no doubt had revenge, very personal revenge, on their minds.

A voice came from up the stairs.

'Arthur, are you coming up or not?'

'Forgot something, be right back,' Lang said, and exited.

His place was now empty. Probably. At least he knew that the lock wasn't connected to an explosive device. He stepped down toward the street, glanced out. The two of them were getting into a one of those big, Nazi-looking Chrysler 300s.

Inside his own place, he felt better. He'd have to start carrying his handgun. He didn't know what, if anything, Rose and Stern would do with the tapes.

He called. Rose was indisposed and he was routed to Stern.

'Your favorite guy,' Lang said.

'All the citizens in our fair city are treated equally, with concern and respect,' Stern said. 'What help might I be to you, Mr Citizen?'

'Lovely. Are you pursuing Kozlov?'

'It is an active case, Mr Lang,' he said with faux politeness. 'I am not permitted to discuss ongoing investigations, especially with a suspect in aforementioned investigation.'

'Four syllables. Nice.'

'Five. Anything else the San Francisco Police Department can do for you?'

'I'm going to make my own tape, Stern. Because if Kozlov and his sole remaining ape kill me, I want the public to know what the San Francisco Police Department was advised that not only did Kozlov kill his wife, but the person investigating it was killed.'

'Keep your panties on, Lang. You gave us a little time to iron this out, OK?'

'Well, yeah, but I came home to find Kozlov.'

'You had a run-in?'

'No, I slithered away when I discovered he was inside. I don't like slithering away. But I don't want to kill him before I find out why he killed his wife. That might be something for your little comedy duo to look into.'

Lang flipped his phone shut.

He called Carly.

'What am I going to wear?' he asked her the moment she answered. What a strange and frightening thing to have on your mind. What was he going to wear tomorrow night? Had that ever been a concern in his life? Jesus. That put him in more of a panic than Kozlov.

One thing led to another. Carly suggested he go to Sacramento Street the next morning. A store there had fine previously owned clothing. She volunteered to go along, but Lang promised he could handle it. A statement he regretted almost the moment he uttered it. There was this strange thing he had with Carly that sometimes caused him to say the opposite of what he wanted to say.

Before he could sort that out, Rose called Lang. He probably wasn't in the same room as his partner.

'We've been trying to find Kozlov. He's disappeared.'

'He was hiding at my place.'

'Your place.'

'Yeah, he broke in. He's gone now.'

'Why didn't you call us?'

'What, have you arrest him for breaking and entering? I want a little more than that. Surely he's not hiding from you guys, his good buddies,' Lang said. 'I already told Stern.'

'Lang, all we have is your comments and a disembodied confession. You still look better for it.'

'I got a body to go with the voice,' Lang said.

'What?'

'I've got two confessions on video. Faces, Rose.'

'Why didn't you send that?'

'Trying to create drama. And if I did, you wouldn't have used the word "disembodied." Probably the only time you've ever used that word. But back to Mr Kozlov and the remaining Russian. Why, do you suppose, are they hiding?'

'Maybe he's afraid of you?'

'That's flattering, but I don't think so.'

'Who is scaring him into hiding?'

'That's a very interesting question, Inspector Rose. Isn't it?'

It was.

Thanh knew where the store was and was willing to go along. Lang, who spent the night in Brinkman's office in an attempt to thwart would-be midnight assassins, met Thanh at Brenda's for a little Cajun energy. The morning was sunny and warming up. The two of them drove over to Sacramento Street.

There they were: in a used-clothing store smack dab in the middle of one of the richest, and most understated, neighborhoods in the world.

'You shop here?' Lang asked as they walked through the narrow aisles to the suit rack.

'If I want something snooty.' Thanh smiled.

'I need something snooty?'

'Yes. Conservatively snooty.'

'Where do these clothes come from?'

'Dead people, I imagine – some of them.'

'Oh, great. If I were superstitious . . .'

'Forty-four, right?'

'Yes. Rich people buy these clothes?'

'Rich people sell them,' Thanh said. 'You are not under the impression that rich people are spendthrifts, are you? In my experience, they squeeze a dime better than anyone.'

'I'm going to report you to the Billionaire Defamation League.'

Thanh pulled a dark suit off the rack and looked at the label.

'Armani,' he said, holding up a suit, looking very pleased with himself. But it had obviously been worn by a very short 44.

'A nice jacket and toreador pants,' Thanh said. 'On the edge of fashion.'

Shopping was interrupted by a phone call. Lang stepped out on to the quiet street.

'I thought you would want to know about the indictment,' Chastain West said.

'I do.'

'Daniel Lee was indicted. Murder one. Statutory rape.'

'Jesus.'

'If you can get the Son of God to testify, that might be the only thing to save him.'

'Sounds like they really want to hurt him.'

'It's a tactic. They want the murder to stick. They think that if the jury is seeing the rape charge that will help settle doubts about the murder.'

'Yeah, but the poor guy's eighteen. She was one year younger. No signs of actual rape. They had a relationship.'

'You're preaching to the choir,' West said. 'He's got a rent-free future.'

'How does he look?'

'If he loses any more weight, there won't be anything left to hold his bones together.'

'I'm trying to zero in on the family.'

'How?'

'Party with them,' Lang said. 'Don't worry, I'm off the clock for awhile.'

'If you get something, you're back on.'

The afternoon went well enough. Lang left with a Zegna suit. He had no idea who Zegna was, but it looked great. They found a pleasant light blue shirt and a slightly adventurous tie that, had Thanh not pleaded and cajoled, Lang wouldn't have chosen.

'C'mon, loosen up. Have fun. You'll be far more approachable wearing this than some stodgy stripe.'

'What are you wearing?' Lang asked.

'I want to surprise you,' Thanh said.

'Just tell me what gender you're coming as?'

'I could come as a boy and we could be a gay couple.'

'I need you to be a ravishing female,' Lang said. 'Remember we're trying to get the Hanover boys to talk and the older one likes Asian women.'

'Don't worry about me.'

That evening, as Lang chanced being back in his own space, he showered, shaved, primped, and dressed.

He wanted to channel David Niven. He looked in the mirror. He didn't look at all like David Niven and he didn't feel, inside, as he imagined David Niven would feel faced with either danger or an evening with high-society. He was, it seemed, channeling the *Taxi Driver*.

Or *Mad Max* – and he was taking Thanh, the gorgeous Asian seductress, to the party.

God, what had he gotten himself into? He had spent hours worrying about what to wear. What to wear! He was worried about what to wear? Who was he? Paris Hilton?

He re-examined himself, took a deep breath. On second glimpse, he kind of liked what he saw. At least he'd be an elegant corpse. He could imagine Rose and Stern standing over his body.

'Damn,' Stern would say, 'I never liked the guy, but who knew he was such a good-looking son of a bitch?'

She was stunning. Covered by a light cape, Thanh impressed Lang when he picked up the talented shape-shifter just off Polk Street. Now in Pacific Heights, in the room, the soft northern light and the chandeliers lit the gild and mirrors in a way that showcased the creature with a thousand identities. Thanh glowed – a worldly elegance. The eyes of the well-heeled guests, male and female, gay and straight, glanced and glanced again. The guests tried to be polite, but they couldn't help it.

The home was almost as stunning. A long hallway led back to a three-room suite. The bar was located in the smaller center room – small being a relative term. A large round table with a huge and no doubt expensive bouquet was in the middle. To the right was a large room with several tables, six monstrous chandeliers and the grandest of grand pianos. It was set up with a microphone and speakers for a speech at the end of the event.

The room to the left of center was a museum. Every surface – tabletop, wall – was covered with art, much of it gold. And Lang knew it wasn't gold paint. There were half a dozen sofas, a larger number of tastefully, if not a little showy, upholstered chairs. Two dozen people could sit comfortably in the room.

All three rooms had a bank of floor-to-ceiling windows. As Lang knew, San Francisco's hills provided many a run-down studio apartment with a million-dollar view. This was a billion-dollar view. The home sat on the uppermost hill. Below was a precipitous drop, with the smaller Cow Hollow and tiled-roof Marina homes below. Then the Bay. The obligatory Golden Gate Bridge, an iconic symbol that refuses to be corny, but also in view the vast land to the north, Alcatraz, Fort Mason Center, Fisherman's Wharf. Lang could only imagine what the view would be when night finally fell.

Lang left Thanh to her admirers so he could review the guests. He was most interested in locating the Hanover boys. Getting in had been easy. His name was obviously not on the list, but it didn't seem to bother the woman who was in charge of the name badges. Apparently Lang's used duds and Thanh's breathtaking beauty – her name for the night was Sasha, the name Thanh had used when they'd first met years ago – suggested they were capable of contributing to the cause. Money was money.

No one seemed to notice the listening device in Lang's right ear. He was electronically hooked up to a small microphone in a brooch on Thanh's gown. Thanh at first objected, thinking that gathering the information and providing it to Lang wouldn't be that difficult, but Lang explained he was recording as well. He'd had such success with the Russians, he wanted to capture any damning conversation on tape.

Sasha talked with a gentleman who was describing his home in Dubai. Lang's invasion of their privacy was interrupted by the first Mrs Hanover, Katherine Wexford.

'Noah Lang, party-crasher,' she said, giving him an air-kiss. 'You'll liven up the place.'

'You're not going to give me away?'

'I wouldn't dream of it,' she said a little too boisterously.

'It just shows that the screen against riff-raff isn't working.'

'You look incredible.'

'Who says you can't make a silk purse out of a pig's ear?'

'I have no idea who said that,' she said, 'but I know the Pamela is working on the idea that it's possible.'

'Ouch,' Lang said.

'I've always lived by Dorothy Parker's words: "If you can't say anything nice, come sit by me."'

Thirty-Five

Wexford disengaged Lang to extract her former husband from the crowd. He had been standing in a corner by himself, probably wondering what he was doing there. Lang looked around the larger room for the boys and spotted the younger one, Jordan. He, like his father, kept to himself. He had a glass of wine and sipped it from time to time as his gaze criss-crossed the room. Pamela stopped for a moment, said something, and continued to gad about.

Lang was still picking up conversation. Thanh, or Sasha, was telling someone how beautiful Hanoi was and that, in fact, Vietnam was one of the most beautiful places in the world. Charming, charming, Lang thought. He went back into the gilded room and noticed Evan. He had his back to the windows and apparently, as Carly confided earlier, his Asian-woman-heat-seeking brain had found the most beautiful person in the room.

But Sasha was now surrounded by three men. That might keep Evan away. Lang decided to intercede.

'I need to borrow my date for a moment,' he said, stepping into the impromptu fan club.

When they dispersed, Lang said: 'Don't look now, but the guy standing alone by the window is interested in you. And I'm interested in anything he has to say.'

Sasha pretended to look around the entire room, not letting her eyes stop at Evan.

'He's twelve,' Sasha said.

'He's going on a quarter of a century,' Lang said. 'Besides, I'm not asking you to sleep with him. Just talk. Talk about family, life and death, morals.'

'All right,' she said. 'He is rich, isn't he?'

'Filthy.'

'I wish it mattered. My life would be so much easier than it is.'

'Your life is tough?'

'No, but it could be easier.' Sasha smiled. She may look slightly different, but Sasha's smile was the same as Thanh's.

'Salmon puffs, sashimi?' the server asked.

'Paladino?' Lang said, grinning. 'Am I in an "I love Lucy" episode?'

'Hi, Carly,' Sasha said.

Carly's reaction was puzzlement before recognition set in.

'Oh my God,' Carly said.

'Cleans up nice,' Lang said.

'I am so fucking jealous,' she said, then embarrassed, she added, 'I'm sorry, but it's not right.'

'Why don't we leave Sasha alone so that Project Evan Hanover can begin?'

Lang and Carly took a few steps in the same direction. 'Salmon puffs?' he asked, his tone suggesting how silly it sounded.

'Thank you, I have some,' she said, before she veered off to feed the hungry masses.

Lang picked up a glass of red wine at the bar, meandered about to see if he recognized anybody famous. San Francisco was a town favored by many well-known celebrities and then, of course, there were San Francisco celebrities – known and revered only here.

He saw Katherine Wexford and Walter Hanover still engaged, only now it seemed heated. It wouldn't be good form to yell at each other in public, especially that public, but the expressions on their faces indicated they were far from exchanging pleasantries.

When Lang heard voices in his ear, he moved back to the gilded room.

'Evan Hanover,' the voice said.

'Sasha Thanh,' came the reply. Sasha had three octaves, one for each gender. She was being gender appropriate.

'Chaka Khan?' he asked.

'If you want,' Sasha said. 'You are the party giver?'

'Kind of,' Evan said.

'And you are?'

'The partygoer, I guess.'

'Are you married?' Evan Hanover asked.

'Not at the moment. But aren't you moving a little fast for a stranger?' Hanover laughed.

'And I might be a little old for you,' Sasha continued.

That was an admission Lang thought he'd never hear.

'The sexes peak at different times,' the young Hanover said.

'Seems to me as if you are used to getting your way.'

Evan Hanover nodded.

'Any more at home like you?' Sasha asked.

'Not any older. I have a younger brother. A bit of a dweeb.'

'What would he say about you?'

'Not a dweeb,' Hanover said. 'He'd say what I told him to say.' He was quiet for a moment, looking intently into Sasha's eyes. 'I'm coming on too strong, aren't I?'

She nodded. 'But you are not without your charm.' Sasha waited for him to feel the heat of her stare. 'Would he kill for you?'

This caught Lang's attention. This was the second surprise line. Subtle, subtle, Thanh, please be subtle, he said to himself silently.

There was silence for a while.

'Yes, he would. He would kill for me. But let's talk about you. Where do you live?'

'I want to remain mysterious.'

'Oh, I like you,' Hanover said.

'So you'll let me be the mysterious stranger and you will tell me everything about you?'

'I'm at your mercy.'

Lang was too far away to see what was going on with their eyes, but he knew that Thanh understood that eyes conveyed meaning, that it too was a language to be used, often in a subterranean way. Would someone as young as Evan Hanover understand what Sasha was doing? Would he care? Lang thought the young man was thinking with another organ by now, and that his brain was silly mush.

Carly appeared with a new tray of goodies, offering them to Lang with a question.

'What's going on?' she asked.

'Interrogation,' Lang said. 'I'm not sure Evan knows what hit him.'

'Can Thanh be as a fantastic a male as he is a female?'

'Yeah. If you like Alain Delon or Horst Buchholz.'

'Horst Buchholz?'

'German actor. His brother operated a restaurant in the Castro.'

'How do you know that?'

'I am not responsible for what clings to my gray matter.'

'Is there anything you don't know?'

'I don't know what these are,' he said, picking up a cracker with something on it.

'I don't either. It's probably caviar. Smells fishy.'

'Can I put this back?' he said, putting it back down where he found it.

'Philistine,' she said.

'You're not afraid Pamela Hanover will see you, or one of the kids?'

'I'm not sure they pay any attention to the hired help. They have money to raise. Anyway, I'm not sure what I can do here. Seems you have things under control.'

'We need to talk to Jordan somehow,' Lang said. 'Can you take him on? Make him nervous. Make him confess.'

'Maybe I can lure him into the kitchen,' she said.

'I'm picturing Hansel and Gretel and an oven.'

'That makes me the witch,' she said.

'I'm sure there were lovely witches,' Lang said as his cell phone moved by itself in his jacket pocket.

He answered, putting the phone to his free ear. Too many conversations going on.

'Hello.'

'This is Yuri.' The thick Russian accent was complicated by the panic in the man's voice. 'You have to help me.'

'You're on your own, kiddo,' Lang said.

'Dimitri is dead,' Yuri said.

Lang didn't know what to say.

'Kozlov killed him. He's going to kill me.'

'The police . . .'

'No, I have family in Russia.'

Lang was tempted to let the man get killed, but eliminating the witnesses was what Kozlov wanted and no doubt what he was doing. The legal system was complicated. It was Lang's guess that the videotaped confessions wouldn't be allowed if he was ever taken to court. But confessions on the witness stand were quite another thing altogether.

'Where are you?' Lang looked around. Carly hovered around him. He put up his finger to say just a minute. He would need her now to finish the work at the party.

'The windmill.'

Jordan might have thought he was rescued. Carly saved him from his island of loneliness in a sea of jabbering guests. But he wasn't. He was about to be grilled.

Lang had hurriedly briefed Carly with what he knew – Jordan's older brother, Evan, had provocatively told Sasha that the younger brother would do as he was told, including murder. Maybe that was macho posturing, but it was worth investigating. He also provided Carly with the listening device and the request that she see Sasha, aka Thanh, home at the end of the evening.

Jordan sat in a corner in the kitchen. The speeches were about to begin so the pace slowed for the servers. There were still a few trays being prepared with various hors d'oeuvres. And there was still some coming and going, but not enough to prevent Carly and Jordan Hanover from talking.

'Today, a young man – I think you knew him – Daniel Lee was indicted for the murder of your sister.'

'She wasn't our sister,' Jordan said, obviously sensing something unpleasant was coming.

'This young man may face life in prison or, possibly, the death penalty.' Because he said nothing and expressed nothing, she added – for dramatic effect – 'Death.'

He remained quiet.

'This is all right with you?' she asked.

'I don't believe in the death penalty.'

'You have nothing to say about whether he killed Olivia or not?'

He looked frightened, but he shook his head. He started to get up.

She put her hand on his shoulder and gently pushed him down.

'Did your brother kill Olivia?'

'No.'

'Maybe some kind of pact between the two of you. Fun. Perfect crime.'

'No.'

'You know what ketamine is? Special K?'

He nodded.

'You know where to get it?'

'Anybody can get it.'

'Did you get some?'

'No.'

'For your brother?'

'No.'

'Did your brother get some?'

'I need to go,' Jordan Hanover said. 'You can't keep me here.' His tone was more appropriate for a petulant five-year-old.

'You knew about the video,' Carly said. 'Did you want to deliver a message? Or did you know who posted it? And removed it. I saw it, Jordan.'

Jordan froze.

'You discovered Olivia's computer. You read what she wrote there, didn't you?'

Jordan looked like he was ready to explode.

'Your mother had the video surveillance removed from your house. She did that because someone was wandering the hallways at night. You knew who and you knew why. You saw, didn't you? You read about it on Olivia's private computer.'

'You can't prove anything,' he said, trying to be defiant behind scared, sad eyes.

Jordan was up and it would have taken physical force to restrain him.

'Jordan, I'm going to the police to talk about the drugs that helped kill Olivia. I believe they came from your house. A member of your family killed that little girl. And it is only a matter of time before we find out who.'

He turned back, but only for a moment.

Carly took off her white serving jacket and went back into the room. She was clearly underdressed in jeans and Peter's blue shirt. Sasha and Evan were nowhere to be found. She could still hear their voices and the conversation seemed harmless enough, but the voices were fading and it was quite likely they were moving out of range.

Thirty-Six

As it happened Carly could use the listening device in much the same way a person can use a Geiger counter. As she moved away from Sasha's transmitter the voices became fainter, the closer she came, the voices grew louder. After a few false starts inside the home ending at a wall with no rooms beyond it, she realized they had gone outside.

Once on the sidewalk, she could see them, standing three or four mansions away despite the dusky light. Evan was angry. Sasha was calm. The way the young man threw his arms about, Carly was afraid it was going to get physical. She went toward them.

'What in the hell are you doing here?' Evan said as Carly came close. His face was white with cold anger. 'You were fired.'

'I wasn't aware your family owned the entire neighborhood,' Carly said.

'We own the whole fucking town,' he said.

'He thinks he's a lot bigger than he is,' Sasha said.

Sasha was goading him on. Maybe, Carly thought, she should have let the woman in red continue. But it was too late now.

'We'll see,' Evan said, heading back to the event, brushing Carly's shoulder as he went by her.

'Steamed.'

'Didn't get what he wanted,' Sasha said.

'Did you?'

'No confessions. Just that it sounds like the Cinderella and her two nasty stepbrothers' story. You'll see from the tape. He doesn't seem to regard other humans with any form of sentimentality.'

Carly glimpsed the view. They stood at the top of a grand outdoor stairway, terraced as it dropped down from the hill, other mansions off to the right at each plateau and the pines and eucalyptus in the Presidio on the other side. Below was the Palace of Fine Arts, keeping the elegant theme of this part of town. A fogless night descended. The waning full moon rose and the lights below began to glitter in the near darkness.

'I think you stole the show,' Carly said.

'Figuring out what the top is and then going a little over, that's how it's done,' Sasha said.

'How do you do that? I mean, being all these people?'

'I learned a long time ago how to be who I had to be,' Sasha said. 'Survival. At first it was painful. Then it became normal. Next a challenge. And now, sometimes, I see it as art.'

'Do you have one person that is you?'

Sasha laughed. 'Yes, but it is not the same person every day. The real me doesn't have to be what other people expect me to be. So that too changes, depending on how I feel. You see the real me whenever you see me not pretending to be someone else.'

'I think I can sort that out,' Carly said.

'I like you. You need to come to work with us. You're just what we need.'

'Thank you. Who knows?'

'Where's Noah?'

'He got a call. Emergency, I think. I can drop you off wherever you need to go.'

'Who called him?'

'I don't know,' Carly said.

'Do you remember anything being said?'

'I heard the word "windmill."'

'I think we should go,' Sasha said.

Lang pulled his battered Mercedes into the lot of the Safeway. He pulled his small handgun from the glove compartment and the long flashlight from the back seat. From the parking lot he crossed Fulton Street and found the dirt and pebble path that led into both the western and northern edge of the huge park. Off to his right and soon out of view was the Pacific, lapping into the night.

He could find his way on the path because of a strangely clear night so near the ocean. As he walked he noticed on his left ominously silhouetted against the sky the huge, unmoving blades of a windmill. Ahead was a tunnel made from brick and timber with darkness in the middle and modest light out the far side.

Cautiously he walked through. In the middle, there appeared to be a full plastic trash bag. As he came closer and the light beam exposed it, the bag was instead the body of the Russian, Dimitri, a bullet through the back of his head. One. Dead center. Lang shut off his light. There was some doubt he had been called to Yuri's aid. Yuri might have been the bait and Dimitri the sacrifice to get Lang.

He pulled the cell phone from his pocket and called Rose. Surprisingly, at this time of night, Rose answered.

'I'm at the windmill at Golden Gate Park. I've got a body. It's one of the Russian kids. The other Russian is in trouble. Kozlov.'

'Crap,' Rose said. 'Get one of the park's cops. They have horses.'

'Help. I don't know how to do that. You get some cops out here. Get someone.'

Lang decided he didn't want to play the fool. He started back the way he came. Back through the tunnel and there was a soft sound — *thoooett*. He was knocked to the ground. It had hit him on the hip. He crawled back in the tunnel, felt for blood. None. He reached in his pocket and there was his cell. It was in pieces, but had perhaps by fortunate angle deflected the bullet. He'd be sore, but he wasn't really hurt. He moved back into the tunnel, where he realized he was a sitting duck.

Better to be a moving target, he thought.

He went back to the other end of the tunnel, looked out. There were a few bushes and then open grass behind what appeared to be a restaurant. There was a dim light inside. Perhaps he could reach help there, but he would have to cross a long stretch of open land in broad moonlight. Nope.

Golden Gate Park was a place large enough to get lost. Little forests, narrow trails, making it easy to lose a pursuer. It was a choice and he chose the latter and moved up the narrow earthen trail that went who knew where. He tried to make his footsteps quiet and he kept to the edges of the trail, letting the growth on the sides slap against him in order to obscure himself as target.

Ahead there was at least twenty feet of nearly complete darkness. He was relieved – unless Kozlov had night vision.

'Jesus.' He stopped in his tracks. He could hear movement behind him. Lang slipped into the heavy row of bushes on the side of the trail. He pulled out his pistol, dropped down on his haunches and took some quiet, deep breaths. He wanted to control his breathing. Whatever it was came closer. In a few more moments he heard the footsteps, soft and slow. In a few more moments he could hear – in all of that night silence – the walker's breath.

Because he couldn't be sure of the person's identity, he declined the urge to shoot first and ask questions later. Instead, as the shadow passed him, Lang lurched forward. He grabbed the body and pulled it to the ground. There were mumblings in Russian; but Lang knew immediately it wasn't Kozlov. Kozlov was a big bear of a man.

'Yuri?'

'Lang?' the man said. 'I'm unarmed. I thought you were Kozlov. I was going to kill you with a stone.'

He still had one in his hand.

'We've got to get out of here,' Lang said, both of them standing. 'Or we could crawl in the brush and wait for the police, or morning at least.'

'No police.'

'How did you end up here?'

'Stepan said to meet us here – Dimitri and me. Now he's trying to kill us.'

'Who is Stepan?'

'You know. The one you put in hospital.'

'Did he set you up?'

Thoooett.

Yuri dropped like a sack of potatoes. Lang dove back into the wall of bushes and crawled several yards before jumping to his feet and moving south and then east. He could try to make it to 19th Avenue and then over to Irving. There should be plenty of people around. But he'd have to break out into the lights and he'd have at least one long, lonely block to go before he found people. And how many people this time of evening? No, he'd have to go where there were guaranteed crowds.

At first he was determined to get to Haight and Stanyan where there would be people and lights and cops. That was, if he could go in anything like a straight line, close to four miles.

He came up to a ridge. Ahead was the polo field, arcs of water glistened in the moonlight as the sprinklers attempted to undo the summer drought. To the left were some buildings. He'd move in that direction, moving along the edge of the path. Down, through the trees, he could see three rectangles of water. He wouldn't go down or back. He would angle around toward the buildings. Perhaps he could take cover there if he needed to. He passed what he remembered now were big barns, housing the park police horses.

There would be a watchman, perhaps. He couldn't yell from where he was and the place was enclosed in a high-wire mesh fence. He went around the building and headed toward what appeared to be the entrance. That's when he felt something hit his ear. He darted forward, dropped down. The lobe of his left ear was missing. He turned and ran through into a stable area – a long row of doors. He opened a couple as he ran along, hoping that Kozlov or Stepan, whoever was trying to kill him, would be slowed by a search.

This trek through the park wasn't working. He wasn't sure exactly where he was, but he decided to move back to Fulton Street. He'd flag down a car. Run through the streets. Surely the killer, with high-powered rifle and infrared sight, wasn't about to follow him into civilization. He smiled. The shooter could stand at the edge and fire away though. He moved quickly. The street wasn't that far and, in moments, it seemed he could see the lights from the homes.

He could hear distant sirens as he hit the street. Perhaps the police had arrived at the windmill. But they were too far away to help him. A bus passed by – the 5 Fulton was slowing as it came to a bus stop ahead of him. Lang ran as fast as he could. He had a chance. The waiting passenger got on too quickly to slow down the process. The lights on the back of bus indicated he was preparing to depart. Lang caught up with it as it slowly accelerated. He pounded on the doors. The driver stopped. As it stopped the electric bus made its usual, strange noise – the sound an elephant in pain.

Lang got on board. The driver had taken pity. Lang did not have the correct change. The driver had apparently run out of pity. After a brief debate, Lang pushed a five through the money slot.

'Keep the change.' He walked toward the back of the nearly empty bus – only a Chinese woman in the seat behind the driver – and was propelled faster by the bus lurching forward. He landed happily in a seat in the rear and to the left, scrunching down to avoid another assassin's bullet. He felt for his ear and found part of it. Most of it. There was little blood, but he pressed a handkerchief against it.

The bus would take him close to home. Tomorrow he'd pick up his car if it wasn't towed. He felt for his gun. It was there. He'd left his flashlight somewhere. Perhaps where he'd been shot.

When the bus stopped at Saint Ignatius at the University of San Francisco, a man got on. A big man. When he turned from the driver to find a seat, there was no doubt it was Theodore Kozlov, hands in the pockets of a tan trench coat as he walked slowly and with a broad smile toward Lang.

He sat down beside Lang, the largeness of his body pressing Lang against the window. With his hand in his pocket Lang pulled the hand and pocket to his lap.

'You don't learn, my friend,' Kozlov said in a friendly way.

'I know.'

'I tried to tell you that you could investigate my wife's death, but not my business.'

'But they are the same thing,' Lang said.

'Yes?'

'You were working both sides – the Native Americans and the Las Vegas interests. They'd kill you if they found out.'

'So you knew.'

'Your wife let you help her people because she thought you believed you were helping. When she found out that you were screwing the tribe over, she was going to tell the world.'

Lang looked to the front of the bus. Because he and Kozlov were on the left side, the same side as the driver, and the driver had a solid divider between him and the rest of the bus, Lang and Kozlov were out of his direct view.

'You know nothing of the world,' Kozlov said. 'You pampered Americans have no idea. You're all fools.'

The bus stopped to let off the Chinese woman, laden with bags. In the brief moment that Kozlov looked away laughing, Lang brought the gun, still in his jacket pocket, to Kozlov's side. He knew that a bullet entering there would find the heart. He pressed the muzzle between the man's ribs and fired. The sound of the gunshot was no more than a muzzled pop buried as it was in Kozlov's clothing and flesh and the sound of the bus stopping. The driver didn't notice.

Kozlov who felt the gun at his side, had already started to turn back, but too late and in his eyes were anger and surprise.

'You were going to kill me,' Lang said.

Kozlov nodded, a movement almost too subtle to notice.

'Did you think I was going to count to three?'

Kozlov nodded, smiled faintly and died.

'You were betting I was a decent man,' Lang said to the dead man. 'I try. I try very hard. In the end, I'm practical. I do what needs to be done.'

Lang reached up, pulled the string and the tone sounded. The light at the front of the bus said 'Stop Requested.' He retrieved Kozlov's handgun and slipped in his own pocket. He wiped off the weapon he used to kill Kozlov and placed it in the dead man's hand, pressing the fingers against the grip and a finger on the trigger, purposely aiming away from the heart. He fired again as the bus stopped. The sound of the electric bus stopping more than covered the sound of the second gunshot. A corpulent, elderly man with a goatee and straw hat got on the bus. The man glanced back, seemed to take no notice. He sat up front, opening a book to read by the dim interior light.

Lang went out through the rear door, went across the street toward and then through the college campus. A young couple sat on a bench between buildings. They ignored him. Lang looked back, saw the bus continue through the intersection and head to its destination – the Transbay Terminal. Lang wasn't too sure about 'Transbay,' but 'Terminal' seemed right.

Lang took off his suit jacket, felt the pockets for anything he might have put in there. He wandered, a little tired and a little stunned, through the neighborhood. Trash and recycling containers were out for morning pick-up. A stroke of good luck. He tucked his jacket just below some plastic bags in one of the containers.

He was about six blocks from home, but home seemed to him days away. He was tired from running, walking. By morning or before he knew he would be talking with the police. When he got home, cut up his pants and little by little flushed them down the toilet. He showered, making sure any gunpowder residue was off his body and cleaned the shower, putting bleach in the drain when he was done.

He wiped off Kozlov's gun, a light olive green SIG P220 that cost more than the one he owned and stuffed in Kozlov's pocket. And betting Kozlov didn't have a license for the SIG since no one could qualify for one, he placed it in his pillowcase. A sniff prior indicated it had not been fired. Kozlov or his hired hand had done all the shooting with a high-powered rifle. Meanwhile he had a gun to protect himself.

Lang was physically exhausted but mentally wired. And he was stuck at home, without music, without TV, without Buddha.

Thirty-Seven

The police wouldn't let Carly and Sasha anywhere near the windmill and tunnel. Blue lights flashed in the night. Carly could smell the sea that was not all that many yards away.

Sasha took a cell phone from the bag and punched the Lang's number on speed dial. It rang and went to voicemail.

'You're here because?'

It was Inspector Rose. Thanh recognized him easily, but Rose had no clue about Thanh.

'Just passing through,' Carly said. 'Just curious. Someone dead?'

'Looks like it.'

'Do you know who?'

'Some Russian guy we arrested earlier in the week.'

'Anyone else?'

'You looking for someone special?'

'Just curious, officer,' Carly said. 'A little walk on the beach in the fresh cool air before heading home. We saw something going on over here.'

He looked at them suspiciously, then acquiesced.

'All dressed up and nowhere to go,' Stern said. 'Good idea. The going home part.'

It was a good idea. Stern was coming toward them.

The knock came a little after 3 a.m. Lang may have dozed off at some point, but if he did, it was fitful sleep. He wasn't rested. His body ached as he climbed down the ladder, Kozlov's pistol in his hand. He suspected it was the police, but the last Russian was still out there. He slipped on his jeans, put the pistol in the waistband in back, and opened the door.

Rose and Stern stood there.

'Please come in,' Lang said, stepping back.

'Thank you,' Rose said.

Lang flicked on some lights, tried to keep his back to them, without being too obvious about it.

'You have a gun,' Stern said. It wasn't a question.

Lang reached back and pulled it out. Stern reached out. Lang gave it to him, grip first.

'License?' Stern was a man of few words.

'No.'

'Kozlov is dead,' Stern said, examining the handgun, finally putting it in his coat pocket.

'I'm not sorry to hear that.'

'And two of his friends,' Stern continued.

Rose meandered about the large room.

'Probably the two confessors,' Lang said. 'The person who's trying to kill me killed them.'

'You know about all of them?'

'You called from the windmill,' Rose said. 'A dead man down.'

'I remember.'

'Another dead one on the path,' Stern said.

'I know that one too. We were talking when he went down.'

Stern scratched his chin. A half smile, smarmy, smart-alecky smile.

'And Kozlov killed himself,' Stern said.

'Good,' Lang said as nonchalantly as possible. 'An appropriate end to his miserable life.'

'I thought you'd see it that way,' Stern said.

'You were there,' Rose said from the bathroom, 'Bus driver remembers a guy getting on with a missing ear lobe. Scratches on his face.'

'I'm not too good at blending in with the crowd,' Lang said.

'Not much of a crowd. Just you and Kozlov.'

'There was a guy in a straw hat,' Lang said.

'And?' Rose asked.

'We talked, Kozlov and I. He wasn't happy. I told him I knew that with the gambling interests he was playing both sides – the tribes and the Las Vegas boys – against each other.'

'For material gain,' Rose said.

'Yes. You just don't do that. If he didn't take his life, somebody would. He knew that apparently.'

'And that wouldn't be you, would it?'

'I thought you said he killed himself,' Lang said.

'The problem is that he shot himself twice,' Rose said.

'Maybe the first one didn't do it,' Lang said.

'That how it went down?' Stern asked.

'You're the professionals,' Lang said. 'Anything else?'

'Oh, kick back, Lang. Got a search warrant coming,' Stern said. 'We'll be awhile.'

'Help yourself. You've already got the only thing that could get me in trouble.' He mustered all his faith in whatever it was he believed in that this was true.

'You keep getting us out of bed,' Stern said.

'You could have waited until morning,' Lang said.

'And have you destroying evidence?'

'Oh, right,' Lang said.

'We hoped this wouldn't get so messy. Three murders to add to the city's tally,' Rose said.

'Hey!' Lang said. 'How many times did I tell you that Kozlov killed his wife? You remember coming down to my office when he brought his gang down from Sacramento to maim or kill me. But he was nice to the cops. So the guy got pass. You know who's responsible for the murder rate, don't you?'

Lang stared directly at Stern.

'Careful,' Stern said.

'So Kozlov died tonight after killing at least two people, and you're here talking to me?' Lang tugged at his foreshortened ear lobe. 'This wasn't a voluntary ear piercing. Go ahead. Put me on the stand, Stern. Let's talk about murders. Let's talk about police competence. I've got a lot to say. Do you want to do that?'

Rose looked at Stern. So did Lang.

Stern finally lost his bluster. He looked sad, defeated.

'A suicide isn't a murder,' Stern said.

'I'll buy it,' Rose said. 'There's the law, then there's justice.'

'That's not supposed to be up to us,' Stern said.

'This would be the first time, wouldn't it?' Lang said to Stern.

'I got your point,' Stern said. 'But you'd be making a big mistake, Lang, if you think that, after this, you have the upper hand.'

'I wouldn't dream of it. You guys have enough to do as it is,' Lang said. 'All these drive-bys and that society murder up at Lafayette Park.'

'That one is solved,' Stern said.

'Don't count on it,' Lang said.

Rose was already on his cell. He was calling off the search. If there had to be punishment for Kozlov's death, it would be the minds of those involved to sort it out.

'Am I going to find anything on the gun?' Stern asked. The tone bordered on the conspiratorial.

'No.'

'You're good,' Stern said.

Lang didn't answer. It really wasn't a compliment.

*   *   *

Carly couldn't believe her luck. They were meeting in the DA's conference room. She couldn't have planned it better if she had planned it herself.

Howard Dane, Assistant District Attorney, in his starched shirt, perfectly tied tie, and well-pressed expensive suit, sat at the head of the long table tapping his fingers on the cheap wood. Hannah Rodriguez, whom Carly remembered from an early meeting with Pamela Hanover, was no longer pregnant. She sat to Dane's left with a look of calm meditation on her face. Gratelli sat on Dane's right. The detective had some files in front of him. As a long-time cop and used to enduring the long wait of bureaucracy, Gratelli had a blank look on his face.

Carly sat at the other end waiting for the shoe to be dropped or for the person or persons they were waiting for to arrive. And arrive, he did. Noah Lang was shown into the room. He was in jeans and a sweatshirt. He hadn't shaved. He looked as if he could have been on a two-week drinking binge.

'I'm very sorry,' Lang said, 'I've had quite a night and quite a morning, thanks to the boys in blue – though I guess they weren't wearing blue. Now, if someone will kindly tell me why I'm here.'

'There is something very troubling going on with regard to the Olivia Hanover murder case,' Dane said after Lang was seated. 'More than troubling.' He made little houses and churches with the fingers of his folded hands. 'It's possible that there is a serious violation of the law and potential criminal prosecution of two private investigators involved in an active murder investigation.'

'I work for the defense counsel,' Lang said. 'I recognize that the constitution isn't what it used to be, but I'm covered as is my partner Ms Paladino.'

'Mr Lang,' Dane said with exaggerated patience, 'you pretended to be someone else to attend a private fund-raiser and Ms Paladino pretended to be part of the wait staff and you both used those ruses to ambush the Hanover children.'

'If you'll look around, Mr Dane,' Carly said, 'you'll see there's no jury here to convince so you might stop the spin. Evan, the predator and his cohort Jordan are not children. They are both legal adults and they may very well be implicated in the death of their sister.'

'The perpetrator has been caught, Ms Paladino,' Hannah Rodriguez said. 'And indicted. You are using your past employment in an unethical manner and your false accusations are causing great personal suffering. I hope your insurance is in order.'

'Let's move on,' Dane continued.

'No, let's not,' Carly said. 'First, I informed Mrs Hanover that if I took the case I would pursue the truth. Was she all right with that? She said yes. Second, there is nothing in the penal code that says we cannot pretend to be someone we're not, unless we take the identity of someone who actually exists or commit fraud through an assumed identity. Even so, I believe Mr Lang gave his name as Mr Lang. And I wasn't just pretending to be a server. I served.'

'Salmon puffs,' Lang said. 'I didn't have any.'

Carly thought he saw the hint of a grin on Gratelli's usually and naturally dour face.

'Don't make a mockery of this,' Dane said. 'This is quite serious.'

'It is very serious. You have indicted an innocent person,' Carly said. 'A young boy, and by your measure, Mr Dane, a mere infant, is about to go on trial for killing someone he didn't kill, someone he loved, in fact. And the murderer or murderers will be able to continue to live a very luxury-filled life.'

'Inspector Gratelli has provided nearly incontrovertible evidence to the contrary. Isn't that right, Inspector?'

'Not exactly,' Gratelli said, his voice cracking a bit. 'Ms Paladino has raised some issues that warrant investigation. The Hanovers had access to morphine. And the boys, young men, especially the older one, frequent clubs where ketamine is as available as bottled water.'

'This is ridiculous,' Rodriguez said. 'This is not why I'm here.'

Dane looked unhappy, but he smiled through his pain. 'You have anything else to add?'

Apparently, the threat in his voice didn't intimidate the old inspector. He continued.

'There's also the matter of the motor scooter. A witness says that the night of the murder and roughly the time and place of the murder, he heard a motor scooter come and go. No one has found a scooter in Mr Lee's possession, nor has anyone seen him on one at any time.'

'So?' Rodriguez said.

'The Hanovers had such a scooter in their garage and there is indication that Olivia had ridden behind the driver somewhat recently.'

'That doesn't mean anything. There are thousands of scooters out there.'

'There was a second video posted to Olivia's website from the Hanover network after Olivia's death. Lee couldn't have posted it. He was in prison. There is no evidence that the young man even knows how to use a computer.'

'Purely circumstantial,' Dane said.

'Which is the same kind of evidence we have against Daniel Lee,' Gratelli said.

'So maybe we should just flip,' Lang said. 'Heads it's the Hanovers, tails it's Lee.' He knew he was being obnoxious. He shrugged. 'Sorry. Lack of sleep and dodging assassins.'

'Yes, I understand,' Dane said, 'you are involved in other nefarious activities.'

'Nefarious? I feel I'm a ne'er-do-well in a Thomas Hardy novel. Thank you.'

'If you can't be serious about a serious matter . . .' Dane said.

'OK. This is serious. I'm representing Daniel Lee's counsel. What you are doing to me – and to Ms Paladino – interferes not just with me, but with the young man's constitutional rights. I think,' Lang said, standing up, 'this meeting is over. And if I were you, Mrs Hanover's attorney, I'd let the family know that the real investigation has just begun.'

Carly, a little surprised by the suddenness of Lang's action and her inclusion in his dramatic speech, was unsure of what she should do. She decided she didn't have a choice. She'd look pretty silly if she stayed.

Outside the conference room, she asked him: 'What are you doing?'

'You were the first one to get snippy. I was just following your lead.'

'I guess I did get snippy, didn't I?'

'I'm impressed. You give me courage, Ms Paladino.'

'What's next?'

'I don't know. All I seem to be able to do is shake the bushes.'

'You know that when Mrs Hanover had the video system removed, she might have had it removed in anticipation of murdering her daughter,' Carly said.

'Go on.'

'She may have done so in order to prevent documenting someone's untoward nocturnal wanderings.'

'Oh,' Lang said. 'There was a secret.'

'Seems so.'

Thirty-Eight

'If I was into the rough-and-tumble type, you would be perfect,' Katherine Wexford said at the door. 'But scratches and bruises aren't attractive before noon. Maybe midnight.'

Her smile said she was amused – by him or herself, he wasn't sure. She stepped back, tacit permission for Noah Lang to come inside. He followed her down the now familiar long hallway to the end room. All the good homes in Pacific Heights, it seemed, were highest on the hill and facing the Bay.

'Rough after-party?' she asked when they arrived.

'You could say that,' Lang said.

'Something to drink?' she asked. 'Oh, don't bother looking at your watch. Even if I believed in traditional conventions, I have a feeling I'm going to need a drink before you say what you've come here to say. Sit.'

Lang was happy to sit, but wasn't sure he'd ever want to get up. He wasn't sure he could stay awake.

It didn't take her long to fix the drink. Liquor and a few ice cubes. She came over to Lang, sat down beside him.

'OK,' she said, 'go.'

'I'm going after your kids,' Lang said.

She didn't seem shocked or angry.

'Why are you bothering to tell me?' she asked.

'Fair warning.'

'Fair?' She shook her head. 'Nothing's fair. I appreciate your gallant attempt Mr Lang. Despite your appearance, you are a gentleman.'

Lang had nothing to say.

She drank deeply from her glass.

'Athletes who want to go to the Olympics train obsessively,' she said. 'Young actors and actresses do whatever is necessary, many of them humiliating themselves, to be who they dearly want to be.' Wexford stood, walked to the window and looked out. 'For some reason – I guess the presumed glamour, the rarefied atmosphere they believe they will breathe – there are people who obsess about being part of what is called "society."'

She turned back. She looked at Lang, a weary sadness in her eyes.

'Evan got Jordan the ketamine because Pamela asked him to find some. Neither knew what it would lead to. She wasn't honest about it. Pamela told Jordan that it was supposed to help with her anxiety. She had been reading about the treatment, she said. And it was true. Pamela was having deeply depressive episodes. Part of it, I'm guessing now, is that she never felt part of the group. She felt like an outsider. Of course she was. I am. We all are. But she didn't know that. She also didn't know that all these old families with money and privilege – all of them, Noah – have deep, dark, embarrassing relatives who do deep, dark and embarrassing things. Olivia was the least of these. No one, outside of Pamela, gave it a second thought. Olivia was merely in another universe, a harmless one, and I promise you that in Olivia's dotage she would have been a lovely old eccentric.'

'Jesus,' Lang said, not that he was surprised at the who-did-it of the puzzle, but the why.

Wexford nodded.

'One day, I'm told, Walter, after enduring the thirty-millionth apology for Olivia's odd behavior, told Pamela that it would have been better had Olivia not been part of the package. He didn't mean anything ominous nor did he believe anything could or should be done. What he was really saying was that Olivia was making life difficult for Pamela because Pamela made it so. Nothing more.'

'How long have you known this?'

'The morning the little girl was discovered in Lafayette Park.'

'And you told no one?'

'Family, Noah. Family. It wasn't as if Pamela was going to kill anyone else.'

'You, the entire family, would let an innocent young man go to prison perhaps to his death because you didn't want what? The public embarrassment? The media coverage?'

'We're not nice people, necessarily,' Wexford said. 'We were waiting to see how the chips fell.'

'You would have intervened at some point?'

'I don't know.'

Lang got up and headed to the hallway.

'Goodbye, Mrs Wexford.'

'Goodbye, Noah.'

As he stepped out on the street Lang reached in his pocket for the cell phone he borrowed from Thanh.

Thirty-Nine

Hannah Rodriguez stood at the door to the Hanovers' home.

'I'm sorry,' Hannah said without a trace of apology in her voice, 'Mrs Hanover isn't seeing anyone this morning.'

'Mrs Rodriguez,' Carly said, 'I'm not here for me. I'm here for her. It's over, Mrs Rodriguez. I need to talk to her. If you have her welfare at heart, I need to talk to her.'

'Let her in,' Walter Hanover said. He looked drawn, pale. There was nothing but emptiness in his eyes, defeat on his face.

Rodriguez looked Carly up and down as if she planned to beat the crap out of her later in the street and stepped out of the way.

'She's in the back. In the garden. You know the way?'

Carly nodded.

'I don't advise this,' Rodriguez said, but it appeared no one was listening.

The sun in summer was able to make its way to most of the garden on the north side of the home. Mrs Hanover sat where she'd sat days earlier signing reminder letters for the fund-raiser. She sat there now without work to do, an empty coffee cup in front of her, a copy of *Vanity Fair* off to one side.

She looked up.

'Carly.'

'Mrs Hanover.'

Pamela wore a big straw hat and sunglasses.

'I'm sorry,' Carly said. It was clear Pamela knew it was over.

'Mrs Wexford called you, didn't she?'

'It's all so senseless, isn't it? Silly really.'

'Your pills,' Gary Gray said, setting down a small silver tray. There was an orange plastic medicine bottle and a glass of water in a clear glass. He didn't acknowledge Carly.

'Thank you,' she said. She spilled two capsules into her palm. 'Helps to level out the moods. God knows –' she took a sip of water – 'she would have been unhappy like me. It's not an easy life and she wasn't as adaptable as I am.'

'Are you killing yourself, Mrs Hanover?'

'As we speak.'

Carly got up and called in. 'Call 911. Pamela's taken something.'

As she called three men walked up the hallway. Carly recognized Gratelli, who was followed by the policeman from last night and another, a big white guy.

'Mrs Hanover has just poisoned herself,' Carly said.

The black cop pulled out his phone. Gratelli went to Pamela Hanover, put a finger on her neck.

'Gone,' Gratelli said.

'A lot of suicide going on around here,' Stern said.

'Catching,' Rose said.

'This one real?'

'Beats me,' Rose said. He turned toward Carly. 'Do I know you?'

'I hang around the Hall of Justice sometimes.'

'You are here because . . .'

'Help her face the consequences,' Carly said.

'I guess you did,' Gratelli said.

Carly walked back through the house toward the front door. On the left, in Pamela's study, Walter Hanover sat on the leather sofa, leaning forward, head in his hands. She walked in.

'There's more to all of this than just embarrassment over Olivia's lack of social skills,' she said.

He looked up. But his eyes engaged hers for half a second. He looked down again.

'Pamela had the security cameras removed not because she was planning a murder . . . not then anyway. She wanted to make sure the cameras didn't catch something else, isn't that right?'

Carly sensed movement in the doorway. She looked back. It was Jordan. He stood there, shaking, eyes glaring at his father.

Walter looked up, stared back.

'What's going on?' Carly asked.

'Time for you to go, Ms Paladino,' Walter said.

'Are you sure all the witnesses have been eliminated?' Carly asked.

Walter didn't look up.

'Your wife is dead,' Carly said. 'She believed her life was over. Why was that?'

'Go away, Miss Paladino.'

'We've got the police here,' she said. 'Maybe we should call them in.' She turned back to Jordan. 'Did you get the ketamine for your mother or your father?'

'Shut up, Jordan,' Walter Hanover said.

'For me,' Jordan said.

'For you?'

'For me to use.'

'On Olivia.'

'Shut up,' Hanover said, standing up.

Jordan nodded.

'You killed Olivia?'

He nodded.

'Jesus Christ,' Walter Hanover said. 'You're an idiot.'

'Why?' Carly asked.

'The family was falling apart,' he said.

'That's was Olivia's fault?'

He didn't answer.

'It wasn't her fault,' Carly continued, 'but killing her was the solution?'

He nodded.

'Because your father and Olivia . . . ? You knew what was going on?'

'The whole family knew what was going on,' Evan said, joining the group. His face was angry, his tone bitter.

'We've got the whole family here,' Gratelli said in his slow, low-key way.

'What's left of it,' Evan said.

'I didn't want to,' Jordan said. 'It was the only way things would be back to normal. And her life –' he began to cry – 'you know . . . was kind of miserable anyway. I made it easy.' He looked at Carly, eyes full of tears. 'She felt no pain.'

'And Pamela Hanover's suicide?' Gratelli asked.

Everyone was quiet.

'Her life was over,' Carly said. 'She saw everything she had and ever wanted slipping away. And Olivia's death really was a family decision, wasn't it?'

Gary Gray was at the front door. He opened it for Carly, but said nothing. His face gave away nothing. She walked out into the sun. The homes up and down the street looked so rich, so respectable.

Poor Pamela Hanover, Carly thought. She thought if she could pretend enough, it would be real.

Forty

Chastain West sat on the arm of Lang's office sofa. No one ever sat in it. There was a sense that if you allowed yourself in that big, soft sofa, you might be swallowed by it.

'I'm sorry I didn't have a chance to say goodbye,' Lang said.

'He said to say goodbye to you and to thank you,' West said.

'Where's he going?'

'He didn't say.'

'Didn't say?'

'Wouldn't say,' West said. 'He no longer has his room. He has a bag and his journals. He's a little thin and I'm sure I saw a few lines around his eyes that weren't there before. But he seems hopeful.'

Lang wouldn't say it, but he admired and was perhaps envious in a kindly way, of Daniel Lee's new-found freedom. The young man would be anonymous again, wandering who knows where – or why. All of this offered about as much freedom as was allowed in human civilization. Lang also believed that there was something in those journals, something eventually translatable, something profound or silly, but something. He wished he knew.

'You have anything for me?' Lang asked West.

'Something is coming up, I think. I'll let you know. It's fairly big. Complicated.'

'I've got a partner now. We can handle big and complicated.'

'Good, I'll get back to you,' West said, as he headed for the door.

Carly stood in the windowless back room of Lang's office. There was a table, a lamp, two chairs and a telephone. On the table she had set the box of her belongings – a laptop computer, a Rolodex, some stationery, yellow legal pads, pencils, pens, stapler, and other office supplies.

Thanh, a casually dressed male at the moment, leaned in the doorway.

'It's like getting in the ocean,' Thanh said. 'You have to just jump in, all the way, so your body will get used to the cold water.'

It was true. She'd made some decisions and she couldn't really go back.

'Yes, I've decided. For better or for worse,' she said.

'In sickness and in health,' Thanh said.

'That too.'

In her mind, she screamed, what have I done? What in the hell have I done?

'It's beginning to look like a family around here,' Thanh said.

Barry Brinkman appeared, an angry look on his wrinkled face. He walked past Thanh and stood in the middle of Carly's new and claustrophobically small office.

'You know what I did?' he asked. He didn't wait for an answer. He shook his head. 'God damn it. God *damn* it. You know what I did? I had my bills in my hand to mail and a bag of scones in the other. I was standing in front of the fucking mailbox and I mailed my scones.'

'Family,' Carly said, smiling at Thanh.

'Family, dear.'

Forty-One

Gratelli sat at one of the back tables at Tosca. He could easily imagine that he was in Europe somewhere, the way the place was allowed to age as if age too was beautiful. Opera came from the jukebox. Chatter came from the bar. Pamela's suicide, assisted or not, passed through his mind for a moment. Gratelli lifted his glass in a salute to the universe.

The thing is, Lang thought, as he changed Buddha's litter box, that when you kill someone, you never know when it might come back to haunt you. He wasn't concerned about ghosts, Kozlov's and the one a long time ago, but the law did concern him. And he didn't know, because there was another Russian thug out there on the loose, whether the would-be killer would finish the job or, as Lang obviously hoped, wanted only to disappear before he too was caught. Lang would have to live with those possibilities and with himself. It wasn't the first time a decision, like the one he made on the Fulton bus, would rest heavily on his mind, or soul if he had one. Buddha looked on with what Lang took as amusement.

Buddha had little inner conflict, Lang thought.

Carly stood out on the back deck of her home. She had a glass of orange juice. She watched Mr Nakamura tending his garden below. He never looked up. If he had, she would have waved, but he didn't. He didn't know his privacy was invaded by a woman who took pleasure not only in the beauty he created, but also in the constancy of his actions.

Because she had identified so much with Olivia, she was surprised that she felt no outrage at the murderer, nor did she feel, as she expected, any satisfaction in seeing the punishment for the crime, such as it was. She revisited, for a moment, the days at Bodega Bay, when she decided to change her life. She remembered that the beautiful white egrets were one vision and the buzzards picking at the remains of a dead animal on the beach another.

Mr Nakamura was meticulous. He put in new plants when others grew old, made sure the bushes kept a pleasant shape, that the dead blooms were removed, that each stone was in its proper place. With her new life, out in the world, she was very happy to know that she still lived in the home of her parents and that Mr Nakamura kept the lovely garden below.